# THINK OUTSIDE THE FOX

ELLEN RIGGS

BOUGHT-THE-FARM
MYSTERIES

# FREE PREQUEL

Rescuing this pup could bring Ivy a whole new life... if it doesn't kill her first.

Discover how big city executive Ivy meets Keats, her crime-solving sheepdog, in A Dog with Two Tales. Ivy Galloway doesn't know how desperate she is to escape the big city and her soul-sucking corporate career until she meets a sheepdog in need of rescue, too.

This short prequel to the laugh-out-loud Bought-the-Farm Mystery series is a page-turner for lovers of animals, humor and spunky amateur sleuths. Join Ellen Riggs' author newsletter at **ellenriggs.com/opt-in** to get this FREE prequel.

Think Outside the Fox

ISBN 978-1-998742-11-0 D2D Paperback
ISBN 978-1-990613-30-2 eBook
ISBN 978-1-990613-31-9 Book
ISBN 978-1-990613-32-6 AudioBook
ASIN B0BCDBJCLY Kindle
ASIN B0CHL1FXYN Paperback

Publisher: Ellen Riggs
www.ellenriggs.com
Cover designer: Lou Harper
Editor: Serena Clarke
2512230121D2D

# CHAPTER ONE

I pulled off my hat, unzipped my coat and loosened my scarf. The late January wind was sharp enough to cut through armor, but my blood was pumping so hard that even my fingers were warm in work gloves.

"It's a thing of beauty," I told Keats, my border collie, gesturing over his shoulder. "Wouldn't you agree?"

He grumbled a sassy retort and turned both eyes—one blue, one brown—away from me. My manure pile was a supreme waste of time in his humble opinion and my new hobby was even worse.

"You heard Edna. Every farm around here has a woodpile. We need to be prepared." I tossed split logs into a heap to be stacked later. "Not for the end times, necessarily. Just regular power outages. I don't trust that generator or even the backup generator. You know I like my creature comforts. Especially coffee."

Much of the advice my neighbor Edna Evans bombarded me with got a hard pass. The octogenarian prepper wanted me to "toughen up" by rock climbing, belly crawling across gravel, and rappelling into caves and bunkers. That wasn't going to happen. Nor was I about to study archery, swordplay or gun handling when mastery of my truck's stick shift was still in question. But a wood-pile? That was something I could get behind. Wielding an ax was plenty risky for me and I made sure my animals stayed well clear.

Chopping wood was better than turning manure to channel frustrations, and I had some of those. While Christmas had been wonderful and the weather was unseasonably mild, business was slow at the inn I ran with my best friend, Jilly Blackwood. She was at loose ends, too, and when I'd burned some wood in the backyard firepit two days ago, she brought out cast iron pans and put her chef skills to the test by making a fine meal over it on a grill.

I had been eager to share the adventure with Edna, but she was preoccupied with her experiential preparedness course. Survival-Dare had been on ice for months, but coincidentally resumed the very day Kellan Harper, chief of police, left town to work on a secret project.

That secret project was the driving force not only behind the current woodpile, but also three others. At this rate, my loved ones would be warm long into the apocalypse, and all because I was worried about my fiancé. The case Kellan was working on was so top secret that I didn't know exactly where he'd gone.

"Down south," was all he'd said.

"Down south" was a big place, and as his fiancée, I figured I should have clearance to know more. Granted, the movers and shakers in the policing arena viewed me as a reckless troublemaker, despite my efforts to put away criminals in our town of Clover Grove and beyond.

Keats mumbled something and I nodded. "Exactly. Our success makes them look bad. Right, Percy?" I glanced up at my fluffy ginger cat in his yellow bomber jacket. He was watching me from the wood-pile with about as much enthusiasm as the dog.

By the end of the day, the stack would reach the eaves of the utility shed and I'd have to start a new one. A couple of storms had brought down some wonderful old trees and after Charlie, my farm manager, worked loud magic with the chainsaw, I decided to pick up an ax and pay my respects to oak, maple and pine.

In addition to being frustrated, I was as bored as my pets. With my sister Poppy and two nephews on the payroll to help Charlie, I'd become overkill.

Keats gave a canine snicker at that.

"What? Overkill is a legit word." I lifted the ax and brought it down with a satisfying thwack. "We're talking chores, not murder."

He preferred to talk murder, or more precisely, solving it. We'd worked together on a string of cases that stretched through five seasons in hill country. My dog and cat liked a challenge and watching me chop wood didn't tap into their impressive skills.

I attacked another log and the ax stopped just short of splitting it. "Kellan asked us to stay out of trouble while he's gone. The substitute chief is a hard"—I smacked the log repeatedly—"nut. To. Crack."

It took four good whacks for the wood to give way. Kellan had used other words to describe his replacement, including "conservative" and "old school."

That was chief of police terminology. A regular boyfriend would just admit the substitute chief was an uptight jerk who wouldn't take kindly to my brand of hobby farmer justice.

I hadn't met Acting Chief Dixon Skowby yet, but I knew what he was like because one of his officers shared a roof with me. My brother Asher's normally unquenchable good cheer had diminished quickly after being deployed to the night shift on highway patrol. Sleeping through the day meant he saw less of Jilly, and they were still in the honeymoon phase. On the plus side, he crossed paths—and spears—with our mother less frequently.

Keats stalked around my little woodlot grumbling, perhaps about the new cop in town. My dog didn't like being confined by arbitrary rules.

"They're not arbitrary to Chief Skowby. They're the law." Propping the ax against the shed, I sighed. "I don't like this either, but Kellan promised it won't be for long. Soon we'll have back-to-back guests anyway. Jilly texted to say a gentlemen's club is coming to stay."

Percy gave what sounded like a sly meow.

"I know, right? What exactly is a gentlemen's club and why would anyone in this day and age describe themselves as such? But with Asher around and in a bad mood, they'll need to behave."

My brother had hoped to be named acting chief, and Kellan had put in a good word for him. Their superiors moved so swiftly to drop Dixon Skowby into the role that I suspected all had been planned before Kellan even knew he was leaving.

Asher probably wasn't quite ready for the responsibility of leading the police in a town with a crime rate as high as ours. That said, he was nowhere near as soft as the brother I once knew. What we'd seen over the past year had hardened him even more than it had me. After marrying Jilly, however, his focus was sometimes as splintered as the wood I was picking up now. Though committed to climbing the ranks to impress his wife, he still couldn't believe his good luck in landing Jilly and wanted to spend as much time as possible with her.

There'd been talk of promoting Asher to a job elsewhere, but in the short-term, Kellan wanted him to hold down the fort here, quite literally. Our living arrangements didn't bother me at all. I'd grown up the last of six kids, and despite having 15 years of big-city independence a crowd felt safe. Jilly, on the other hand, had to make the usual adjustments to married life, while living with me, our guests and worse, my mother. Mom had her own apartment in town but didn't use it often and the term "gentlemen's club" was likely to serve as a magnet. Unlike her five daughters, Dahlia Galloway loved flirting.

Goosebumps started on my forearms and quickly covered my

torso. At first I blamed it on the breeze, but then I sensed someone was watching me.

A joint growl from dog and cat confirmed it.

I turned quickly and found the spy wasn't a someone but a some*thing*.

# CHAPTER TWO

The most gorgeous red fox I'd ever seen was sitting in the driveway, fluffy tail wrapped neatly around delicate paws. A white tuft at the end of its long tail was so full and bright that it made Keats' similar tuft look scrawny.

Keats grumbled, seemingly over being compared unfavorably to this lesser canid.

"Hey there, Red," I called. "The driveway is no place for a fox, even if you're as cunning as the old stories. You'd best be on your way."

The fox tilted its head quizzically.

"I'm serious, young lady." Its glorious fur suggested youth but the gender was just a guess. "And don't get anywhere near my chicken coop, either. I heard about you."

Jilly's cousin, Janelle Brighton, had seen the fox while visiting the inn at Christmas. I had watched for it ever since, finding only paw prints in the snow.

The vixen seemed to do nightly rounds, circling pasture and barn repeatedly. Keats had initially shown interest but I guessed there was no immediate threat because he let it go. Regular wildlife wasn't a particular worry to him. Byron, our livestock guardian dog, wasn't concerned, either. The fox was unlikely to be a threat to anything larger than a chicken and my feathered friends were well secured.

Percy meowed again and I pursed my lips. Was the fox a risk for the cats? Percy, probably not, but what about the regular barn cats? There were half a dozen flitting in and out these days. They wanted little to do with me, probably because of my assertive sidekicks. They were fans of my father, however. He fed them and often shared their sleeping quarters in the loft, despite owning a large home nearby.

"You're right, Percy. We need to look out for the smaller critters. I suppose this vixen could take down Elaine the emu, since the bird can't run like she would in the wild."

The fox tilted her head the other way, as if to suggest she could feed herself just fine without tackling a very large bird.

"What then?" I asked. "You're hanging around for a reason and I'm all ears."

Keats mumbled something rude. He didn't plan on taking directions from wildlife.

The fox unfurled her tail, stretched like a cat, and then turned to walk toward the field. She looked at me over one shoulder and the afternoon sun danced off amber eyes.

It was an invitation.

Keats must have agreed because he mumbled a decided no. My sheepdog shifted uneasily and I wondered if the fox was leading us into trouble. More likely, my dog was embarrassed about his down-filled black winter jacket. Members of the local herding club told me he didn't need a coat in winter. That might have been true but I didn't trust any of them. They'd shielded one of their own after she murdered someone on my property, thereby giving her a chance to try her moves on me. When it came to my pets, I made my own decisions. Keats and Percy were outside with me all day and I couldn't risk losing my buddies to hypothermia.

That reminded me to zip up my own jacket. I tightened my scarf and started walking after the fox.

She was out in the field already, her brisk but steady pace telling me to get a move on it. Trotting up a hill, she threw me another amber glance before disappearing over the crest.

"Game on, lady," I called, picking up the pace. "Where you go, I go."

I probably wouldn't have been so hasty in committing if I'd realized the fox would turn into the woods so soon. She passed the old orchard, and then the dump where I had fainted once. We were off my property now. Long ago, this land had belonged to the Harlow family, and I'd visited before in a similar adventure. That time, a beautiful painted bunting had lured me to an old barn and a cache of letters. The land had changed hands often but was vacant during my tenure at the farm. Maybe it had more secrets to reveal before it would be habitable by some of the homesteaders eager to put down roots in the area.

Perhaps that's what our mission was about today. The fox had dropped back now, probably so I wouldn't lose sight of her. She was taking me somewhere.

Keats trotted a few yards ahead, grumbling the whole time. Percy added his commentary from my shoulder. There had been a few inches of snow in the fields but it was never as bad in the woods. That was the only good thing I could say about the miles and miles of dense forest that still covered much of hill country. When I came home, it surprised me that more hadn't been cleared, since real estate prices had soared in neighboring Dorset Hills and satellite communities like Clover Grove. Maybe I wasn't the only one who sensed the menace. Right now, I felt like Little Red Riding Hood, with no idea whether a wolf grandmother in a bonnet might greet me at the other end.

A snuffle of laughter slipped out. My own grandmother,

Gardenia Swingle, was a tough lady with a slightly wolflike demeanor, but she was a puppy dog underneath.

Keats circled back and poked my leg. The hackles on the back of his neck rose and fell, and then repeated the cycle, trying to make a decision. It was enough to make me pull out my phone.

"Hey, Jilly." I heard the expected clatter of utensils at her end. The kitchen was her happy place, just as the barn was mine. "Whatcha doing? Making a mess or cleaning it up?"

"Messing," she said. "My usual menus won't fit the bill for this so-called gentlemen's club. They'll want more red meat."

"Probably. You've got your favorite stew recipe." It happened to be a favorite of mine, too. I ate far less meat now that I'd come to love my cows, chickens and yes, even my feisty pig. Sometimes, I pretended meat was just tasty fuel. That was another lesson from Edna. Surviving an apocalypse wouldn't happen on chickpeas alone.

"I'm testing chili today," Jilly said, with the familiar clank of cast iron. Sometimes I caught her patting her favorite pot with the same fondness she showed Percy. "Always a crowd-pleaser."

"Awesome. Good thing I'm working up an appetite."

She clanked some more. "I noticed. There's a lot of puffing at your end and no thudding of the ax. Did the manure lure you back?"

"Not yet. We're on a little adventure."

The clanking slowed as her friendship navigation system recalibrated. "Adventure? That's a bold word on a cold day. What are you doing?"

"Just taking a walk in the woods. No biggie."

"You hate the woods."

"True." I stared around and then shrugged. "Marginally less in winter. Without leaves, it's a little brighter. Oh, look!"

"I can't look, unless you video me in. Which isn't a bad idea since you're out there alone."

"Never alone when you've got a cat, a dog and a wild dog." My voice trailed off a little at the end. Mostly on purpose but partly because I'd bent over to see the tracing of tiny paws in a sprinkle of snow. "There are all these sweet little footprints. Probably belong to mice."

"Ivy. I may be clattering and you may be chattering about mice, but I heard your reference to a wild dog."

"Exactly why I'm calling. I thought you'd want to know I was out on a jaunt with a wild dog."

Her exasperated laugh still qualified as amused. "Yes, that falls under the friendship code. Although when I signed on back in college, there was no wild dog clause."

"Let alone a reindeer or emu. That agreement needs an overhaul. Why don't we know a lawyer?"

"We should know a lawyer. Let's put that on the plan for this year."

"Along with reviving the Clover Grove Culture Revival Project. Maybe a lawyer would turn up for arty events. They've got cash to spare."

"So... back to the wild dog. I presume we're talking about the fox that's been lurking around. I doubt you'd take the pets any closer to a coyote or wolf."

"There used to be wolves around here, according to Buckley Brackens. Now even a fox is a rare sighting."

"It's the soaring crime rate," Jilly said. "Even the carnivores are moving down the range." She went back to clanging, satisfied that a fox wasn't much of a threat. "What's this guy doing?"

"I think it's a gal, actually. She's small and built like a ballerina. Probably young."

"Probably starving. Even a mild winter is hard on animals."

Black-tipped ears peeked over a stump as the fox waited for me. "She's in good shape. Plenty of mice to eat, judging by the tracks."

"Well, what does she want with you?"

I loved that Jilly understood and accepted that this fox did indeed want something from me. I'd suspected as much for a month but feared it had been as prosaic as eggs or the creators of them.

"Unclear, but she's led me onto the old Harlow property. Not sure who owns it now."

"Where Picasso took us? You walked through the swamp alone?"

"No, thank goodness, although it's frozen anyway. Veronica preferred to enter near the old dump." I shuddered. "You know. Where I found the evidence to convict Myrtle McCain."

"I hate that dump and I've never even seen it. And I assume Veronica is the vixen? That's a lot of syllables for a young fox."

"She looks like a Veronica. Suits a ballerina." I started forward again. "There were motors over this way earlier in the week but it was hard to hear over Charlie's chainsaw. Maybe it was snowmobiles and someone ended up falling into a bunker. Buckley says there are plenty of skeletons to be found."

"Buckley says too much," Jilly said. "There's no shutting him up at family dinners."

"The topics aren't as savory as your food, but he's an untapped source of intelligence about old crime. I was trying to tell Kellan that, but his head was full of new crime and then he was... well, gone."

"Kellan isn't gone in the way your tone suggests." Jilly sounded more confident in this familiar section of the friendship code. "He's on a business trip, that's all."

"Cops don't take business trips like corporate executives who go to Vegas and party too much. He's been deployed on a dangerous mission."

"You don't know that."

I plodded through a clearing with deeper snow, wishing I'd stopped to grab my go-kit, which held snowshoes, trekking poles, rope and other necessities for the daring farmer. "Kellan was probably hand-picked for his expertise in solving complicated crime."

Jilly was quiet for a moment. "They should have hired you, Keats and Percy, too. Kellan's record is extra stellar because of you."

"And you, my friend. We're a team. All of us."

The water started in the sink back home. "Then why am I here doing dishes when you're wandering in the bush?"

"I didn't think it was a—well, a security issue. Still don't. Looks like we've gotten where Veronica wanted to go."

"And where has this vixen dropped you off?"

I looked around the clearing. "It's a woodlot. Like my spot behind the barn, only huge, and with machines." Moving forward, I ran a work glove over the top of a long rack of neatly stacked firewood. "Wow, this is stunning."

"The woodlot?"

"Not the lot, per se, but the stacks of wood. I've spent days arranging mine and they're a mess compared to this. It's the work of a professional. Make that plural, since it probably happened fast." Keats moved forward and I followed. "The stacks are neat but otherwise the place is a disaster." Walking around the perimeter of the clearing, I stared at a swathe of stumps. "A lot of trees have died for some cause. I hope it's worthwhile."

"Maybe someone's planning to build there. It's been vacant a long time."

"I guess. That could be why Veronica's upset. They're clear-cutting her territory. Pushing her out, as well as other wildlife."

"It's a shame your dad didn't buy the land first. Asher said he was looking to spend some of his bunker fortune but the Harlow property wasn't available."

"He was? How come I'm always the last to know? Or is this a secret from the marital bed?"

She laughed. "Definitely not, since we rarely share one these days. I just figured Calvin had mentioned it because you two chat often enough."

"We chat about livestock and barn cats, mostly. Important stuff. Not trivialities like property acquisition."

"Well, from what I understand, he wants you to have room to expand. Plus keep riffraff out of the farm radius."

"Like a land moat surrounding a castle?"

"Exactly."

The fox strolled along a log and then hopped onto a picnic table. She used one black paw to knock a tin can off the top. There was litter on the ground below. Cardboard boxes from takeout joints in town. Seeing garbage strewn around annoyed me almost as much as it seemingly did Veronica.

"Pigs," I said.

"Pigs?" Jilly's voice had a note of alarm and the water shut off. Wild pigs were making a resurgence in hill country and we knew enough about their ferocity to be cautious.

"Of the human variety. They've left garbage all around. There's a tub from the fried chicken place. Bones like that can hurt wildlife."

"Want me to come and help clean it up?" Jilly was already on the move because I heard the jangle of keys. "Or is this something we should mention to Asher?"

"It's private property. I guess they have the right to do what they please."

Veronica left the picnic table and started walking on a pile of snow that had been cleared by a plow of some sort. She was light and there was enough of a crust that her paws barely broke through.

She tilted her head one way and then the other. Since there was nothing to see, she must be listening.

I was listening, too. Somewhere in the distance was the roar of a motor and it sounded like it was headed in my direction.

"Uh-oh," I said, backing away.

Veronica leapt in the air and dove into the drift. When she emerged, covered in snow, something small and limp hung from her jaws. She had caught an afternoon snack.

"What?" Jilly asked, as the fox scampered off with her prize.

"The fox left me holding the bag." I had to raise my voice over the ATV emerging from the bush. "There's a man driving this way and he doesn't look neighborly."

"Don't hang up," Jilly said. "I'm coming. I'll follow your trail."

"It'll be fine," I muttered, letting the phone drop to my side.

"That's what you always say." Her voice was tinny and faraway. "Is it ever true?"

# CHAPTER THREE

The ATV pulled up beside me before I had a chance to debate Jilly's point. I wanted to say that things usually worked out fine in the end. It was the middle we needed to worry about.

I was preoccupied by middles because the middle-aged man who jumped off the big ATV was decidedly portly. He was wearing a scowl and a red-and-black checked lumberjacket that didn't quite meet around his belly. I could see his blue plaid shirt in the gap and a gold medallion on a heavy chain. Aside from the medallion, he was the cliché of a woodsman, starting from his fur cap with flaps and ending with heavy work boots that looked brand new.

"Real fur," I muttered, touching Percy gently with my free hand. "Not our people."

He stomped over to me across a thin layer of snow. "What did you say?"

I pulled a human resources smile out of my mental closet. It had been a while since I used one and it felt like it didn't quite fit my face anymore. The ends of my mouth resisted and my upper lip refused to rise beyond half mast. That wasn't good. I depended on my HR armor to get around people like this fake lumberjack. When this was over—whatever this was—I'd have to go back to the smile gym and work out.

Clearing my throat, I focused on vocal modulation. Tone was going to mean a lot with a man like this, I suspected. "I was admiring your hat. Looks like raccoon."

He turned to flick the striped tail that dangled over his collar. "What was your first clue?"

Keats gave a snarky mumble at my side and my gloved fingers dropped to touch his head. The dog probably wasn't going to check my attitude but he still served to ground me. My lips cooperated as I applied more muscle to my smile. "It would have been perfect for a typical Clover Grove winter. This has been the mildest on record."

His eyes were so small I couldn't get a fix on the color as he stared at me. "Why are you standing here with a cat on your shoulder talking about the weather?"

I laughed. "You must be new in town. We always talk about the weather here. Even if there's something important to say, we package it in a weather sandwich. In farm country, nothing is more important than the weather."

He shrugged beefy shoulders. "It's winter. You dress for it. End of story."

Oh, it was just the beginning of the story. I could sense it. "As for the cat on my shoulder, everyone talks about Percy and me. More proof you're new to town."

"I've been around long enough to know it's best to mind my own business if there's any hope of other people minding theirs."

I shook my head gently, so as not to dislodge the cat. "There's somewhere close to zero chance of that happening, Mr. ...?"

"Croaker. Dawes Croaker. Owner of the property where you're currently trespassing."

"It's not trespassing when you're just out for a walk with your pets," I said. "At least, that's how most people think in hill country. You must be from the big city."

"And you must be from someplace where it's okay to pry into someone's business."

My smile was warming up to the task. "Actually, yeah. I was an HR manager for a big company before moving back here. Making small talk was part of my job."

"You call it small talk, I call it nosy. Since we've established there's no welcome mat, how about you get going, missy?"

"Missy? I've been called worse, I guess. My name is Ivy Galloway."

He blinked a few times and it looked like his mental processing chip was laboring as hard as my smile. "Oh, right. I should have known. You're the weirdo they warned me about."

I felt a vibration under my fingertips as Jilly growled into the phone. The lumberjack looked down, likely thinking it was Keats rather than my elegant best friend. "Yep, I'm probably that weirdo. Who sang my praises?"

He turned and walked away, head swiveling, as if assessing whether we'd done any damage.

"Read about you in the paper. The Clover Grove Prattler."

"Tattler." I couldn't help snickering. "But I like your version better."

He ran his fingers over the closest stack of wood. "The reporter sure has it in for you. Seems like there's an Ivy angle to everything."

"You're not wrong, and Justine Schalow conveniently forgets I've saved her life. Honestly, if I did half the things she says, I'd never get any work done."

"That's another reason you're unwelcome here. We don't need attention from your personal paparazzi. There are already people hassling us for clearing our own property. My wife and I want to build our dream home here."

"Nice," I said. "That's exactly what this land needs... a happy ending. Long ago, there was another couple whose love story—"

He slashed a glove at his throat to cut me off. "No time to chat, like I said. I'm expecting company."

Ignoring the dismissal, I examined a rack of firewood. "How do you get these lined up so straight? I'm new to woodpile management and no matter how I try, everything ends up crooked and eventually falls over."

He turned, brushed past me and grabbed a rifle from a compartment at the back of the ATV. "Move it, chatterbox."

"Mr. Croaker, there's absolutely no need for a rifle." I raised my voice so that Jilly would know what she was walking into. "We're neighbors."

His piggy eyes landed on me. "You've never heard the expression 'good rifles make good neighbors'?"

I backed away. "I believe the word is 'fences.'"

"Guess I'll need one of those, too, if you're going to come over and poke around. Something with a charge, to give you and your furry friends a little wake-up call."

I forced a light laugh. "I've got coffee for that, sir. Why so hostile?"

He stared around again and I got the sense that while I was a handy target, I wasn't his only worry. Sweat ran down his cheeks and he braced himself for a second on the ATV.

"It's just one thing after another. All I want to do is clear my land and build my wife a big house. She deserves that and more. But the plant people and animal people are on my back."

"Plant and animal people? What do you mean?"

He gestured with a big glove to keep my voice down. "The wild-flower society or some such foolishness. And the owl advocates. A man can't make a move on his own land without running it past tree-huggers these days."

"I didn't even know we had wildflower and bird enthusiasts in Clover Grove. But I did want to speak to you about something related." I gestured to the pile of garbage. "Cooked chicken bones splinter and could puncture an animal's guts. Maybe you could pick up a secure trash container."

He threw me a glare and then wiped his forehead with his checkered sleeve. "Now I have to run the trash past you? Forget it, lady. Get off my property."

I wasn't sure the change to "lady" was an upgrade or downgrade from "missy."

Just beyond the last rack of wood there was a flash of red. I hoped Dawes Croaker would miss it, but his head swiveled and the rifle came up.

"There it is! Been trying to shoot that thing for weeks." He shook off his glove, raised the gun quickly and pulled the trigger.

The booming sound made my ears ring but I held my ground. "Hey! Don't you dare shoot my fox!" My voice was shrill. "Thank goodness you missed her."

He took aim and fired again. The vixen flitted away, not seeming too fussed about it.

When he turned, the muzzle also turned until it was pointed in my face from uncomfortably close range. "Your fox?" he asked.

The gun barrel had an obvious wobble, as if the weapon was too heavy for the strapping man. He leaned against the ATV but kept the rifle trained on me.

"Veronica, yes. And I'd thank you to lower your gun." A squawk from my phone made him step back but the gun was still raised. "My friend Jilly is on the line and I may ask her to text my brother. He's a police officer and he hates it when people shoot at me. Especially when he's trying to sleep off a night shift."

The gun came down. "I did not shoot at anything."

"Your word against mine. Jilly heard it all."

"You bet I did." My friend shouted but my glove smothered most of it. "Get out of there, Ivy."

I backed away slowly, torn between keeping Percy and Keats safe and staying to watch over the fox. "Mr. Croaker, I'll be going, but if Veronica isn't home for dinner, you can expect a visit from the wildlife society."

He backed away, too. "Which is it? Pet or wildlife? Can't have it both ways."

Keats herded me out of the woodlot and I called back, "You're new, sir. I expect you'll see soon enough that the dividing line between tame and feral is mighty slim in Clover Grove."

## CHAPTER FOUR

E dna Evans normally wore fatigues but today she was in safari-style tan pants and a matching jacket. Her permed hair frizzed from under the edge of a puffy tan hat with earflaps, one of which she flipped up rather rakishly. A camera hung around her neck and binoculars stuck out of her pocket.

"Point me in the direction of the fox killer," she said. "I'm armed and ready for action."

I was glad only weapons of surveillance were visible. In a situation like this, it was best to disarm with charm, or failing that, guile.

Jilly had dressed to charm, with her best green wool coat that made her equally green eyes pop. Blonde curls cascaded onto her shoulders under a cute navy blue hat adorned with white knitted snowflakes and a big pom-pom.

I hadn't bothered changing for the return trip to the woodlot. Having already failed miserably with charm myself, backing Edna with guile was better done in overalls and a parka. Our fierce friend had hoped to roar in on her all-season ATV, but it didn't fit with her cover story. Instead, we trudged through the fields, with Keats in the lead, his tail cocked at an officious angle. Percy elected to ride back on my shoulder, although Jilly's arms were available to cradle him like a precious fur baby.

Generally, the cat rode with me for business and Jilly for recreation. I appreciated his discretion. His intelligence surpassed that of any feline I'd known.

"Did you hear the Harlow property had changed hands?" I asked, trying to keep up with Edna but eventually falling back into the trail she left. Though I was taller, she had a longer, powerful stride. Bigger feet, too, although she was as skilled on the dance floor as she was in the bush. An apocalyptic prepper apparently needed to be a chameleon these days. "There are a lot of trees down."

She shook her head. "I didn't, and that's unusual. Why can't that pesky reporter write about something useful for a change? The Tattler's turned into a rag."

"And Justine only likes to spotlight Ivy," Jilly said. "Last week she reported that a new goat joined Runaway Farm. Hardly news, unless you know the Rescue Mafia liberated the goat from an abusive owner. Thankfully, Justine doesn't."

The Mafia, a band of animal rescuers from neighboring Dorset Hills, more commonly known as Dog Town, regularly deposited livestock at my farm. Most critters stayed, but I suspected this goat would be rehomed since her pretty face had appeared in Justine's online periodical. Someone might recognize the goat and come to reclaim her. It was hard not to get attached to every animal in my care but I learned to hold something back with Mafia placements in case they really were temporary.

"I wish I could catch Justine trespassing," I said. "She's gotten more skillful at evading security feeds."

Jilly pushed her hat back and grinned. "Let's set a trap. Bait it with farm scandal. Then Asher can run out and lower the boom."

"I like the way you think, my friend. Let's do just that when this fox situation is resolved."

"Focus, girls." Edna picked up her pace even more, leaving us lagging. "We know this faux lumberjack has a rifle. And while that's not unusual here, if he missed the fox, he's an amateur. I'd rather deal with a good shot any day of the week. More predictable."

"I'd rather not deal with a gun-toting neighbor of any kind," I said. "I'm surprised you didn't notice the clear-cutting, Edna. Normally you don't miss much."

She flipped up her other earflap. "Been busy. I can't always hover at the window watching over your farm like a guardian angel."

More like a vulture, but there was no question her surveillance had helped me out of some tough situations. "Busy with the course that takes naïve seniors out in the bush in the dead of winter? I thought you parked SurvivalDare because it was too much work."

"I parked my course because your fiancé put himself on my board of directors, when there's only one director. Me."

"Ah, I see. When the chief's away, the mice will play."

She puffed out a dismissive sound. "My students are far from naïve and by the time we start field training, they're extremely prepared. That's the point of a preparedness course, after all. The experiential part is just a reward at the end."

Jilly was yards behind now so she had to raise her voice. "Thank goodness my gran can only join online. It would worry me sick to think she's out in the bush freezing."

"Let it worry you sick she's trapped in a gated community like a caged wolf," Edna said. "Bridie Brighton is not the mild-mannered sheep you think you know." She stared around and pointed at a fresh stump. "It's common to clear deadwood in winter around here. Most folks mark their trees in early fall and do the heavy work when the leaves are down. I had an arborist in myself for a few days."

The smirk she tossed over her shoulder told me she'd cleared even more trees to guarantee an unobstructed view of Runaway Farm. That used to annoy me but now it was reassuring. Whether there was trouble with an animal or someone was accosting me personally, Edna was usually the first to arrive.

"This wasn't a little pruning," I said. "There's hardly a stick left in a large tract of land. No house—no matter how big the dream—requires that many trees to die."

Edna finally slowed and waited for us. "How do you want me to play this? Naughty or nice?"

"Haughty with spice," I said. "The birding folks have been giving them trouble, so the naturalist society should, too."

She pulled down her earflaps as the breeze picked up. "Must be a new club. There have been iterations of birding groups over the years but the last one exploded in fuss and feathers over who was the first to see a rare warbler. I thought the members aged out and died. Ambling around taking pictures won't fend off the grim reaper. Only hard training can do that."

Keats gave a ha-ha-ha from my side. The very mention of the grim reaper made me cringe. That had been the much-loathed title my former boss, Wilf Darby, assigned me for my skill with downsizing staff. How ironic that the reaper cut Wilf down in his prime at my farm. Hopefully the nickname he gave me died with him, because I was all about a growth mindset now. My passion was fertilizer, after all.

Jilly stepped in to help Edna firm up her game plan. "From what I overheard of the conversation with Mr. Croaker, he cared about public opinion and was worried about privacy. If you're high-handed about the risk to wildlife and throw in the mayor's name, he'll probably stand down on shooting animals."

"I bet he doesn't have the right permits for the work he's doing." Edna moved forward again. "He'll likely want to avoid formal complaints. I'll be sure to work that angle."

I sent Keats to circle around and keep her with us. "Sounds good, but remember to let Jilly try her charm first. He's one of our closest neighbors and I'd prefer to be on good terms."

Jilly jerked her head toward her backpack. "That's why I

brought jars of chili and stew. Not the usual housewarming gift, but there isn't a house yet and it seemed appropriate for a lumberjack."

"Faux lumberjack," I corrected. "There was a price tag hanging off his collar. It wasn't from Norland's Hardware but a high-end men's clothing store in Dorset Hills."

"He must have money if he's planning to run water and power out here, and build a palace," Edna said. "We don't get many like that. Folks with coin tend to settle in Dorset Hills. And the homesteaders who'd like to live in the woods can't afford to build or get the zoning committee onside."

I blew out a breath and watched it float away. It was only four o'clock but the sun was already behind the trees. Darkness fell early in the bush. "There was something fishy about the operation. Everything was new except the old tractor thing. Who buys all that equipment just to clear space for a house?"

"You don't," Edna said. "You hire contractors, unless you plan to keep on clearing and earn enough from quality wood to pay for the machinery. It doesn't come cheap."

"Exactly. There's more to the story and I sure hope Edna Evans, head of the Clover Grove Naturalist Society, can find out."

"Ivy, you think too small." She held out her phone. "Take a look. I formed the *Hill Country* Naturalist Society the minute you called. There's a webpage already, with a photo of your fox on it."

I stared at the screen. "Veronica?"

"Whatever you call her. She was posing on your woodpile one morning, so I took her up on the offer. Nice portrait, too."

"Sounds like everyone had seen her except Jilly and me, until today."

"Foxes always have an agenda," Edna said. "Nature of the beast."

"We'd better figure out what that agenda is before she gets herself shot."

Jilly's gloved index finger pointed off to the left. "There she is. Maybe she'll make this easy on us."

The vixen stood on top of the tallest woodpile, sunlight glinting off her burnished fur. It was hard to look away.

At least, it was for me. Edna's eyes had dropped to Keats. "Look sharp, girls. We got trouble."

The dog had gone into a point. His tail was up and bristling, but he wasn't looking directly at the fox.

"Not good," I said, as he grumbled a warning, echoed by Percy in a higher pitch at my ear. "Maybe Mr. Croaker has a gun trained on us."

Edna shook her head. "I'd sense that. Prepper's intuition."

"Happens that often?" Jilly whispered.

"Often enough to know. And I don't feel in imminent peril. Other than from the looming apocalypse, which is business as usual."

We proceeded with more caution. Keats tried to take the lead and I called him back. I didn't want Dawes Croaker refining his gun skills on my dog.

When we finally walked into the woodlot, everything looked pretty much as it had two hours ago.

Except for one thing.

"The old tractor has moved," I said. "It was parked on the other side of the clearing."

Edna pulled out her binoculars and took a look. "At least he followed regulation and left the blade down. So many fools don't." She lowered the binoculars, rubbed her eyes, and lifted them again. "Looks like your new neighbor left his jacket behind. Maybe I'll collect it for the bunker clothing bank. High-end outerwear will be priceless after the end times."

Percy jumped down from my shoulder and started leading us over a mix of dirt and light snow toward the tractor sitting among the stumps.

"Why would he leave his jacket on his tractor?" Jilly was walking so close to me I felt a shiver run through her. "It may be a mild winter, but it's still January."

"That's not a tractor," Edna said, as we got closer. "It's called a cable skidder. Built to winch logs out of muddy, swampy areas."

There was a blade at one end and a short cranelike contraption at the other. Chains covered its large wheels. "You mean it's a fancy tractor," I said.

At first I couldn't see Mr. Croaker's lumberjacket, but Keats guided us around the front of the machine. It looked like the cheery fabric had been caught under the blade.

Percy was already there, giving elaborate sweeps of his paw over the sleeve of the red-and-black checkered coat. Perhaps it was too late for the jacket. Had it been ruined already?

The cat stretched to make a pass over a work glove lying a few inches away and then looked up at us with gleaming green eyes to make sure we noticed what *he* noticed.

If the collective intake of breath was any indication, we all did.

Sticking out of the coat's cuff was a bare white hand curved in a claw.

# CHAPTER FIVE

J illy made the call, as usual. It was kind that she spared me the unpleasant task, since Bunhead Betty, the police receptionist who dined on gossip—especially gossip about me—wouldn't get to hear it straight from the farmer's mouth. No doubt she'd still quote me directly, possibly even to Justine Schalow. Some of the news stories in the Tattler had colorful detail that may have come straight from Betty's lips. The receptionist had never quite gotten over my appearing in front of her desk carrying someone's femur. "Brandishing a bloody bone," according to her account of the tale, when in fact the femur in question was old, dry and sticking out of my bag.

Still, I could see how it came as a shock. Not the first deadly care package I'd delivered to police and apparently not the last. The only good news was that Kellan was away and didn't have to deal with the current situation, which had once again put me in the wrong place at the wrong time. It wasn't my fault.

Or was it? My eyes fixed on the slender red fox, still visible in the shadow at the edge of the remaining trees. Edna was directing a flashlight around the dimming clearing and I saw the glint of amber eyes before Veronica retreated. If she had led me here purposely to save Dawes Croaker, I had failed her. And failed him even more.

Edna jabbed my shoulder. "Don't stand there reminiscing about past crimes. We've got work to do on the present one."

I turned away from the fox just as her white tail tip vanished. "We don't know it was a crime. It looks like Mr. Croaker died by his own blade, as it were."

She smirked at my turn of phrase. "Good one. But unless he could be in two places at once, that's impossible. Someone needed to be in the driver's seat to pull the lever. It's run by hydraulics."

Jilly finished her call in time to hear that. "Maybe it was a malfunction. That machine is as old as the hills."

"Hardly." Edna gave her a withering glance. "I'm as old as the hills and I know a good cable skidder can rival me for stamina. The color and model tell me this one hails from the sixties." She held up her hand. "Before you ask, I know because I treated a few loggers when I was a traveling nurse. One told me more than I wanted to hear about equipment following a worksite incident."

"But it could have been a malfunction," Jilly persisted. "I mean, why would Mr. Croaker get anywhere near that blade if the machine was running?"

We all moved away from the skidder and turned our backs on the fallen man. There was no need to add to the deep reservoir of trauma we all had from witnessing other crime scenes. Only Keats and Percy kept moving.

"Maybe this Dawes was looking at something in the soil," Edna said. "Such as it is. The ground should be frozen and digging slow progress. Strange time to start construction."

"I wondered about that myself." I glanced around for Keats and found both animals exploring the area. Finally, the dog caught my eye with his blue one and went into a point about five yards from the body.

Walking over, I knelt beside him. Half-buried in light snow was a gold medallion. The severed chain lay a few feet away. It would have taken a struggle to break links that heavy.

Hearing sirens in the distance, I pulled out my phone to snap a few photos. "If only I could get a better look without disturbing the evid—"

Before I could finish the word, an orange paw took care of the problem. The snow and dirt shifted to give me a good view of the piece.

"Oh, Percy," I said, pushing myself upright. "You're terrible. And also amazing."

Jilly leaned over to look at the medallion, too. "He left claw marks. The police are going to know."

I took another photo of the chain. "Yeah. Nothing like getting off on the right paw with the new chief. But I do come well recommended."

Edna and Jilly both snorted and I turned in time to see four streams of steam coming from their nostrils.

"If this new fella were the type to heed recommendations, your brother wouldn't be ticketing speeders," Edna said. "We'll likely need to take the substitute chief down a peg."

"Edna!" Jilly heaved off her backpack, made a move to set it down and then reconsidered. "There will be no hazing of the new chief."

"Acting chief," I reminded her. "The position has a full-time occupant."

My best friend gave up and slipped her arms through the straps of the backpack again. "Currently held by someone with power over my husband. Asher has been so bummed about this and night shifts are taking a toll."

"Jilly's right, Edna. We need to look out for Ash." I took the backpack and shouldered it myself. I was used to carrying heavy loads now. In fact, I packed more onto my back than any animal on the farm. If the donkey thugs were more obliging, I'd consider training one to help on missions.

Keats gave a pant-laugh, perhaps knowing I'd end up trampled, like Dawes Croaker.

"We need to look out for Kellan's reputation, too," Jilly said, although I could barely hear her over the noise.

ATVs rolled ahead of the police SUVs over a rough-hewn road that undulated among hills and stumps. It was pocked with rocks and deep, semi-frozen mud puddles.

The uniformed men on ATVs hopped off but waited at a discreet distance, muttering among themselves. Their eyes flicked to me a few times and my face got a little warm for a chilly evening. For all I knew, Kellan's staff might already be texting him about his lady's latest quandary.

I didn't have much time to worry about it as the first police vehicle pulled up quite close to us. Closer than Kellan would normally get to a crime scene. So close, in fact, that we had to move out of the way or risk getting whacked by the driver's door.

A man I didn't recognize got out and walked over to the cable skidder without bothering to acknowledge us. He signaled to his staff and quietly issued orders. The truck that pulled up last disgorged the main investigative team and their equipment. A cop carrying one of the big lights gave me a smile, but the rest looked away as they passed. Maybe they had orders to freeze me out, but it still hurt. I knew these people well from both crime scenes and police socials.

Keats came back from his own investigation and offered his ears to my fingertips. Shaking off my glove, I went for the full sensory experience. There was nothing in my world quite so comforting as my dog's ears.

A thump midback, followed by pinpricks that pierced my down parka, put the lie to that thought. A purring cat head-butting my cheek was the epitome of comfort, too.

And that wasn't all. Jilly and Edna had clearly picked up on the crime scene vibe because they moved in on either side of me. Jilly looped her arm through mine, squishing Keats slightly, but he didn't complain. On the contrary, he mumbled something insolent, likely directed at the substitute chief as he turned to us.

"Miss Galloway, I presume. I've heard about you."

Edna took issue with his tone, although there was nothing overtly hostile about it. "No doubt, young man. She's in the news often. Justine Schalow from the Tattler has an unhealthy obsession with Ivy."

He stared at Edna. It probably wasn't easy to intimidate this man, but the way he scanned my senior friend suggested he hadn't seen anyone quite like her. There wasn't anyone quite like her—and she wasn't even wearing camouflage.

Before Edna could say anything more, I held out my hand to the chief. "We haven't met, sir. Yes, I'm Ivy Galloway and I presume you're Dixon Skowby."

"Chief Skowby," he corrected. Ignoring my hand, he gestured to the two men who'd come up on either side of him. "This is my deputy chief, Tye Fenway. And Officer Joel Gibbons."

Fenway and Gibbons shook my hand and each found a smile. They were new, so I had to assume Skowby had brought his own staff to back him in his role. I supposed that wasn't unusual, although we'd never had a deputy chief in Clover Grove. What *was* unusual was how similar the three men looked. All had sandy hair with hazel eyes, at least from what the limited light showed. Dixon Skowby was the tallest, then Fenway and finally Gibbons. It reminded me of my sisters, so alike we resembled stackable Russian nesting dolls. Had Skowby intentionally hired replicas? It would speak volumes about his ego.

Some women would find Skowby attractive, but his nose and chin were sharp and his air of superiority off-putting. I persisted with my hand, and he finally gave it a single listless pump with a Gore-Tex glove. My bare fingers dropped again to Keats' ears for a warmer reception.

Chief Skowby had established a boundary without saying much

of anything. It was a skill I admired while working in HR, and one I shared in those days. A serious concussion had eroded that ability, however, and I didn't really mind. A lack of boundaries might be why I understood my animals so well. The membrane between us was practically permeable.

He flicked his fingers. "I'd thank you to move back a few yards. We need a clear radius to investigate."

His car was parked within the normal radius, but it was his right to break with protocol. The thought made me smile. When I first came home, I had teased Kellan about writing a crime scene etiquette guide for civilians like me.

"What's so amusing, Miss Galloway?" the chief asked. "According to your friend's phone call, a man experienced a fatal accident here." He glanced at his staff and got a bunch of nods. "Did you even try to revive him?"

Edna took a step forward. "Young man, I'm a retired nurse with field training and this man was at least an hour past reviving when we arrived."

"You're so sure you didn't bother trying?"

My prepper friend took another step toward him and while he didn't back up, he leaned slightly away. It was a win and Edna smelled it. "I hope you're not suggesting dereliction of civic duty, Mr. Skowby."

"Chief Skowby. Or 'sir,' if you prefer." There wasn't room to offer his hand, even if he wanted to, and I doubted he did. "I've heard about you, too, Miss Evans."

"Then you know I'm an upstanding member of this community who'd never neglect a patient. Make no mistake, Mr. Croaker had already shuffled off this mortal coil."

Jilly pulled Edna back. "I'm sure Chief Skowby appreciates that we discovered this tragic situation and promptly drew it to the attention of the authorities." She directed her brightest smile at him. "I'm Jilly Galloway, by the way. Officer Galloway's wife."

She didn't use her married name often and when she did, it was strategic. But her fetching smile earned something resembling a smirk. "I know your husband, of course. He's keeping our highways safe."

Now Jilly bristled and I pulled her closer. Percy stepped onto her shoulder, judging her more in need of his services, no doubt.

"Let me elaborate on what Jilly said on the phone, sir," I began. "While I was out walking my pets, I ended up here, where I met Mr. Croaker. He accused me of trespassing—"

"Because you were trespassing," the chief interrupted. "As is your habit."

Keats mumbled something intended to be calming. The new chief was coming on a little strong, but I'd have to play along so it didn't blow back on Kellan.

"Dog-walking in the woods is pretty normal here and there are no fences. This land hasn't been occupied in decades."

"Go on. What happened when you arrived on Mr. Croaker's property?"

"I introduced myself and tried to be neighborly. He asked me to leave, and I did."

He crossed his arms. "As simple as that?"

"Well, not quite. Somewhere between hello and goodbye, he shot at a fox of my acquaintance and then directed his rifle at me."

"A fox of your acquaintance?" He tilted his head and his top team of two men fought grins. "Is it a pet?"

"No, sir. I run a hobby farm, so my hens would object. But a fox was no threat here, so I stated my objection to the shooting."

Jilly jumped in to redirect the conversation. "I was on the phone with Ivy the whole time she was here. Mr. Croaker was already quite agitated." She swept her hand around and Percy took the opportunity to jump down and sit between her feet. "People have been hassling him about all this."

"All this?" Chief Skowby seemed perplexed.

"The clear-cutting," I said. "Advocates for plants and animals have given him a hard time about the impact on the environment."

"A concern I share," Edna said. "So I came back with Ivy and Jilly to speak to Mr. Croaker about sparing wildlife in general and the fox in particular. Vulpines have an important niche to fill in controlling rodents."

He took off his hat and rubbed a gloved hand through very short hair. I had the sense he kept it that way to avoid a hint of personality, but it probably helped reduce static, too. "Are you saying Mr. Croaker was so upset by the hubbub he stumbled in front of his own machine?"

"Perhaps," Edna said. "It's hard to say exactly why he was on the ground. What I do know is that someone deliberately released the blade, which comes down with hundreds of pounds of force. A swift end, at least. And then they took the key."

"He may have been dead already," I said. "If you look over there, you'll find a broken chain and a medallion. Mr. Croaker was wearing it when I met him so I'm guessing he got in a fight."

"No signs of dragging, though," Jilly said. "He walked over on his own."

I nodded. "True. He must not have understood how the machine worked, either, or he wouldn't have trusted someone behind the controls while he poked around."

Chief Skowby cleared his throat. "Excuse me. Are you done?"

Edna gave him a cheerful smile. "As done as we can be for the moment. Take it from here, young man. We've given you a head start."

"Chief?" Fenway looked perplexed. "This speculation is... unconventional."

Skowby ran his hand over his hair again and then pulled his hat back on. "Most definitely, but I was curious about where it would go. I heard Harper ran a lax operation but I had to see it with my own eyes to believe it. I take it they walked all over the site with those animals?"

"They did," Gibbons said. "Footprints, paw prints, scratches and a clump of orange fur. Just on first glance."

Fabulous. We'd walked into a trap designed to make Kellan look bad in front of his former staff and perhaps beyond. Skowby was smart enough not to badmouth him without proof and now we'd given it to him. Shame whooshed from my heart and traveled through me in a hot wave.

"I see what you're doing, Dixon," Edna said. "We were sharing our observations with the best of intentions. If you want to twist that for your own gain, go right ahead."

"Edna, we should leave the chief to do his job," Jilly said.

"Acting chief." Edna directed a smirk his way. "Substitutes always need to prove themselves."

"Miss Evans, this chief requires neither collaboration, nor speculation," he said. "I'll run a textbook investigation and draw conclusions based on evidence. What you've left of it, anyway."

"I'm sorry we walked across the crime scene, sir," I said. "We were flustered."

"If it is a crime scene—" he began.

"It is," Edna interrupted. "Feel free to call me when you need my help."

"I won't." His tone was terse.

"Don't be hasty. I'm willing to wager none of you knows how to run a cable skidder and I do."

"That's what Google is for," Gibbons muttered.

Edna gave him a scornful glare. "More power to you then. The grieving widow will be glad to have googlers at the helm."

Chief Skowby's lips pressed together in a thin line and his eyes closed for a second, too. I wanted to turn and run before the hailstorm of righteous indignation struck. Instead, I took a deep breath and held my ground. We had stomped around his turf and he wasn't the first chief to take issue with that. At the rate we were going, we'd be blackballed in every town throughout hill country.

Keats gave a ha-ha-ha, and that's when the chief's eyes popped open.

"Miss Galloway, you and your friends and your pets will leave this property immediately. If you return, I will have you arrested."

"For what? Trespassing?" I tried to call up an HR smile and failed. "If so, you'll be a busy man because it's common practice here."

"Stop babbling before you say something foolish." Skowby glanced over at the cable skidder again. "I hope Miss Evans isn't the only one capable of operating that tractor. For her sake. And yours."

The veiled accusation caused a ripple of energy through Kellan's staff. They'd always been extremely loyal to him. He was a good boss and an inspiring leader. But he was also gone and there was no telling when he'd return. Dixon Skowby was piloting the ship now.

"Cable skidder," Edna said, breaking the silence. "You'd best remember that if you want to look it up online, young man."

"Just go," he said. "Before I stop being so nice."

## CHAPTER SIX

K eats gave a low growl I was confident only I could hear, because it was more of a vibration under my fingertips. Jilly tugged at my sleeve but my boots wouldn't budge. I desperately wanted to find a way to dispel the new chief's ire before he made waves for Kellan. This was a huge overreaction on Skowby's part but he was obviously trying to prove something to his officers. That worried me more than anything. If he cared that much about their attitude, maybe he was planning to stay awhile and knew more than I did about Kellan's posting. Or maybe he was bucking for a promotion in another jurisdiction and wanted to make a big impression in a short time. Either way, his fierce expression told me he wasn't going to back down. Someone had to make peace, and that was me. Surprisingly, Edna was the quickest to retreat but also the loudest, muttering insults under her breath. All I caught was "impudent upstart."

Jilly followed Edna but turned back suddenly. "Percy? Come!"

The cat had been sitting near our feet but was no longer in view.

Chief Skowby lurched forward suddenly and I knew before seeing the fluffy orange evidence that Percy was also trying to make a big impression. The chief spun and sure enough, the cat dangled between his shoulder blades, just out of reach. Percy was a master at finding that precise location on anyone. Hands and harsh words flew, but when that didn't work, the chief spun again on the spot. Once, twice, three times. He seriously underestimated my cat. Percy had basically swung on a trapeze while clutching a man's face before. Today was child's play. Or kitten's play.

The game sent a grin racing around the circle of Kellan's officers, although most tried to hide it. Some even looked down at the body to regain their composure. Even Skowby's special task force of two fought smiles.

When the spinning stopped, Chief Skowby gave me a furious glare. "Get this thing off me before I have him euthanized for assaulting an officer of the law."

"Let me," Jilly said, but someone beat her to it.

There was a rush of air as my brother hurtled toward the chief. "Sorry, boss, sorry. I got this," Asher said, slowing on his approach. Percy disengaged and launched himself from the chief to Asher. After landing lightly on my brother's shoulder, the cat gave him a few head butts. His fondness for Asher was surpassed only by his adoration of Jilly.

"Officer Galloway, what brings you here?" Chief Skowby said, brushing his shoulders and sleeves. "Your shift starts in"—he made a show of checking his watch—"under an hour."

Percy crossed from shoulder to shoulder across Asher's face. Normally he took the back route but he was obviously determined to keep the party going. Smiles flitted through my brother's comrades and this time they were more relaxed. Ash was the most popular cop on the force among colleagues and civilians. His natural effervescence had subsided somewhat of late, probably because he wanted to be taken more seriously, but you couldn't take the charm out of Asher and the sheepish grin he gave the chief now proved it.

"I'll clock in on time, sir. I was worried about my wife." A quick frown in my direction left no doubt he blamed me for getting Jilly into this situation. "And my sister."

"What about me?" Edna said. "We were always so close."

Asher shook his head a little too hard. "Miss Evans and I are not close. Not at all."

"Now, now, Asher," Edna said. "Is that any way to speak of a bridesmaid at your wedding? And the godmother of your unborn child?"

"Unborn child!" Asher turned quickly to Jilly. "Did I miss something?"

Jilly smothered a grin with her glove. "I'd have texted, at least."

"It's a good thing you're here now," Edna continued. "Because your boss seems to be laboring under the impression we run around assaulting people."

"You do assault people, Miss Evans," the chief said. "I've seen your record."

She chuckled. "Not while running, or at least, not often. Young as I look, I'm still in my eighties."

Both men ignored that and Asher moved closer to his boss. Percy prepared to make his ascent to my brother's head. The cat loved that move, made far easier by winter hats. Asher tried to intervene but when Percy made up his mind, nothing could stop him.

Well, nothing except Jilly, who ran forward now to start detaching the cat from my brother's woolen cap, claw by claw. "Do not make a laughingstock of my husband, Percy."

"Too late for that," Chief Skowby said, glancing around at the staff. Evidently he missed the subtle difference in their expressions. They were laughing *with* Asher, not at him. "Miss Galloway, I asked you to leave, did I not?"

"You did, sir. You also threatened to throw me in jail and euthanize my cat."

Asher's eyes widened. "Chief?"

"Your sister was obstructing justice with her friends."

Someone in the rank and file caught Asher's eye and gave a slight shake of the head.

"I'm sure she wasn't doing that," my brother said. "Right, Ivy?"

"On the contrary. We were offering helpful advice to the chief, after which he suggested we might have murdered Mr. Dawes Croaker."

"Croaker?" My brother's voice got a little tight and I hoped he wouldn't succumb to laughter that would only irk his boss more. "I don't know anyone by that name."

"Guess you never will," Edna said. She was enjoying this far too much. "The poor man is no more."

"Edna," I said. "Respect, please."

Chief Skowby turned to us again. "And yet you're still here. Respect, please."

Asher managed to dislodge Percy from his head and handed him to Jilly. "Better go home, honey. I'll check in on you soon."

"You'll accompany them, Officer Galloway. Then get on with your highway shift."

"Highway patrol?" Asher was incredulous. "My investigative skills are excellent, sir. Check my record. You need me here."

"The highway needs you more. I hear you're a real hero out there. Your record is full of commendations for your rescues. Now get out there and keep those roads safe." Skowby's lips twitched just enough to make Keats growl again. "That's an order."

Asher joined us reluctantly, looking as bereft as when Huckleberry Marsh swallowed his cherished Superman figurine. That was a bind even the man of steel couldn't escape. And my brother couldn't escape this one, either. He was being sidelined by his new boss, either because of his association with Kellan, me or both. The knot in my stomach tightened as I considered the collateral damage my exploits cost.

I muttered an apology but I doubt it reached Asher's ears

because the big police lights showed a couple of Land Rovers coming up the road.

"What now?" Chief Skowby grumbled, as the two vehicles pulled up and five men jumped out. "This is turning into a circus."

A man of about fifty, with silver hair peeking out from his dark cap, walked over and stuck out his hand to the chief and I couldn't help but notice he got more than a cursory pump. "Fleet Jurgen," he said. "Crew chief for this operation." He scanned the clearing. "I have a meeting with Dawes Croaker."

"A meeting now?" The chief looked skeptical. "It's nearly dark."

"We just arrived in town and want to get our marching orders," Fleet said. "Serious logging starts tomorrow at o-seven hundred."

"New marching orders," the chief said. "You're on hiatus till further notice."

"Hiatus?" Fleet sounded incredulous. "Dawes brought us in from Orono County. It's a long drive."

"He couldn't find loggers closer to home?"

"Not like my team. We're freelance forestry experts. Travel all over the state."

Fleet glanced back at his men, all of them younger, taller and reasonably handsome. Two were dark, one fair and the last a redhead. They had nicely trimmed beards and would have fit the stereotype of a woodsman perfectly, had they worn lumber jackets. Instead, they were in regular parkas. The redhead looked over and gave me a smile. I returned it, but kept it at HR level, in case he got the wrong idea. I was a happily engaged woman, but I had sisters who weren't.

Chief Skowby considered his words. "Hmm. Well, your meeting's been canceled. Mr. Croaker is—uh—"

"Indisposed," I said. The word was out of my mouth before I could stop it.

"Permanently," Edna added.

Fleet was understandably perplexed. "Why didn't he cancel

before we drove all this way? We booked accommodation for the week at a local motel called Runaway Farm."

"It's an inn," Jilly said. "A luxurious one at that. But we look forward to welcoming you." She introduced herself and then me. "We're your innkeepers. And I suppose you're the mysterious 'men's club' who paid in full."

The redheaded lumberjack laughed. "That's just a joke but we're a fun crew. You'll see."

He caught my eye again and this time his smile really was a few degrees too warm. The snow was probably melting around him.

I slipped off my left glove and rubbed my cheek, hoping the diamond ring would catch his eye. No point getting off on the wrong foot. He probably left broken hearts after every clear-cut. On reflection, I hoped he'd spare my sisters.

Asher must have picked up on the vibe because he dropped his arm over Jilly's shoulder and pulled her close.

Gesturing to the Land Rovers, the chief said, "You might as well retire for the evening and I'll speak to you tomorrow." He sent a sneer my way. "Mr. Croaker is not indisposed, but dead."

"Dead! How? I spoke to him a few hours ago from the road." Fleet swept off his hat and ran his fingers through abundant hair. There were plenty of women around who'd like to charm him, too. Starting with my mother, unfortunately.

"A site accident," the chief said. "I'm sure you're no stranger to those."

"I run a very tight ship. Never lost a finger, let alone a man." Fleet sighed. "I told Dawes to leave everything to us but he was in a hurry. Speed is the enemy of safety, and I suppose he learned that for himself." His blue eyes traveled the clearing and landed on the group around the skidder. "I guess we know what happened."

"We know what happened but not how and why," the chief said. "I'll make haste to find out. You'll need to stick around Clover Grove until we do."

"Why? There's no work for us."

"And an inn is no place for a men's club," Asher said, pulling Jilly even closer. "The Have a Nap Motel might be a better fit. There's a casino over in Brenton, too."

"They'll stay at Runaway Farm until further notice," Chief Skowby said, flicking an index finger at Asher. "Under your watch, Officer Galloway. When you're not keeping our roads safe."

"We're happy to host you," Jilly said. "Wait till you see my—"

Asher released Jilly suddenly and walked over to the men. "I'll drive you back. My wife rides shotgun."

All the woodsmen grinned, except Fleet Jurgen.

Keats gave a pant-laugh, too. This day had been too dull by half for my ambitious dog before we met Veronica, who was currently standing on a rock beyond the circle of light. I could see her outline, without much definition. Now life had become everything a sheepdog Sherlock could wish for, with the exception of a good man in the lead.

It was almost as if Chief Skowby read my mind, because as I walked to Asher's truck, he called after me, "I run a very tight ship, too. Understood, Miss Galloway?"

"Of course," I said. "We'll make sure our guests enjoy every second of their stay in Clover Grove."

"That's not what I—"

Keats gave a sharp bark to drown him out and earned a good scratch behind the ears. The occasion called for insolence, but only one of us was free to deliver.

# CHAPTER SEVEN

I grabbed the phone on the first ring. "Hi!" Putting it on speaker, I set it on a stack of logs and went back to working out my frustrations. "Great to hear your voice," I added, between puffs of steam. "Miss you."

"Miss you, too," Kellan said. "What on earth are you doing? It sounds like an ax-throwing contest."

"You're not far off." Except that he was, quite literally. Too far off for my liking. "Just chopping some wood."

"Ivy, it's past ten your time. Hardly the hour to wield an ax. You could lose a foot."

I held the ax over my head. "My time? You're in an entirely different time zone? I thought you were just down the range."

"I was. At first. They sent me on some out-of-state research. Just for a week or two. I'll be back before you know it."

The ax came down with a little more force than needed and sent split wood flying. "Out of state? Does this case have any relevance to Clover Grove at all?"

"That remains to be seen. But even if I knew—"

"You couldn't tell me. I know." I set another log upright on the stump. "I don't understand why they sent you instead of this Skowby guy. He's. A. Jerk." I punctuated my words with thunks of the ax.

"Maybe so, but not because he asked you to stay away from a case he's investigating."

I rested the ax and leaned on it. "You took Asher's call and not mine?"

"Business over pleasure," he said. "Sorry. Now I'm calling to see how my fiancée is holding up."

"I'm chopping wood at bedtime. That should give you an idea."

He paused, perhaps considering the best way to handle me. "Ivy, every chief has his own style. I happen to be more relaxed than many. And you know I'm never okay with you tampering with potential evidence."

"I didn't." Thunk. Thunk. "Percy did."

"The pets are an extension of you, and obviously Skowby knows that. There's plenty of information available about your amateur sleuthing, thanks to a certain reporter."

I kicked split wood aside. "Guy doesn't even know how to operate a cable skidder."

Kellan laughed. "I don't know how to operate a cable skidder. That's not covered in chief school."

"Well, he didn't suspect it was a murder till Edna explained. And then he had the gall to suggest we had something to do with it."

"Ash said you had words with the deceased. Over a fox, as I understand it."

I raised the ax again. "Dawes Croaker tried to kill Veronica. Before he was deceased."

"I don't believe I've met Veronica." There was a smile in his voice. "Tell me more."

He was handling me and I decided to go along with it. I was angry at the situation, not Kellan after all. I wanted him here with me, running the investigation and letting us help him. Or at least not stopping us from contributing in our unique way.

"She's a young vixen who's been hanging around the farm since Christmas. Today she introduced herself and invited me to take a walk over to the former Harlow property, where a faux lumberjack tried to shoot her."

"That was uncalled for. What provoked him?"

"He said she was eating the trash he left behind. Leaving food scraps is a free pass for wildlife."

"So then you told him where to go?" He was smiling again. I could tell.

"I may have raised objections, yes. Nothing that justified getting the muzzle of a rifle stuck in my face."

Kellan sighed. "There's almost never a justification for sticking a gun in someone's face. But when you knew his temperament, mightn't it have been better to have the discussion later?"

"I cut it short and came back with reinforcements. That's when we found he'd been murdered."

"No one's confirmed it's a murder, remember."

Keats gave a saucy mumble. He had been keeping a safe distance from the flying wood but wanted to weigh in on the conversation. Percy added a meow from the woodpile.

"There's your confirmation," I said, shifting to stacking wood. "That blade didn't just drop itself. Percy and Keats called it."

"Maybe they're wrong. It's bound to happen sometimes."

Keats dove in and nipped my calf. "Ow! Keats, I will not be proxy. Save the fangs for the man calling your genius into question."

Kellan laughed again. "There is one benefit to being away. You get the bites. But I still miss the kisses."

"Yeah, me too. I wish you were here. Skowby scolded me like a child in front of all your staff. They don't like him, you know."

"I know. Asher keeps me in the loop, obviously."

Still stacking logs, I smiled. "Did he tell you about Percy? Scaling Mount Skowby? Took the guy down a peg."

There was another pause and I pictured him fighting a laugh at the expense of his counterpart. "Not a great idea with a guy like Skowby." He raised his voice. "I know you can hear me, Percy."

"I thought you'd never met him. Skowby, that is."

"I haven't. Don't know much about him, either. His second-in-command seemed like a decent guy, though. Tye Fenway. Met him at a retirement party for a cop near Thistledown a while back."

"Skowby brought reinforcements and they're edging out your staff. Aren't you worried?"

"About their loyalty? No. They're professionals and they'll do their job."

I shoved logs into spots too small for them, causing a ripple through the woodpile. If I wasn't careful, the whole structure would collapse. It was all about balance. "Skowby's trying to prove something, Kellan. Maybe he's after your job."

"No one wants my job. Sometimes *I* don't want my job. It's tiring and thankless. I've paid my dues and could move on, if I wanted. That's probably what Skowby wants, too. To pay some dues and move up."

I adjusted the logs more gently. "Well, I have a bad feeling about it."

"And I have a bad feeling about not being there. For you and my staff. Without me, you'll need to tread carefully, Ivy. Sounds like Skowby rules with an iron fist. He won't like being shown up by amateurs, let alone pets."

"He's not an animal person. You know what that means. Poor character."

Once again he offered the laugh I loved so much. "I'm not a pet person by nature and you're marrying me anyway."

"Only if you come home." I left the pile and got the next log set up. "Ideally before anyone else dies."

He waited until I finished the split. "Hopefully you haven't been swept off your feet by a hunky lumberjack before then." And then, "Ugh. Did I just say 'hunky'?"

"You did. And there's zero chance of that. Keats doesn't like any of them."

"Oh? Why not? Asher said they were very affable."

"Ash would never use a word like 'affable.'"

"I never thought I'd use 'hunky,' either. But he told me a certain ginger woodsman was eyeing my girl."

"Did he also tell you I flashed my gems at said woodsman? I'm an affianced innkeeper keeping my distance. No need to worry, Chief Hunky."

"I thought it was Chief Hottie."

I gave another log a whack. "Both apply. Wear your nicknames with pride." Picking up more split logs, I headed for the woodpile. It was already too high. Percy's ears nearly brushed the eaves. "Anyway, the so-called gentlemen's club is currently enjoying the fruits of this woodswoman's labor. They have plenty of distractions from the current situation."

"Like what? Cards? Video games?"

Stacking the pieces, I shook my head, forgetting he couldn't see it. "Games are afoot, most certainly. All my sisters came for a surprise visit after dinner. Then Teri Mason arrived with Mandy McCain."

"Even Mandy? She's so shy."

I headed back for another load. "I think Teri duped her into coming. Mandy's so petrified she's helping Jilly in the kitchen. There's never been so much giggling under my roof. Mom was utterly eclipsed by the volume."

"Uh-oh. She won't like that at all."

"Her pout drove me out. The only age-appropriate man was keeping to himself anyway. Fleet Jurgen, the crew lead, made a lot of calls out back. Now he's working at the dining room table."

"But the project's scuppered."

"I guess they'll roll on to the next one after Skowby clears them to leave. Doesn't seem like they know anything."

"Ivy. You haven't been questioning them, have you?"

Keats mumbled his "duh" sound. "Just small talk over a heaping helping of Jilly's chili," I said. "I was warming them up with some hot sauce and planning to crack open the best scotch after dinner to see what spilled out. Then the estrogen bus arrived and all hope was lost."

"Good. Let Skowby do his job."

"*Your* job. While you're off on some secret mission." I set a log on the stump and then gave it a good kick. "Doesn't the timing make you curious?"

"The timing of a man dying under a cable skidder? Can't see how it would have anything to do with me."

"Even a murder? What if someone planned this because you're gone?"

He paused, perhaps giving it some thought. "Well, it's not like I left the door to the henhouse unlocked. The chickens of Clover Grove are well defended by an acting chief my superiors respect."

"If no one else. Poor Asher is stuck on graveyard. That's personal."

A deep sigh told me he agreed. "Skowby probably knows Asher wanted his turn at the wheel and feels threatened."

"I suppose that's why he seemed unfazed by what happened to Dawes Croaker. It's a chance to prove his mettle."

"A chance to run a high-profile investigation, perhaps. If it is indeed deemed murder."

"The orange paws of death deemed it so. It's just a matter of time before the evidence catches up."

"Ivy, can you please stay out of Skowby's way? If he feels threatened, he'll be heavy-handed with all my staff. I can't risk losing good officers. There's a shortage across hill country and they won't have far to go to find another job."

"I'll stay out of his way." Keats gave a mumble of protest. "Sorry, buddy, we have to. For Kellan, Asher and the rest of the police force."

This time Kellan's sigh was different. Relieved. "You promise?"

"Sure." I looked at Keats and crossed my fingers. "I'll stay out of Skowby's way. My hands are full with the woodsmen and their fan club anyway."

"I know ladies love men with axes."

"This lady prefers using her own ax. And I'm glad you're okay with that."

"Very much so. At the rate you're going, you'll fuel us right through the apocalypse."

"That's a sure thing, now?" I set the head of the ax between my feet and clasped my fingers over the knob at the other end. "I mean, the apocalypse. Did they give you more deets during this top secret cop mission?"

He blew me a kiss across the miles. "Couldn't tell you if I knew, sweetie. But keep chopping. It'll keep you out of trouble."

Keats let out a sassy mumble as if to say, "Fat chance of that."

I let the dog have the last word and blew Kellan a quick kiss as I hung up.

# CHAPTER EIGHT

The next morning was so balmy I took my coat off while doing my rounds. It was the kind of weather a girl could get used to, but that would be a mistake. I'd been duped by mild winter days before. The cold only nipped harder when it circled back. No point wasting good energy hoping.

Energy that was in short supply this morning, as I'd been too busy observing our guests at dinner to eat a second helping of Jilly's hearty chili. All I learned was that they called themselves "the choppers," and seemed to be the best of buddies. Fleet, the crew lead, was more reserved. Aside from an occasional eye roll at his men, he seemed mostly lost in thought, while still managing to put away a lot of food. I hoped to have better luck with him later, after Chief Skowby had come and gone.

Keats herded me up rather hastily and I wondered if the chief was already on his way. Percy waited on the hood of the truck, green eyes fixed on an auburn spot beyond the donkey and camelid pasture. Veronica was apparently watching over us and since she didn't approach, I had to assume she was happy to see us get on the road.

I didn't need to put any thought into our destination as I drove down the lane and turned onto the highway. We were going where we always went when there was a puzzle to solve.

The lights were on in Mandy's Country Store and she stood at the door with her thin arms crossed over her apron. The smile on her face as we pulled into the parking lot told me she was waiting for us. While the cops were doing their postmortem, Mandy and I usually did the same, only verbally, over coffee.

And in my case, pie.

"Apple or cherry?" she asked, heading behind the counter. "There's chocolate chiffon, but I'm guessing that's a little much before eight, even for you."

I waggled my fingers, grinning. "Bring it on. All of it."

"Ah, you never disappoint, my friend. Maybe others will take a chance on that pie once there's a piece missing. People have conservative tastes around here. Fruit pies are the big sellers but I'm getting bored in the kitchen."

I headed for my usual stool at the counter by the window, and set Percy's carrier on the floor. Keats normally sat like a statue beside me but today he roamed through the café-style tables, sniffing. Catching my eye, he gave a casual point with a white paw. There was something of more interest here than delectable baked goods, just as I'd grown to expect.

Mandy was back so fast she must have already had the pie plated, including the chocolate chiffon. She also set the coffee pot within easy reach so she didn't need to leave when I drained my cup. It was steaming but I was usually in such a hurry that I'd built up a tolerance for heat. My days of leisurely coffee chats were long gone. There was always something that needed doing, even if no one had died in suspicious circumstances.

Still, I made a point of savoring a mouthful of chocolate chiffon pie and complimenting the baker before diving into the conversation. "What's up? Normally you join me."

She hovered anxiously and then slid onto the next stool. Her cheeks were flushed, as if she'd been bent over the oven. "Nothing. Everything's good."

I eyed her for a few moments and then looked to Keats. "What's got Mandy's heart rate up, buddy? Do you think she hit it off with one of the choppers last night?"

Her eyes widened and her fingers went to her throat, as if I'd accused her of a terrible crime. "Nothing like that. There had just been a death. It would have been so inappropriate."

Keats' pant-laugh told me I was on the right track. "Which one? Big Red?"

"He's very handsome, but he only had eyes for you in spite of the bling on your finger. Clearly not my type." She twisted her mug on the counter. "Not that I have a type anymore. Lloyd put me off men forever. My 'picker' is broken."

"That's why I keep telling you to let Jilly set you up with one of Asher's carefully screened friends. With her headhunting record, she knows a good fit when she sees one."

Mandy's cheeks burned even more. "I couldn't handle a cop. Too dangerous. If I ever date again it will probably be a plumber or something like that. Nothing more exciting than snaking out a drain."

I laughed. "Okay, but everyone loves a lumberjack, or so I'm told. My sisters certainly did." After pausing for a moment to let her worry, I added, "I heard someone had you cornered in the kitchen, and was telling forestry war stories. Rock, right?"

"Rock? Really, Ivy?" She rolled her eyes. "It's Rob Snooks. You know the names of your guests."

"Rob is as boring as fruit pie. The name, that is. Doesn't suit an arboreal acrobat at all. Chopping is dangerous work, too, you know. But they do get paid well for it. Better than cops, I hear."

"He was very nice," Mandy said. "Quieter than the others. Still scared me speechless, but I liked hearing him talk."

"Do they all live in Orono County? It's not a big community."

"Apparently so. They do extreme sports together, like rock

climbing, kiteboarding and cliff diving." Mandy took a sip of coffee and sighed. "I could never be with someone so daring. The biggest risk I take is trying a new recipe." She gestured to the chocolate chiffon pie. "Look where that got me."

I carved off a large chunk and popped it into my mouth. "To heaven, Mandy. At least, that's where it got me. My goodness, it's rich."

"Too rich?" Her brow furrowed. "Be honest."

"There's no such thing as too rich. I mean, come on, it's pie. No one wants a low-fat pie." I glanced over at the counter. "Do you have another one?"

She nodded. "You think the lumber crew would like it? Jilly didn't include it on her list. Maybe it doesn't suit her menu."

"This suits any menu. It's not just for extreme palates."

Finally, the tension in her shoulders eased. "Thanks, Ivy. It's so tough for me to try new things and be judged. I wish I were more like you."

I continued on with the pie. "You wish you were gearing up for what Kellan calls a 'reckless pursuit of justice'?"

She laughed and it lit her up from within. "Not quite that. Just a little braver is all. Mostly, I'm happy to sit here on the sidelines and feed you pie and information."

My eyes left my plate in a hurry. "Information? Serve that up next, please."

"It's not much, but I thought you might like to know that the gentleman who died—"

"He was no gentleman," I interrupted. "He tried to shoot my fox. Veronica." Keats mumbled what sounded like a suggestion to focus on the matter at hand, so I added, "Sorry. Go on, Mandy. What do you know about Dawes Croaker?"

Her thin lips pressed together for a moment. "A dreadful name, given the circumstances. He was polite both times he was here."

I put my fork down. "Tell me more."

"The first visit was about a month ago, when he met with Fleet Jurgen. It seemed like a business meeting. Mr. Croaker said they'd finally got the green light and then they shook hands. I didn't think much of it because business meetings happen here all the time."

"Did they seem to be getting along?"

She squinted out into the parking lot. "Not really. After the handshake, their voices got a little louder. It was about the budget. Mr. Croaker was trying to negotiate the cost down. He said he needed funds for equipment, like ground thawing blankets. Thousand a pop, apparently. Fleet said, 'Then don't do a winter dig. No one digs in January unless they're burying bodies. Are you burying bodies?'"

I slid right off my stool. "Burying bodies! What did Dawes say?"

"He got all huffy. Said the details were none of Fleet's business. He was only hiring him to chop, not dig, and if he didn't want the work, someone else would."

"And then?" My voice was high enough that Keats mumbled a "simmer down" kind of sound. It didn't pay to get too excited. You lost nuance that way.

"Fleet laughed and said, 'Good luck with that.' According to him there isn't a better crew in all of hill country and most don't want to work up this way. He said there are rumors about our woods."

I hopped back up on the seat. "I'll bet there are. Buckley Brackens says there are plenty of bodies out there and maybe Dawes was planning to add a few more."

"He denied it, anyway. Said he was just getting a head start on the foundations for his new house. End of story." She let me eat the last bite of chocolate chiffon and start in on the cherry pie. The contrast made my tongue tingle more than the hot coffee. "His wife corroborated that story when I met her."

My fork tinkled on the plate as I set it down even harder. "Mrs. Croaker was here? When?"

"Just a few days ago. Dawes told her my carrot cake was the best he'd ever had and she wanted to try it. He helped her with her coat and pulled out her chair. That's why I thought he was a gentleman."

"And what was she like? His wife?"

"Nice enough. She said she loved the cake, too. Told me to call her Marlene and said she'd be back soon, because they're staying in a rental until Dawes gets the new house built. She touched his arm and called him 'my honey.' They seemed fond of each other and I'm sure she's devastated about what happened. Now she'll never get her dream house. They were going to retire here."

I glanced down at Keats and his blue eye told me to eat fast. "Did she say where they were staying?"

Mandy paused long enough to let me shove an enormous forkful into my mouth and chew. "Marlene started to say something and Dawes cut her off. It started with 'Mac,' though."

I reviewed my mental map of Clover Grove's suburbs while finishing the pie. The town had grown since I left for college and I made a point of touring when I had errands. As Edna said, you never knew when you might have to make a quick getaway. "Mackelby Lane, I bet. It's on the outskirts." I glanced at the counter. "I believe I see that famous carrot cake. I'll take one to go."

"Ivy, you can't show up on Marlene's doorstep today. She just lost her husband."

I jumped off the stool and grabbed Percy's carrier. "You mean I can't show up on her doorstep empty-handed. It's perfectly appropriate to deliver food to someone in mourning. In fact, there's a long tradition of it, especially in Clover Grove."

"Casseroles, yes. Carrot cake, no. It's for weddings, not funerals. You'll hit all the wrong notes."

Keats grumbled at me to stop debating etiquette and get going.

"Well, what have you got that is appropriate, Mandy? Because according to Keats, we're going, one way or the other."

Mandy sighed as she left her seat and headed for the counter. "Quiche. It's not ideal, but it might get you in the door since

Marlene liked that, too." She tied a box with string and then handed it to me. "Please share my sympathies. And maybe ask about her ring. It's quite a gem and she never stopped playing with it."

I let Keats herd me up and headed for the door. "You've outdone yourself this time, Mandy. And your prize is more time with Rock the lumberjack. See you at dinner."

Until then, I would have pegged Mandy as least likely to hurl a spoon at me. But I'd have been wrong.

# CHAPTER NINE

Keats panted happily, paws on the dash as we headed toward Mackelby Lane. Even Percy, now out of his carrier, looked bright with anticipation. Of course, his orange fluff was always bright but his ears were forward and his eyes big and blazingly green. The pets were brimming with anticipation.

"Have you boys no shame?" Elation started hissing out of me like a leaky balloon. "Intruding on a grieving widow makes us no better than Justine Schalow, quiche notwithstanding." I checked the clock on the dash. "Especially this early. Mandy was right."

The dog mumbled his disagreement. It was exactly the right time to be indelicate.

"I know it's a good place to start but the ends don't necessarily justify the means. That's what sets us apart from the shady reporter." I shrugged. "That and the fact that we solve crimes instead of serving up dubious details to the public in the media."

Keats panted again, his tone changing to amusement. He followed that with a "you-got-that-right" sort of mumble.

"This had better be worth it, because you know Jilly would disapprove, too." I turned the last corner onto the lane, surprised and relieved that there were no police cruisers in sight. "That's why I'm not calling her. I feel bad but she has her hands full with the guests and doesn't need more stress. Plus, if she gives me a hard time, Asher might overhear. He'd rat us out to Kellan, guaranteed."

Keats pounded his white paws in the canine equivalent to "wrap up the angst."

"Fine. I'm doing this anyway. Obviously. But I'm allowed to feel compunction about it."

He turned to shoot me a look with his blue eye as if to say, "I know what compunction means." No doubt he did. He was a genius, after all. And if this genius really thought I should be accosting a grieving widow, I guess I'd have to roll with it.

On the other hand, it would be a relief if she weren't home. There were only five houses on the short street and three of them had toboggans, hockey nets or melting snowmen out front. That left two homes, one in advanced disrepair. It was easy to deduce the rental, but also a waste of energy since Keats had already indicated his choice—without compunction.

He spared me a pant-laugh as I pulled into the curb.

"It's odd that there are no cars in the driveway. What are the chances Marlene Croaker will be alone after hearing such news?" I turned off the truck. "I hope for her sake she's got support. What a hard time to be in a new town and temporary digs."

Keats offered a grunt that sounded like, "Stalling."

Flipping down my visor, I checked the mirror. Still me, thank goodness. I half-expected to see Justine's weasel-like features reflected back. Trusting my pets had never led me astray before so I'd need to take the leap now.

Another pant-laugh made me chuckle, too. Trusting my pets had led me into plenty of trouble but there was always a way out. That's what I actually trusted.

Carrying the quiche in one hand, I clutched the railing on the way up the front stairs. Dozens of big boot prints had frozen into slushy grooves. Those prints belonged to police-issue footwear. I'd seen enough of them on my own paths to know.

At the top, I prodded the bell with a gloved fingertip at the same moment the inside door opened. A woman in her late forties with highlighted toffee-colored hair and blue eyes stared at me through the screen. "Are you selling something? Because this isn't a good time."

I shook my head. "Gifting something. Are you Mrs. Croaker?"

Her lips pressed together and she looked down, smoothing what looked like a cashmere sweater. It matched her eyes, while her pants matched her hair. "I am. I mean, I was. I suppose I'm not a 'Mrs.' anymore. Obviously word's gotten out about what happened to my husband and someone's sent what appears to be a pie to fill the horrible hole in my life." Her eyes came back up and met mine with a fierce stare. "I hate small towns."

"I get that." I lowered the quiche since the door hadn't opened to receive it. "When I left Clover Grove for college I swore I'd never come back."

She ran her index finger under one eye to rub away the mascara ring. "Yet here you are, on the doorstep of a grieving widow."

"Being neighborly. It's tradition around here to deliver food for happy or sad events. When I moved home, my house filled with pies, preserves and especially eggs." Holding up the box again, I smiled. "Never a quiche like this. Mandy McCain said you enjoyed it when you came into her store."

"Mandy? Yes, what a sweet girl. I didn't realize you're a delivery service. I'm sorry to take things out on you." The door opened and she accepted the box. "Come in and I'll find you a tip."

I debated letting her think I was paid to deliver but Keats nudged my hand as if to remind me I was after another kind of tip. It wouldn't pay for her to discover later she'd been duped. That was a bigger crime than intruding at such a time.

Stepping inside, I said, "Mrs. Croaker, there's no tip required. You see—"

"Nonsense," she interrupted. Setting the quiche on a glass console, she rifled through her purse. It gave me a moment to glance around. The house was nicely decorated in neutral tones to accommodate people on short-term stays. I'd seen the look often while traveling for business. Stripping a place of personality helped guests feel more at home. "I always tip," Marlene continued. "Dawes and I were very fortunate and it's important to let that trickle down to those who have less." Turning, she offered me a handful of change. "Call me Marlene. I'll probably go back to my maiden name, Whiffle. I never liked Croaker." Her eyes darted from side to side as she thought about how that sounded. "I mean the name. Obviously, I loved my husband."

I cupped my left hand and the coins landed in it with a jangle. "Mandy said you were so sweet together. Like newlyweds. Had you been married long?"

"Nearly twenty years. Dawes was much older than me, but he swept me off my feet. He was so romantic." She fiddled with a large sapphire ring. It was on her right hand, whereas the traditional set was on her left. "At least back then. It faded over time. I suppose that's inevitable."

"I hope not." I turned my hand without thinking and coins rained onto the floor, rolling in every direction. Stooping to retrieve them, I saw a flash of orange in the dining room as Percy explored.

"Don't worry, I'll get them later and find more for you," Marlene said, gesturing for me to get up. Grabbing a few coins, I took a good look at the sapphire ring. It had a unique and intricate setting. When I rose and set the recovered coins on the console, she eyed my own rings—the traditional diamond and the band of hill country garnets Kellan had made from his grandmother's brooch. "Ah, I see. You're a newlywed."

"Not yet. Just happily and belatedly engaged to my high school sweetheart. I'd like to believe this feeling will last forever."

"It won't." She nudged the coins into a pile. "I'm sorry to be so blunt but my filter is gone."

"Mine's been out of commission since I had a concussion nearly two years ago. Sometimes I forget the niceties, which is why I hope you'll forgive me for not introducing myself sooner. I'm Ivy Galloway and I own the property next to yours. I understand you were about to build your dream home."

Her eyes became more calculating and I knew she'd heard about me. Then her gaze dropped to Keats. She probably hadn't noticed the ginger cat now cruising along the back of the sofa. "Ivy. Of course. I should have known from the dog. Everyone talks about you."

My trademark HR smile snapped smartly into place. It hadn't taken facial calisthenics, after all. "I'm sure they do. Like food deliveries, gossip is part of that small-town charm."

"No doubt, but it wasn't the rumor mill that warned me about you. It was the chief of police. Dixon Skowby told me not to speak to you. He said you didn't know your place and that his predecessor, the former chief, turned a blind eye to your lawbreaking."

The comment was like a hard kick in the gut with a police issue boot. Not because Skowby thought ill of me, but because he called Kellan his 'predecessor.' That made this situation sound permanent. Surely if Kellan thought he'd been transferred for good he'd tell me. There was no way I could ever leave the farm to join him out of state. We'd have to do long-distance until the winds changed again.

Keats moved closer to me and nudged my hand. I realized I was the one absentmindedly twisting a ring now. He mumbled something both reassuring and rallying. It wasn't the time for romantic speculation. Kellan and I would work things out, as we always did. Maybe Chief Skowby was trying to get under my skin, and sadly, it worked. He'd underestimated my dog, however, who urged me on now.

"Marlene, the acting chief wasn't wrong about me, but my fiancé didn't turn a blind eye to my attempts to help solve crimes in town. Far from it. But some took place on or near my property, including what just happened to your husband. That always makes me worry for the safety of my livestock, as well as the guests at my inn. I do know my place and I protect that place in the best way I know how."

Marlene took a step back and crossed her arms. This wasn't going as I'd hoped. I'd worried about distressing the grieving widow and instead I was offending her.

"Ivy, you should go," she said. "You're scaring me. I don't believe it was a crime at all. Chief Skowby said it will likely turn out to be a worksite accident. Dawes didn't know the first thing about clearing land and it makes sense that he fell under that machine."

It was probably best for her to think so. There was no use telling her my pets had pronounced it foul play. Nor did she need to understand that a cable skidder couldn't drop its own blade or remove the key.

"Maybe the acting chief is right about it being an accident," I said. "But that's not why I'm here. I wanted you to know that I spoke to your husband shortly before he passed away."

Her blue eyes widened and I noticed they weren't particularly bloodshot. Nor were her lids puffy. The mascara rings said she'd shed a few tears but not enough to leave the trail mine always did. "Really? What did he say?"

"The discussion started okay but unfortunately, didn't end well when he took a shot at my fox. Veronica." Every time I said the name my face got a little flushed. I was largely immune to embarrassment over pets and livestock but naming wildlife felt different. It definitely filed me on the community shelf under "e" for eccentric.

"Your fox? You must not feed her well enough because Dawes said she was hanging around every day looking for scraps. That wasn't the first time he shot at her. She must have more lives than a cat."

"Sounds like it." I caught a glimpse of Percy climbing the stairs with stealth. He had used up his first nine lives and was into double digits. "Putting that grievance aside, I wanted to let you know that Dawes was thinking of you up to the end. I hoped it would help."

"Oh?" She went back to twisting the sapphire ring. "What did he say?"

I stared up, trying to remember his exact words. "That he had to get this house built for you. And you deserved only the best. It seemed urgent."

"That was sweet of him to say. This was supposed to be a fresh start for us, after a rough patch. He wanted it to go well but there were so many roadblocks. Dawes had been trying for years to buy that land and get the go-ahead but the town's planning committee refused to approve a build until recently."

"There are plenty of properties available, many with better views of the hills," I said. "Why was he so set on the old Harlow place?"

She shrugged but her eyes dropped to the ring. It really was quite impressive. I loved mine, too, but any woman would have a hard time not gazing into the blue depths of that stone. Blue of another shade was trained on me. Keats thought the time for soft-pedaling was over.

"I don't know," she said at last. "There were so many stories about it. Some quite tragic, of course. I guess we wanted a place with history."

Keats put a paw on my boot and pressed. "I wish you could have brought that land a happier ending, Marlene. It must be doubly heartbreaking to give up on the house of your dreams."

Her head tilted slightly and her eyes flicked up. "Perhaps I won't give up entirely. In time, building there might feel like the best way to honor my husband's memory."

"That sounds wonderful. We may still be neighbors yet."

"For the moment, I just want to be alone with my grief. If you don't mind, Ivy."

She gestured to the door and the sapphire, or the diamonds around it, caught the light and showered rainbows on Percy as he came toward me with his tail up. He flicked a couple of coins across the floor to announce his arrival.

"Oh, my. Where did this cat come from?"

He leapt at me with the expectation that my arms would be waiting, and they were. "This is Percy. Sometimes he slips in behind me. Moves like a shadow—if shadows were orange."

Marlene gestured to the door again. "I don't really like animals."

That would explain why neither of them seemed to like her very much. Both had kept well back and their ears spent more time down than up.

"We'll be on our way, then." I shifted Percy's weight and reached for the handle. "Marlene, I can't help but notice that gorgeous ring. My mother would absolutely love a piece like that. Would you mind telling me where you bought it?"

Her right hand balled into a fist and she clasped her left over it, as if fearing I'd make a play for the gem. "It's a priceless antique, Ivy. A gift from a very dear friend. They don't make rings like this anymore."

"I know a jeweler who could probably design something similar, if you'd let me take a picture."

"It's meant to be one of a kind. Please go." Marlene stuck her right hand into her pants pocket and gave me a little shove with her left. "And if I do decide to continue building on the Harlow land, I'd ask you to keep your fox at home."

I responded to her push and walked outside. "I don't actually own the fox, Marlene, but I have a soft spot for any animal."

"Well, good luck." She closed the door behind me and I barely heard her last words. "Because I'm a better shot than my husband."

# CHAPTER TEN

I pulled a U turn in the truck and roared away. "Did you hear that? What kind of woman threatens to shoot an innocent animal just hours after her husband dies in suspicious circumstances? I don't care if she's distraught."

Keats' mumble suggested he expected no more from the widow Croaker, and Percy concurred by making a single sweep over the passenger seat with one paw. The cat was dismissing her as nothing more than litter box filler, a category currently occupied by Justine Schalow and the Langman sisters, among others.

"I don't feel so bad about intruding now. She can't be too grief-stricken if she's already thinking about reverting to her maiden name. Well, she'll always be a Croaker to me."

I took the corner a little too fast and Keats mumbled a warning. "Got it, we're good." I corrected course just in time to swerve around a beat-up sedan also going too fast. The driver flipped me the bird, even before recognition dawned.

"Oops," I said. "I want Justine Schalow gone, but there's no point killing her after saving her life."

Keats gave a pant-laugh and Percy repeated his litter box sweep —a move that was getting a lot of practice.

"Turns out we are better than Justine in one way. We're faster."

By the time we hit Main Street I'd calmed down. Our next move eluded me and Keats hadn't issued directions. He was sitting back in the seat looking pretty chill.

"What are you smiling about?" I asked. "We're on a case. This is normally when you keep bossing me around."

He lifted one white paw as if to say, "Wait for it," and pretty much on cue, my phone pinged. Then pinged again. And again. So many pings it could only mean one thing: a Butter Tart 911.

"Ugh. Seriously? I don't know if I have the stamina to deal with my family in person. Maybe we could call in."

Keats mumbled a you-know-the-rules sort of sound. For a family emergency, you showed up in person unless you were fully incapacitated and had a doctor's note to prove it.

Sighing, I turned the truck around and headed toward Daisy's house. There was no point checking the phone. That was the meeting site and always would be, even after a zombie uprising.

"They're never truly emergencies, have you noticed?" I slowed to delay the inevitable. "Someone's always overreacting about something. Usually something I've done. Or want to do. Those meetings are a constant reminder of how it feels to be the youngest of six. I used to think that's what made me a hyper-responsible exec, but then the dam burst and now I'm probably the most reckless of them all."

Keats' mumble confirmed my title as the most reckless Galloway. It wasn't an easy win, as Asher, Poppy and Mom were extremely reckless, and Dad certainly was in his youth. Even Daisy, our true matriarch, had a spectacularly reckless moment once with long-term repercussions. Come to think of it, only Iris and Violet came up roses in this strange family rivalry. Jilly, now a Galloway by marriage, had a blemished record, too.

I was relieved to see my best friend standing on Daisy's porch as I pulled up. She could have begged off without proof of hospitalization simply by way of being honorary family. The pressures of having so many guests—and big eaters, all of them—would have been a legit excuse. But she was there, and I suspected it was to support me, because Asher's truck was in the driveway. He'd gotten out of bed for this meeting after his overnight shift. All signs pointed to me being on the chopping block.

Turning off the truck, I continued to grumble. "What have I done? Other than visit a dead man's widow, which no one knows about yet."

Keats stepped onto my knee and pawed at the door, tail fanning a "let the games begin."

Jilly came down to greet me and my voice was plaintive when I asked, "Do I have to?"

"It's never as bad as you think." She looped her arm through mine. "Sometimes it is quite bad, granted. But this time it'll be fine."

"This is about Asher, right? He's getting squeezed by Skowby. That guy is such a jerk."

"Ash wouldn't say and don't think I didn't try. My wifely wiles don't work as well when he's exhausted and stressed."

Keats trotted ahead with Percy and both tails were up. Obviously some people—and to me, the boys were people—loved family gatherings. The more dramatic the better.

Inside, all were in their usual places, with Daisy buffing and polishing in rubber gloves. The tenser the vibe, the harder she scrubbed. Her aggressive use of vinegar spray as I walked into the kitchen suggested we were at a level eight. We'd all be pickled in Galloway brine before this meeting was done.

"Finally," Asher said, pushing himself off the refrigerator. "Did you walk from Mackelby Lane?"

Keats arrived under my fingertips panting happily. We were caught but could rally.

"A Butter Tart 911 is an emergency, darling," Mom said. "Look at me. I didn't even take off my uniform."

Mom and Iris were both wearing smocks that read, "Bloomers."

Iris' was floral, to suit the name, but Mom's was a clinical white. Her clients were generally men looking for the barbershop experience and she wanted them to feel comfortable. Besides, floral prints made her look even shorter than five feet tall.

Looking around, I let myself marvel briefly that her tiny body had produced this strapping clan. I was the tallest of the Galloway girls, but all of them were in average range, and Asher was over six feet. Mom didn't like to speak of it, but she had worked feverishly to stay trim and fit. In some ways, she was a good role model. In others... well, the reckless gene came from somewhere.

"Ivy?" Asher pressed. "You haven't answered my question."

"No, I didn't walk from Mackelby Lane. But I stuck well within the speed limits, which I'm sure you'll appreciate, being an officer of the law."

My brother's blue eyes were a little dazed, probably from sleep deprivation. He was pretty sharp, on the whole, and getting sharper by the day, thanks to Kellan's leadership. The thought gave me a pang. No doubt we were both missing Kellan, albeit for different reasons.

"You know what I mean. Why were you over there in the first place?"

"Well, that's a different question. And here's one for you: how did you know?"

"I don't have to answer that. As you pointed out, I'm an officer of the law."

I looked him up and down. "In civvies. At a Butter Tart 911, you're just Asher, controlling big brother."

Mom fluttered fingertips meticulously manicured in her signature scarlet. "Darling, we don't leave our identities at the door. Our careers are part of who we are and I'm proud of each and every one of you."

"Why are you being so nice, Mom?" Poppy asked.

"Because it's not her on the hot seat," Iris answered. "For a change."

"Darlings, stop. I just want us all to get along. Asher's under a lot of pressure, with Kellan gone."

"And I'm not?" I asked. "I don't even know where my fiancé is right now. He's been deployed somewhere on a special mission that's probably dangerous. We're stuck with a pretender as chief of police."

"That pretender is my current boss, whether I like it or not," Asher said. "He found Justine Schalow staking out Mrs. Croaker, and guess who threw you to the dogs?"

"Jealous," Jilly said. "Justine is sore because Ivy got in and she didn't."

Asher turned his blue stare on his wife. "They got in and you didn't tell me?"

A bit of color rose in her cheeks, but not much. "I don't know that for a fact. I'm surmising from the pep in the pets' step."

Her husband rubbed his forehead. It was harder for him to hassle me when Jilly took my side. "Is she right, Ivy?"

I gestured to Keats, whose tongue lolled cheerfully. "Read him and weep."

Asher turned to the only one he could count on for help. "Daisy? Are you just going to stand there scrubbing when Ivy's been hassling grieving widows?"

"Only one," I said. "Don't make it sound worse than it is."

Our sister gave the counter an extra spritz of vinegar before speaking. "Ivy, it's always dangerous to interfere in an active police investigation."

"Kellan wouldn't like it," Mom said. "Do you really want to jeopardize your engagement?"

Five female voices fired out "Mom!" and "Dahlia."

Mom tapped her fingernails on the counter, drawing them back quickly when Daisy shot vinegar at them. "I'm just saying that relationships are hard enough even without distance and murder. Wouldn't it be wise to sit out this one criminal investigation, Ivy?"

"For Asher's sake, if nothing else," Daisy said. "He's the one on the front lines right now."

I thought of half a dozen comebacks but by sheer force of will, held them in. My reward came by way of Jilly.

"It isn't really a criminal investigation, though," she said, smiling at her husband. "Is it, honey?"

He glanced away from both of us. "It's still an investigation."

I crossed my arms. "What do you mean it's not a criminal investigation? Dawes Croaker was murdered."

"Not according to Chief Skowby," Asher said. "What happened was a jobsite accident. There's no evidence to prove otherwise."

"There was plenty of evidence." My throat tightened, making my voice reedy. "The cable skidder's blade didn't drop on its own and the key was gone. Plus there was the broken chain, suggesting a fight."

My brother shook his head. "Nothing conclusive. The area was contaminated by feet and paw prints."

"Edna said the cable skidder's blade only drops manually. Does Skowby think that lever moved itself?"

"That's exactly what he thinks, and experts on the machine said it could happen." Now my brother's eyes met mine and I saw that he didn't necessarily agree. "Edna's opinion held no weight with him. Nor would declarations from your pets."

My brain wanted to lash out at him but my heart saw he was in a tough position. I let sisterly love win and spoke more kindly. "He's wrong, Asher, and that leaves a killer at large. I know you don't run the show, but it's a problem."

"If it's a problem, it's Skowby's to solve," he said. "Interfering will get me fired." Raising a palm, he added, "Before you argue, those were his exact words. I interfere, I get fired. You interfere, you get tossed in the slammer."

A collective gasp went around the kitchen and Daisy gave an involuntary spritz that sent a cloud of vinegar toward the ceiling.

Jilly was the first to find words. "Is he deliberately burying this?"

Running his hand through fair hair, Asher shrugged. "He spent the night examining the crime scene closely. Spoke to the mayor this morning, and called it done."

There was a moment of silence before someone rarely heard in these discussions cleared her throat. "The Croaker project begins again tomorrow," Violet said.

Even Asher was shocked. "What? Where did you hear that?"

"Mandy McCain. She called half an hour ago and said Fleet Jurgen had commissioned her to cater and she needs my help. They're expanding the crew and there will be a lot of mouths to feed."

That startled me even more. I'd just left Marlene and she hadn't let on the build was going ahead, let alone growing. It couldn't be a surprise to her.

My brother's cheeks flushed with what was probably a mix of fury and wounded pride. He was hearing official police information from his part-time caterer sister. What a terrible disappointment given his ambition to scale the ranks. It saddened me to add to his burden by sharing a report from Marlene Croaker, but I did it. "Mrs. Croaker said Dixon Skowby described Kellan as the 'former chief' and 'his predecessor.' He was framing it as if this is a permanent gig."

Keats moved under my fingertips again and Jilly pressed closer, too. "I hope he didn't hear that from the mayor," she said.

"Meryl Martingale has to be the one who approved the dig continuing," Daisy said. "Although why on earth would a woman want to build her dream house on a site where her husband died so horribly? I'd move away fast if something like that happened to mine."

"I'm not that surprised about Marlene, given that she was

already contemplating taking her maiden name back. But I am surprised about the mayor."

Asher straightened out of a gradual slide down the fridge. "Don't bug Meryl, Ivy. That falls into Skowby's slammer category."

"Did he specifically say you'd be fired if I spoke to the mayor? Because he can't stop me from speaking to our civic leader."

He rolled his eyes. "It was implied under the general category of not interfering."

I snapped my fingers to summon Percy from the living room, where he was no doubt keeping an eye on my nephews' ferrets. "Clutch your badge, brother, because Meryl and I are good friends and I owe it to her to do *my* civic duty."

# CHAPTER ELEVEN

Turned out Mayor Martingale and I weren't quite as close as I thought. Meryl had stayed under my roof with her family for Christmas twice and enjoyed Jilly's fine cookery on any number of other occasions. She'd deployed my pets to do her bidding without giving me a say in the matter. On top of all that, Keats had saved her life. But our generous hospitality couldn't get me an appointment when I called City Hall after our family meeting.

The mayor's assistant knew me well and normally patched me through without hesitation. Today she asked me to repeat my name. At first I thought she was experiencing a medical issue. After my head injury, I forgot names sometimes and wasn't quick to judge. Three repetitions later, I was forced to acknowledge this was deliberate and possibly even part of mayoral protocol. When someone was blacklisted, names might be deleted from corporate memory, like a computer file.

"We're not taking this lying down," I told Keats and Percy as I headed into town. "Meryl can't include me in family photos and then sideline me at her convenience." Keats mumbled something and I clenched the steering wheel tighter. "Fine, she could. She's the mayor and I'm just an innkeeper. But remember how she forced

Bocelli and me to sing in the Christmas choir? We made that holiday merry and now she's giving me the slip."

The dog rumbled what sounded like a reminder that she owed him even more.

"That's right, buddy. You've helped her cover this town's butt over and over. You, too, Percy. Dissing you boys is worse than dissing me."

Keats didn't look nearly as indignant as I felt. His paws were on the dash and his mouth hung open despite the cool breeze coming in through the open window. He lifted his muzzle, gave a good sniff and then mumbled again. It sounded like, "Relax. We'll find her."

That took the edge off my frustration as I pulled into the parking lot at City Hall. Showing up at reception with a cat on one shoulder and a dog by my side was bound to resurface some memories for the mayor's assistant. Many had told me we left an indelible impression —chief among them my mother, although she didn't mean it as a compliment.

I wasn't wrong. When I pressed the buzzer at the glass doors to the mayor's suite, the assistant—a big fan of Percy's—started to smile before she remembered she didn't remember us. Her face became a blank slate so I buzzed a second time. And then a third.

A voice came over the intercom. "Mayor Martingale isn't receiving guests today."

"Fine," I said. "I'll book an appointment for tomorrow."

The intercom spoke again. "I'll check her schedule and... sorry. She's booked for the rest of the week. The whole month, actually."

"Really? Well, tell her she can clear her schedule on Easter, too, because dinner at Runaway Inn is cancelled."

Keats wasn't one to back away from a snarky moment, but he gave my leg a poke to tell me to let it go. The guidance probably came less from political savvy than his plan B. His perky ears suggested he had one.

Still, I gave the buzzer a last jab before leaving, a move I regretted even before my boots hit the sidewalk on Main Street.

"Jilly wouldn't have liked that unseemly display," I said. "Especially not in the office of a high-profile guest. There's probably a security camera showing me pounding that buzzer like a nutter." I took a deep breath and looked around to ground myself. "I've been making good progress controlling my temper but that set me off for some reason." Keats was trotting ahead of me but I continued aloud, "I can't believe the mayor doesn't want to hear my thoughts on the Croaker investigation. We've given her good reason to trust our instincts, and no matter which way the political winds blow, I believed Meryl had public safety at heart. She seemed like that rare politician who really cared."

Keats fell back and offered his ears, perhaps as a reminder not to badmouth the mayor in public to a dog. Or anyone. I shouldn't need a reminder about that, and it told me I'd do better to enlist Jilly's support, no matter how busy she was. After my accident, my best friend had become my human filter. While I needed that service less these days, it seemed like I was backsliding. A rumble under my fingertips directed me to the cause.

"Yeah. It's about Kellan."

My righteous indignation covered a fear deep in my heart that Kellan's position was truly under threat, and worse, that my activities had put him in the crosshairs. If he lost the job he loved because of me, I could never forgive myself. Serving as chief of police in Clover Grove was his passion. His calling. If he were removed from that role, he could never come home and take another job. There was no other job of similar rank for him on a small-town police force and he couldn't very well shift to something else when policing was in his very bones. That meant his only option would be transferring to another jurisdiction. Then I'd have to make an impossible decision about leaving my farm—*my* passion and calling—behind.

Keats had used up his sympathy. It was never in abundant

supply with a border collie. A lab would be more indulgent. Instead, the dog fate had dropped in my path was herding me along with nudges that quickly escalated to pokes and then a sharp nip.

"Hey, what gives?" I lurched ahead of him and Percy had to dig in for balance. "I'm hurting here, pal. Don't add injury to insult."

He mumbled a sharp reproof. A moment of sadness was allowed, but not wallowing. Nor was giving up too easily. When the going got tough, the tough stopped for coffee, apparently, because the dog ended his assault on my calf outside the Berry Good Café.

"Coffee? Really? I mean, there's never a bad time, but—"

Instead of herding me in the door, he drove me around the side to the rear courtyard.

"It's January, buddy. The patio won't be open."

Only it was. Since my last visit, the café had installed half a dozen propane heaters, cleared the stones of snow and erected an awning. I figured it would still be a hard sell even on a relatively mild day, but two customers at the corner table were braving the elements. The one with her back to me had meticulously highlighted blonde hair under an uncharacteristically subdued black hat. Normally Meryl Martingale had a little flash. Considerably less than my mother, but still, she liked to be noticeable in a crowd.

Not today. It was like she was incognito and I may have overlooked her had it not been for Keats, who was underscoring his point with an actual point.

"Got it, buddy," I muttered, crossing the stones. "Good job." I waited till I was right behind her to turn the volume way up. "Well, hello, Mayor! So sorry to interrupt but my calls keep going to voicemail and your assistant has sudden onset amnesia."

Meryl jumped but by the time I came alongside the table, her expression was a neutral mask. I'd learned that same skill in HR and it still served me well when I was more regulated. "Ivy, hello. Please don't take anything personally. My assistant was just doing her job. I'm exceedingly busy today." She gestured to her companion, a middle-aged man in a fedora. "This is Feldon Cork, an associate of mine. Feldon, please meet Ivy Galloway. She owns Runaway Farm and Inn."

Feldon didn't have the gift of neutralizing and a mix of emotions showed on his face. His ears flushed a rosy pink under the black fedora. "Hello, Ivy. Nice to meet you."

"Greetings, Mr. Cork. How wonderful to run into the head of the town's zoning department at last. I've been trying to reach you for ages by phone, email, and even snail mail. Could we please book an appointment to talk about repurposing some of my land?"

"Yes, of course." Feldon was nearly stuttering. "I'll ask my assistant to set something up."

"Let's do it now. I was obviously drawn here for a reason today."

He pulled his phone from his pocket and didn't ask for my number. A notification came to my phone, anyway. I was in his contacts, just not worthy of being contacted before. "I must be going," he said, as his ears burned even brighter. "Thanks for the coffee, Meryl."

The mayor gathered her purse as if to join him but I slid into the seat Feldon vacated and Keats parked beside her. Her face remained stony but her eyebrows rose a little. "Yes, Ivy? There's clearly something on your mind."

Percy dismounted from my shoulder and sat between us on the table, clearly deciding outdoor winter dining had relaxed rules about cats. Meryl grabbed her coffee mug, frowning, but she didn't shoo him away. In fact, she seemed to realize his fluff provided a good screen and adjusted her position to put him between us. Although Percy very much liked being in the middle, he moved to accommodate my stare.

"Mayor, you're avoiding me. That's hurtful, given our history. I'm in your family photos in front of the Christmas tree."

"It's not personal." She moved her chair again to block me with orange fluff. "I just have pressing business today."

I countered her move by shifting my chair. "Today and every day for a month, your assistant said. You have no time for me—for us." I gestured from the cat to the dog at her side, and Keats offered an indignant mumble on cue. "We've always been happy to step up when you asked and all we wanted was a conversation today."

Her lip twitched as she glanced at Keats. "Oh please, Ivy. That's not all you want. Chief Skowby told me about your hijinks."

"Hijinks? All I did was take my dog—the very dog whose talents you've enjoyed—for a walk and run into a new neighbor. Dawes Croaker tried to shoot my fox and I beat a hasty retreat before he did the same to me. It was terrifying."

"So terrifying you went right back with Edna Evans, well known for deescalating any situation. You went to pick a fight."

"On the contrary. Jilly Blackwood, the soul of discretion, was poised to talk Mr. Croaker down. Regrettably, he was already down. For good."

She took a sip of coffee that certainly wasn't steaming. "This is no joking matter, as amusing as I generally find the three of you. It's tragic that Mr. Croaker fell under the blade of that monstrous machine but Chief Skowby assures me it was an accident. He's investigated the matter thoroughly."

Each time she used that title it was another pinprick in my heart. "Acting chief. Or substitute chief. And how thorough could the investigation be in less than a day?"

"Dixon Skowby pulled in resources from Dorset Hills and Thistledown, and everyone agreed it was accidental. I understand the site was sullied by paw prints and claw marks."

I hated to concede the point but perhaps I could turn it in my favor. "Isn't our trampling the crime scene reason enough to spend more time there?"

"It's not a crime scene, and he's quite satisfied with his conclusion. The machine that killed Mr. Croaker has been decommissioned."

"And the person who pulled the lever? Have they been decommissioned, too? Because Edna says that's the only way the blade works."

Her carefully lined lips pressed together as if choosing her words carefully. "I cannot take advice from Edna Evans on logging equipment. Or much else. I'd most certainly come to her if I were in the market for a bunker."

Keats trained his warm brown eye on me and it kept my temper in check. "She'll be happy to hear that. But in the meantime, I'm concerned you're allowing the job site to reopen. Someone else could be hurt."

"A safety inspector has been assigned to monitor the work. You don't need to worry at all about your livestock or your... what is it this time? A fox?"

"Veronica. A real beauty." I wasn't falling into her trap, though. "You're so confident this is resolved that you're allowing Marlene Croaker to continue building her dream house in the dead of winter?"

She slouched behind Percy. "The project will continue, yes."

"The project? Oh, wait a second! That's why you were meeting with Feldon Corker. To discuss rezoning the property."

Meryl glanced up at a propane heater and shivered. "I meet with Feldon often. We talk about many things."

"Including my hopes to expand? If you can accommodate a newcomer, surely you could back a local business. Someone who's contributed so much to Clover Grove." I coughed in my glove to muffle the next words. "And saved your life."

Her eyes darted at me and back to the heater. "I honestly wasn't aware of your requests to meet with Feldon. I'll have a word with him."

Keats directed a mumble of rebuke at me. I'd veered away from our mission and worse, put myself in the compromising position of being silenced with a building permit. That wouldn't do at all.

"Thank you, Mayor, but today isn't about me. It's about justice for Dawes Croaker. You've trusted me before. You've trusted my pets before. We believe more needs to be done. What am I missing here?"

Her fingers stretched out to Percy and he leaned into her hand. He wasn't much for gloves, but anything for the cause. "Ivy, listen. I'm very grateful for all you've done, including saving me from the gingerbread killer. But sometimes it's wise just to let things go."

She had dropped the "you" and I suspected it was because the advice applied to her, too. Her eyes were fixed on Percy, now working his fluff hard. What was really going on here?

"Mayor." I gestured to catch her attention. "Meryl. Are you getting pressure from Dixon Skowby into letting this go? Because Kellan would never do that."

Her jaw set and she folded her hands again. "Chief Skowby isn't in a position to pressure me."

"Is someone else? Someone higher up the chain? I don't even know who's higher than a mayor."

She permitted a small smile. "So many. A small-town mayor has very limited powers in the big scheme of things. Regardless, the Croaker build will continue tomorrow."

"And expand into what, exactly?"

The shoulders of her fine wool coat went up and down. "I'm not at liberty to discuss the project."

"Zoning decisions aren't classified information. Don't I have a right to know what's going up next door? There was no public hearing. It could be a danger to my animals. A power plant, for example. Or an opium farm."

Her smile became more authentic. "Poor climate for poppies or I'm sure someone would have tried it already."

Keats mumbled again and moved to my side of the table. There was a time for humor and a time to get real. Percy evidently agreed because he launched lightly onto the mayor's shoulder, making her gasp.

"Okay," I said. "So some big gun wants to build something right beside my farm, no matter who dies to make it happen." Pulling off my glove, I ran my fingers over the dog's sleek back. "And that's why you sent Kellan away."

Meryl tried to shove Percy off and he clung like a burr. Moreover, he rubbed against her coat, working some ginger into the fiber. "What a terrible thing to say, Ivy."

"That wasn't a denial. I spoke to Kellan last night and he certainly believes this is a temporary assignment."

"It is temporary. At the moment, Skowby is the chief of police in Clover Grove. That wasn't my decision, either. As I said, I have limited powers and take my orders just like Kellan does. For the moment, others think Dixon is the right man for this job, while Kellan is right for a special mission."

I leaned across the table and grabbed the hand still trying to scrape off Percy. "Meryl, please tell me when Kellan is coming back to the position he loves. He's done more to clean up crime in this region than the last ten chiefs put together."

"Agreed. I admire and respect Kellan Harper and you. But I don't know the answer to your question."

A chill sank into my bones and ice formed around my heart. "Don't know, or won't tell?"

She sighed. "Lately I'm fed information on a need-to-know basis. Even though I've signed an ironclad confidentiality agreement."

My eyes filled with tears. At least they wouldn't freeze in the warm bubble of the courtyard. "He's my fiancé. We have a right to know his future. Our future. We've both earned that, haven't we?"

"If I could share more, I would. I don't know what was so special about Dawes Croaker but decisions are happening above my paygrade. All I can do is promise to stand up for Kellan—and you—if the need arises."

She got up and darted away, Percy still firmly lodged and in it for the ride. Keats pursued and managed to nick her leg. A high-pitched squeal was the only satisfying thing about this meeting. "Sorry," I yelled after her, and then more quietly, "Good boys."

"I'm taking your cat," she called back.

"Enjoy! His scalp massage is legendary."

"Ouch! Would you— Ivy Galloway, call this cat off or I'll charge you with assault." Her voice got louder as she came back up the alley and stopped at the patio entrance. "Imagine how much Chief Skowby would like that."

I signaled for Percy to jump down. "*Acting* Chief. And if that title changes you won't be presiding over my wedding."

She headed back up the alley. "Fine. Saves me worrying about the perfect wedding gift for the farmer who has everything."

Meryl Martingale was hard to hate, but I intended to keep trying.

# CHAPTER TWELVE

The fog was so dense the next morning I could barely see Veronica out beyond the pasture shared by the donkeys and llamas. Since she clearly wasn't afraid of me, I had to give her credit for knowing better than to come closer. My trust in animals was high —some said too high—but I wouldn't happily put my hens at risk. Choosing the pasture she did may well have been deliberate. She probably realized the donkey thugs would make short work of her and relish the job. They didn't like any livestock but they'd defend them just the same. Veronica was telling me she knew her limits. But she was also trying to tell me more.

Given the distance, she had to get creative about delivering her message. She ran a few loops, stirring up the thugs, and then repeatedly turned toward the Harlow land—now the Croaker land, whether I liked it or not. Finally, she threw her head back and yapped. It sounded more like a dog than I expected. Not my dog, but some dog somewhere. I realized I'd heard the sound before and mistaken it for the little mutt down the road. How long had Veronica been talking to me before I listened? A good month, probably. Perhaps since Janelle had told me about her at Christmas. With

Kellan leaving, my focus had been elsewhere and now there was a problem. A big one.

"Note to self," I said to Keats, as I backed out of the pasture and closed the gate. "Never ignore the messenger, no matter what coat she wears."

"What's going on?" Edna asked, coming up behind me. She had walked through the trails today, wearing plain clothes instead of fatigues. Her down jacket, hat and scarf would have fit in well in any gathering of the town's senior citizens, and it was jarring. That wasn't the Edna I knew, the fierce apocalyptic warrior. Technically, it was, because this was a disguise, of sorts. Today she didn't want to scare anyone. "Is she intentionally taunting the livestock?"

I shook my head. "Just wants us to get a move on. She's a fox on a mission."

Edna gave Veronica a wave. "Hold your donkeys. Our chariot hasn't arrived."

"Won't be long now." I could hear an engine hiccupping out on the highway. This chariot needed a tune-up.

Jilly was coming down the front stairs carrying a basket of pots and pans. She added it to the coolers beside the driveway.

"What's all that?" Edna asked, as we walked over. "I thought Mandy was catering."

"Joint effort," Jilly said. "She's covering morning and afternoon break and I'm doing lunch. This is actually last night's dinner. My classic beef stew went uneaten because our guests didn't have the courtesy to let us know they'd be dining elsewhere."

"Ah. Dahlia must have been disappointed," Edna said. "Not to mention the rest of the town's population of single women. Myself excluded." She patted her fringe of permed curls. "There's much to be said for aging. A crew of lumberjacks does nothing at all for me. I put my hormones in a cooler like that decades ago and never felt more at peace."

Jilly laughed. "I think it's fun. When Hazel Bingham lamented the lack of eligible men in hill country I thought she was exaggerating, but she isn't wrong. I'm so glad the man of my dreams was standing right here waiting when I arrived."

"It's a shame you had to settle," Edna said. "A fine woman like you deserves a hero, Jillian."

"He is a hero," I said. "Even if he's assigned to highway duty. Asher would risk his life for you."

"I'd like to see him try. I'm as capable of thrashing him as I was when I gave him his first vaccine."

"Only because he's carrying childhood trauma from that very incident," Jilly said. "Now's as good a time as any to remind you of your obligations as the bridesmaid at my wedding. No talking smack about my husband."

"It's my favorite hobby," Edna said. "Besides prepping for the apocalypse. And that's what worries me. The way Asher's taken his reassignment lying down suggests he'll be little help to us when the end comes. I'm willing to carry you and Ivy, but not that big lug."

Jilly's cheeks flushed. It was rare that Edna got under her skin but like me, she was rattled by the current situation. "He hasn't taken it lying down. He's depressed."

"Exactly. We won't have the luxury of indulging our moods in the end times. Better to pack them in a cooler now, with your hormones."

"Edna, stop," I said. "There's nothing Asher can do right now. I told you about my talk with Meryl. There's political pressure from above to have Skowby and his minions here."

"So the Croakers must have friends in high places," Jilly said. "It didn't sound like Dawes was the type."

Keats had been silent, keeping a wary eye on Veronica, but now his muzzle came up to give me a piercing look with his blue eye. "Maybe it's less about high places than the place itself. There's always been speculation about the Harlow land, according to Uncle Sterling. Could this be another treasure hunt?"

"Quite possible," Edna said. "If the so-called gentlemen's club was away, I presume you came up empty?"

Keats gave a mumble of disgust that said it all.

"If it weren't for Violet, we'd be totally in the dark," I said. "And here she is now."

The vehicle rolling slowly up the lane huffed, puffed and blew off a mysterious mauve cloud before coming to a stop beside Jilly's coolers.

"Where on earth did this relic come from?" Edna said.

"You talking about me, old friend?" Gertie Rhodes chuckled as she jumped down from the driver's seat. She was wearing her usual brown poncho, although the distinctive shape of Minnie, her rifle, was missing underneath. A long braid nearly reached her knees and if Gertie cared about scaring people, it didn't show. "I'm five years younger than you."

"Only on your forged passport," Edna parried. "But you're in good shape for your vintage, unlike this wreck. Did you pull it from the museum of food trucks?"

"Buckley hooked us up," Gertie said. "For a hermit who never answers his phone, he's surprisingly well connected."

The window at the side opened and my sister Violet's head appeared. Her long brown hair, just a shade lighter than mine, was tucked under a baseball cap that read "Mandy's Catering." The same logo—a pie wearing a bashful grin—graced her apron. "Ready for action?"

"You bet," Jilly said, lifting the first cooler. "Stew for a crew of hungry men. Any idea how many?"

"Fleet told Mandy to prepare for twelve," Violet said. "I'm so glad you guys could help. Mandy can't leave the store for long and I could never handle three meals alone."

"Wouldn't have it any other way," Edna said. "There's something fishy going on and the only way we'll find out is by getting in there."

"This stew will loosen lips," I said. "Guaranteed."

Jilly loaded the first cooler into the back of the truck. "Maybe it'll win Violet a boyfriend."

Edna and Gertie did the rest while I touched the faded red lettering on the side of the big truck. "Chippies. That's an unfortunate name. Shame we don't have time to paint over it."

"Priorities," Edna said, gesturing to me to climb into the kitchen in the rear. "We'd better hustle if we're going to get there for morning break. I'll ride shotgun."

Keats rounded me up and delivered me to the passenger door. "Overruled, Edna. Sorry."

She grumbled while walking to the back. "It's not like you can help if Gertie expires at the wheel. This thing takes an experienced handler."

I laughed. "Yeah, one with a license. I could get us there. It's not far, even going around the long way. Besides, it's more about Keats wanting a bird's-eye view."

"Come along, Percy," Jilly said, crooking her arm to receive him.

"You can't bring a cat onto a food truck, Jilly," Violet said. "It's unsanitary. Mandy has standards."

"And I don't?" Jilly asked. "I cook fine dinners with this guy around and no one's ever complained. No man getting a whiff of this stew will even notice the cat."

"Besides, he'll be off exploring with Keats," I called, as the rest got into the rear of the truck. "What we can't do under a safety inspector's watch, they can."

Keats mumbled agreement to that. Veronica must have endorsed the plan, too, because the last thing I saw as the truck pulled out was a flash of auburn and a white tail tuft disappearing into the trees.

"Is there a plan?" Jilly asked. "Or are we winging it?"

"Winging it is a plan," I said. "Follow the fox, annoy the acting chief if he shows up. That's it for me so far."

Edna cackled behind me. "Setting achievable goals is important but you could aim a little higher."

We were only halfway down the lane when a sudden lurch forced me to amend my plan. "And learn to change a tire. Fast."

That goal proved out of reach of this former city girl, but two skilled octogenarians had the job done in about 15 minutes. It would have been less if they hadn't fought over the honors. In the end, Gertie's poncho proved her undoing because it snagged her arms and Edna, even in her sensible senior attire, was able to manhandle the spare into position and tighten three of the bolts.

"I'll leave the last one to you, old friend," she said. "Just so you don't feel outclassed."

"Never will as long as you can't drive," Gertie said, grabbing the wrench. "I suppose we should have made this a teachable moment for the kids."

"This kid will take a pass," Jilly said. "I'm all for being an independent woman, but you don't marry a man like Asher because you enjoy breaking a nail."

Gertie held up her hands to show two broken nails and a lot of grime. "Fair point."

"You can't serve food with those hands," Violet said. "Mandy—"

"Has standards," I finished. "We know. Keep in mind she couldn't have taken this gig without our help."

"Unpaid help," Gertie added, firing up the chip truck again. "It's not like we have nothing better to do. I cancelled a fencing lesson to be here."

"Oh, please," Edna said. "Like you'd be anywhere else. You were dying to show off your stick handling."

Gertie piloted the truck with assertive yet gentle care. "True enough. It's good to feel needed."

"We always need you," Jilly said. "Both of you."

I turned and grinned at Edna, who was riding in a flip-down seat that would never pass current road safety checks, while my sister and Jilly tried to stay upright while clinging to frayed vinyl handles. It was a good thing we weren't going too far. "Absolutely. And my chances of achieving my goal are higher with you here. I'm guessing Skowby will visit and we may need to work fast to get him annoyed."

"Fear not, bestie," Jilly said. "Just seeing you will do the trick. You're a living, breathing reminder that he's sloppy seconds in the chief role. Even with his high-profile backers, he'll never match Kellan's accomplishments."

"You mean Ivy's accomplishments," Edna said. "And ours, Jillian. It astounds me how you modern women still want to stand behind your men."

"Not true." I kept my hands on Keats and turned my eyes to the side of the road. Now and then I saw a flash of rusty red. This parade float had a grand marshal in vixen form. "Kellan and Asher wouldn't even want us standing behind them and the very fact we're here proves we don't."

"Kellan asked you to stay away?" Gertie said between clenched teeth. It was taking all her focus to keep the old wreck on the road. The truck was very much inclined to drift into the ditch and die a peaceful death in a dirty snow drift. Thank goodness there was no ice or I wouldn't like our chances of making it to the site by break time.

"Of course," I said. "He also asked me not to provoke Skowby. And yes, he called him 'chief.' Maybe even more often than the mayor."

"So, the former Chief Hottie is taking his fate lying down, too." Edna had to shout over the combined clanging and rattling of the truck's engine and the cookware. "Sounds like I'll have two big lugs to carry when the end comes. Good thing I've started weight lifting."

I ignored the taunt. "If Kellan is worried he didn't let on."

"Chain of command," Edna said. "They're trained to do what they're told when they're told. Eventually a learned helplessness sets in."

Jilly took over for me. "Kellan is far from passive. He breaks plenty of rules around here for the sake of the public. Asher, too."

I thought about the night Mom and I caught them drag racing on the back country trails and smiled. "Not all of them for the sake of public safety. They go rogue more often than we probably know. But there's not much Kellan can do from wherever he's deployed and Asher understandably wants to keep his job."

I turned to look at Jilly, who continued to hold Percy while swinging wildly. She managed a tight smile and a nod. "It's on us. All of us."

"Not me," Violet piped up. "I'm just here to cater."

"That's right, sis. You're here to cater to a fox, a brilliant dog and a fearless cat. But it all starts with serving food and lowering inhibitions. Can you do that?"

She laughed. "I accept the challenge."

"Throw in some flirting," Edna said. "It galls me to suggest it but there's a time and a place to exploit youthful good looks. Interrogating a male work crew at a crime scene is one of those times."

"I've texted Poppy and Iris, too," I said. "Unlike me, some of the Galloways have picked up feminine wiles from Mom."

"You landed the chief of police," Jilly reminded me. "You're no slouch."

"More luck than skill, I'm afraid. But we can all work our charms to see what we can pull out of these guys."

"What little I have is draining fast on this truck," Gertie said, as we turned into the long and exceedingly rough new road from the highway into the worksite.

"Happy to take over," Edna said. "My organs are rearranging themselves back here, under your leadership."

A few minutes later we pulled into the open area where Acting Chief Skowby had hassled us two days ago. It seemed fitting to park the chip truck there and take our stand. There was no one to complain. If the safety inspector the mayor mentioned was around, he wasn't in sight.

"Deploy," Jilly said. "Ivy may not have a plan but Violet and I do. There are hungry mouths to feed and that's what I do best."

She ordered the rest of us around in very tight quarters and I was glad Gertie had left Minnie at home or someone might have blown out the floor. I sent Keats and Percy out to explore, deciding it was more dangerous inside than out. Keats was gone before I had a chance to change my mind.

By the time Iris and Poppy pulled up beside us, we were ready to roll, all of us in aprons and caps except Gertie. Turns out she had standards, too.

Jilly opened the side window all the way and leaned out to ring an old school bell Edna had apparently liberated from my elementary school. It clanged loudly and Fleet Jurgen came out of the bush to find out what the racket was about.

His silver eyebrows rose in surprise. "What are you ladies doing here?" There was just the slightest hesitation over the word "ladies," when his eyes fell on Gertie, who hopped down after me. "We ordered catering from Mandy McCain. No slight to your cooking, Jilly. It's just that the police chief banned you and Ivy from the site. Or so Skowby told me."

"That's when it was a crime scene," I said, heading toward him with a tray of steaming quesadillas. "When it was cleared so quickly, Mandy hired us to deliver since she has a store to run. My sister Violet is on Mandy's team but it's a bigger job than she could manage alone. And since the gentlemen's club hasn't been around much, we had the time, expertise and groceries to spare."

His brows came together. "I don't think Chief Skowby would be—"

"Have a quesadilla," I said. "I hope you don't mind grilled chicken, because beef is on tap for lunch. There are mini pizzas, too. Triple cheese and bacon. Best thing ever!"

He glanced around at the men surging out of the trees. I counted four beyond our paying guests, and every face lit up at the smell wafting toward them. Shrugging, Fleet took off his work gloves and helped himself. After swallowing, he pronounced the food "very good," and showed his teeth in a real smile. It was a nice set of choppers, even with red pepper studding a few.

The men gathered, and as I'd fully expected, my sisters proved to be popular servers. It was hardly a sacrifice, since even the guys who were technically average-looking had a rugged appeal.

While the cheese and carbs pumped happy chemicals into their bloodstream, I let Keats guide me around from one set of boots to another. None of the rank and file seemed to warrant more than a cursory sniff. Fleet, however, was another story, and that's where my dog ultimately dropped me off with mumbled orders to "do my thing." My thing was to put what Keats was smelling, hearing or otherwise sensing into more concrete form.

Proffering my nearly empty tray, I directed my best HR smile at Fleet. I couldn't flirt but I could be the hostess with the second mostest, since the primary cook was still filling trays in the truck. "You guys were missed last night—particularly by the single women of Clover Grove, my mother included."

Fleet smiled again and the bits of pepper were gone. "Your mother is charming, as are your sisters." His eyes moved to his men. "Word to the wise, though. My choppers are all good guys but we never stay long enough to set down roots."

"Roots. Clever." His puzzled stare told me the play on words hadn't been intentional. "I'll warn the ladies not to get too attached. Meanwhile, can you tell me where you found a better meal than Jilly had ready and waiting for you?"

"Not better, certainly." He bit into another quesadilla and swallowed before saying, "She's a fine cook. But sometimes the men need to cut loose so we hit a pub in Dorset Hills and played pool."

"St. Bernard Billiards?" To my knowledge, there was only one pub in Dog Town with pool tables, and it was a holdover from before their city council began pushing a more upscale tourist experience.

"That's it. Right." He smiled again and red pepper once more marred his perfect teeth. "It's been a strange few days, with the project off and then on and now expanded." His smile faded as he glanced around again. "I prefer keeping things small and tight, even if it takes a little longer. But it isn't my call."

"No, I suppose with Dawes gone, it's Marlene Croaker's call. She must be a resilient woman to carry out her husband's vision so quickly. Perhaps she's still in shock."

He locked his upper lip over the pepper bits. "Probably. Who wouldn't be? I suppose a lot of us feel obligated to live out our loved one's legacy."

I made a show of looking over his shoulder. "You're clearing so much land that I'm starting to worry."

"Why? Are you one of those tree-huggers?" The lip went up again and this time the pepper held tight. It was a bit unnerving to see flecks of red the size of blood droplets.

"Not really. The woods around here spook me a little. They're full of secrets and, if you listen to gossip, dead bodies."

"I don't listen to gossip, although I've heard my share of urban myths." He shrugged. "In this case, rural myths."

I waited till he took another bite to ask, "Have you ever dug up a body?"

He nearly choked on the quesadilla. "A body? Well, I don't do the digging. We clear the land and contract out excavation."

A deft evasion. "I bet you have, though. Because I have, and not so very far from here."

Now he backed away from me a couple of steps. "Is that what you're worried about? More bodies so close to home?"

"No, although bodies aren't good for business, as I learned the hard way. It's taken us ages to bounce back from an early crime at Runaway Farm. I'm worried about a different kind of threat—a competing business. From what I see, you're clearing enough land for a big resort."

He backed away more. "I'm not privy to the housing plan, but Marlene said nothing of a resort."

"Housing plan... does that mean it's multiple houses? A condominium? As the closest neighbor, I'd really love to know."

"I'm hired to oversee chopping and digging." He was now a couple of yards away. "The details are above my paygrade."

That was the second time I'd heard the expression in two days. It grated on me because my former boss spewed it around our corporate offices whenever he wanted to withhold information.

"Someone will know. Nothing stays a secret long in this town."

He stopped walking. "For the record, my men sign confidentiality agreements. We wouldn't be the most in-demand crew in hill country if we left a mess behind."

Jilly's food had left a mess behind in his mouth. "Got it. Happy chopping! See you at lunch."

I hadn't planned to follow him but Keats had gradually eased me in Fleet's direction. The lead hand gave a shrill whistle for his crew and they faded into the trees, leaving me standing beside the long rack of firewood I admired on my first visit. It still gave me woodpile envy.

Percy's weight shifted on my shoulder—a signal he planned to take off and make the stack his personal catwalk. I lifted a glove to stop him and then pointed at the white tuft of a tail on the other side of the rack heading to the far end of the pile. Following, I peered over it just as Veronica sat down a few yards away and wrapped her fluffy tail neatly around her paws. Up close, she was stunning, with amber eyes that seemed to bore into my soul. "Hello, there. What news have you?"

The "news" sat in a cubbyhole where a log should be, just a few feet from the end. It was full of leaves that were oddly green for this time of year. I was curious enough to pull them out and then gasped. Tucked in behind was a box of poison.

I'd seen this brand before and knew it was intended for mice and rats. Here on a woodlot, there was no reason for pest control—unless someone considered a fox a pest, and a rifle wasn't getting the job done. Poisoning that fox's food source might be an alternative strategy.

Pulling a bag from my pocket, I filled it with the cubbyhole's contents. "I hope your nose can detect a rotten rodent, Veronica, because the fresh leaf disguise suggests Fleet has picked up where Dawes left off." I shoved the bag into my pocket. "I'll find a way to bring it up with our guests without offending them." Meeting her eyes again, I smiled. "I've got your back, girl."

The pretty fox lifted her muzzle and yipped. Keats yipped back, making me wonder if there was any overlap in their canid language. It seemed like a congenial exchange, and even Percy added a meow from my shoulder.

"Thanks for the heads-up," I told the fox, before heading back to the chip truck. "The last thing we need around here is another murder."

## CHAPTER THIRTEEN

After we cleared the decks from one meal and prepared for the next, everyone hopped out for a break. There were too many bodies for the small space and even Jilly wanted to get away from a two-burner cooktop that made the stove at the inn look like the height of luxury. Still, those burners were sufficient to heat one very large pot of beef stew and a small one of a vegetarian dish. I doubted she'd get many takers on the chickpeas, but my best friend always covered her bases. There were a couple of quiches if all else failed.

We walked around the woodlot together and I showed them where we'd discovered the poison. Then we followed the sound of chainsaws and found the crew in an even larger clearing. They were so busy razing trees they didn't realize they had an audience. Rob Snooks, the worker Mandy admired, was harnessed and dangling from a crane, looking rather like bait on a fishhook. We had crowded so close together that I could feel shoulders shaking. The lumberjack allure faded quickly, at least for me.

Gertie signaled for us to leave just as Rob started what looked like an uncontrollable and uncomfortable spin at the end of his tether. No wonder these guys got danger pay. As someone who feared heights, I thought it looked like the worst job ever. Still, I was riveted and wanted to watch where he landed. His colleagues were scattered around the clearing, some lower, some higher. The raucous din continued and the earth trembled underfoot as wide trunks came down in large pieces. There were bellows of warning I was surprised anyone could hear through ear protection.

"It smells nice, but something's fishy," Gertie said, as we walked back to the truck. "Even more than that lad on a fishpole. No one clears so much land for a house."

"Even a palace," Edna said. "I'll be speaking my piece to Meryl Martingale. Whatever they're doing, it's far too close to my property for my liking."

"Good luck with the mayor," I said. "She told me this is above her paygrade."

"Not above mine. I'm a colonel in my own army. How many can say that?"

Edna cackled and we joined in. I was glad we could still find humor in this strange situation.

Jilly headed inside the truck and rang the school bell again. This time the men came almost at a run. The magic combination of her cooking and Mandy's had won fans.

Fleet not only kept his distance from me at lunch, he also circled his crew like a human sheepdog. The regular sheepdog worked hard to divert him and mainly succeeded in disrupting Fleet's meal. At this rate, I'd learn very little about what was happening here, but at least the crew put away all of Jilly's famous stew. Only two of them turned down beefy goodness in favor of the quiche and I was surprised the number was that high. The chickpeas got a hard pass.

Keats was finally making headway in bringing the men and women together when Fleet put fingers to his mouth and issued that sharp whistle again. With sheepish shrugs, the crew followed him through the stumps and into the trees.

"Maybe we'll have better luck at afternoon break," Jilly said.

"We'll lean heavily on sweets to loosen tongues. Mandy added real bourbon to the sauce for the bread pudding."

"I'll need that bourbon if I can't figure this out," I said. "Fleet is definitely hiding something and his crew must know enough that he's keeping them from mingling."

"This time we'll have a better plan," Edna said. "Because you might not get another chance."

Jilly sighed. "They'll probably skip dinner and go back to the pool hall tonight."

I flashed my phone at her. "Fleet lies as well as evades. I asked Remi Malone to find out if a bunch of lumberjacks were at St. Bernard Billiards last night and her source said no. He checked the other pubs, too, and no dice."

"They'd be hard to miss," Jilly said. "At least they paid us in full and I'll be able to use some of the food I ordered to cater their meals here."

"Tomorrow I'm coming in fatigues and crawling through bush to see what we're missing," Edna said. "I can tolerate a lot for a cause but never boredom."

"You won't be bored for much longer." I pointed to the bumpy road. "There's a cavalcade coming our way."

I figured it would be the police. *Should* be the police. A man was killed here so recently, and no matter how it happened, it warranted a security presence beyond what my friends and I provided. Even the safety inspector the mayor mentioned was a no-show.

The vehicle in the lead wasn't a police SUV but a Land Rover with the sunroof open. A dark-haired man was at the wheel while a senior in the passenger seat held his safari hat down with one hand while gesticulating at the other vehicles to back off.

They weren't backing off. A Jeep was close on their fender while a sedan built for more sedate outings pulled up the rear.

When the Land Rover stopped, the young man leapt out of the driver's seat and ran around to get the door for his mature companion. They reminded me of the hosts on that old TV show about wildlife. Asher and I used to watch the recordings Dad left behind when he vanished.

Edna offered the elderly man a mock salute. "Melvin Yardine. Fancy meeting you here. Shouldn't you be out tracking Sasquatch? That's about all that's left in hill country for wildlife fans. Slim pickings for the Dorset Hills Conservationist Society."

"Stand down, Edna," Gertie said. "I believe Melvin's driver is the fellow who wrestled a wild boar out of a culvert in Brenton."

"You don't say." Edna scanned the younger man from head to foot, perhaps assigning him space in her future bunker. "I apologize for dismissing you as a Ken doll. Wild boar are fierce fighters. I bet Mel sat in the car shouting stage directions."

The old man took the bait. "Wild pigs are precisely the reason we're here, Edna. That's all this land will be good for by the time this work is done. If you climbed off your ATV more, you'd know there are plenty of foxes and coyotes. I've seen lynx and even cougars. Haven't seen a wolf in years, mind you, and never will after the casino goes up."

"Casino!" I let Keats herd me in front of Edna. "They can't build a casino here. It's zoned for residential builds."

"Exactly," said the woman in a khaki jacket and hat who was standing beside the Jeep. She was likely in her seventies, as was the man with her. "My husband and I are nearly all that's left of the local birding club and we're here to protest the build. I heard it was a saloon, but a casino is even worse. Gambling away the lives of birds already near extinction. Did you know we're the only ones who saw a rare pair of purple gallinules in the marsh here last year?" She smiled in triumph. "Something you'll never see, Edna, although I heard you started your own nature club."

Edna leaned around me. "Settle down, Claudette. I thought you and Pierre had gained your wings and someone had to take up the cause."

Gertie snickered and I gestured for both to let me speak. "Where did you folks get your information? I spoke directly to the mayor and she wouldn't give me a hint of what this project is about."

A woman with sharp features and dyed red hair came forward from the sedan. She was about my mother's age and height but that is where the similarities ended. This woman had dressed for long forays in the bush and looked capable of dealing with wild boar, too. "I heard it was a massage parlor. We all know that's code for brothel."

A gasp rippled through the small crowd, including my sisters and even Jilly. Edna was fighting a guffaw and losing the battle, so I jumped in quickly. "It's not a brothel, of that I'm sure. Meryl Martingale would be thrown out of office."

"That's crazy talk, Aster Crooks," Edna said. "Have you been smoking some of your own weeds?"

Aster directed a scowl at Edna that would have withered most people but earned only the threatened guffaw. "As head of the Clover Grove Wildflower Club, I can assure you I protect our native foliage instead of using it for illicit ends. I'm quite sure ginseng is behind this project."

"Ginseng?" I asked. "How so?"

"It's a hot commodity on the black market," Aster said. "Everyone knows that. But few seem aware of how much wild ginseng grows in our area. It requires mature deciduous trees to thrive, including ash, maple and oak. They've decimated hundreds of those trees here already. And for what?"

"You must stop this atrocity right now," Claudette said. "For the gallinules and other waterbirds that need the wetlands you'll dry out and drain."

"Not to mention the wildlife you're driving higher into the hills, where there's precious little food and shelter," Melvin echoed.

"And the ginseng is just the most marketable of many plants being murdered in their sleep," Aster said. "Stop the carnage now."

Five fists came up and five voices began chanting. "Stop the carnage!"

Edna bellowed over them to be quiet, giving me just enough of a gap to say, "Folks, we're concerned about this build, but I took my voice to city hall and you should, too. We're only here to provide catering."

"If you're catering, you're caving," Aster said. "No one who truly cared about the environment would feed these killers. I'm going into that forest to strap myself to a hundred-year-old oak. Who else needs rope?"

"Me," said Melvin. "We'll strap in, too."

"Ready, willing and able," Claudette said. "Let's call all our friends. Make this a real protest."

They pulled out their phones and Melvin was the first to strike gold. "My poker club wants in but they don't drive." He turned to the younger man. "I'll pick a good spot while you head over to Sunny Acres Retirement Villa. Grab anyone who's fully mobile. Terrain's too rough for walkers and wheelchairs."

"Don't discriminate," Claudette said. "The infirm can dominate the parking area. I called that reporter. She's a weasel but she'll get our faces in the news."

Aster's gloved hands thudded together. "This will be a protest like Clover Grove has never seen before."

"That's for sure," Edna muttered, amusement giving way to concern. "A bunch of frail seniors strapped to trees is a bad idea. I'm the first to back the elderly but someone's bound to go into shock or fall. I should go home for my medical kit."

I looked over at Jilly and found her texting with savage jabs. "I keep trying Fleet Jurgen and he's not answering. It's their problem to solve."

"It'll be ours soon," I said. "We can't stand around while people put themselves at risk."

Finally, a whistle made us turn to see Fleet coming out of the woods, followed by a trickle of men. The sound wasn't nearly as sharp as it had been earlier and they were moving slowly. Fleet was on the phone, probably briefing Marlene Croaker, the wallet behind this operation.

I was reasonably confident Jilly and I could puncture this balloon before it burst and hurt people, but wanted Fleet to take the first swing at it. He was normally confident and composed but now he mopped sweat out of his eyes. His ruddy cheeks had paled, too. Was he really that scared of a bunch of environmental activists? Maybe the powerful people pulling the mayor's strings would call Fleet on the carpet for bringing bad press.

Bad press personified arrived in the form of Justine Schalow. She must have already been en route when Aster called. Pushing through a small crowd she could have easily walked around, she demanded, "What's going on? Who's in charge here?"

Fleet Jurgen started to raise his hand and stopped. He reeled a few steps, clutching his midriff.

"Fleet?" Jilly said. "What's wrong?"

The crew leader didn't answer. Instead, he dropped his phone and fell over backwards.

## CHAPTER FOURTEEN

The rest of the team also fell one by one, until only two choppers were left standing.

"All dead," Justine announced, more excited than dismayed. "It's a massacre. Ivy Galloway, what did you do this time?"

The protestors started screaming again but at least the jumble of words did not include "stop the carnage."

"Not dead, you idiot." Edna shoved Justine aside and knelt beside Fleet. "Make yourself useful and call an ambulance. More like three ambulances. Gertie, any chance you brought your kit?"

"Sorry, no," Gertie said. "Just tools and a fire extinguisher."

"I did." I turned in surprise to see my sister Poppy running to her car. "I travel heavy now. Something Edna taught me."

"See, girls?" Edna didn't look up from checking Fleet's pulse but I knew the comment was directed at Jilly and me. "That'll teach you to mock my classes." Releasing his wrist, she checked her watch. "We don't have long for this to work. It's already been forty minutes."

"Forty minutes since what?" Jilly asked.

"Take Violet and check on the others," Edna told her. "Make sure they stay conscious and sit them up if you can." She waited till

Jilly was on the move and whispered, "Ivy, hang on. Grab this." She managed to nod toward Fleet's phone while continuing to loosen his scarf and jacket. "Then keep the crowd back."

"Fleet's alive," I called out, discreetly sliding the phone into my side pocket. "Rob. Rob!" He was one of the two choppers standing, but both were gaping in shock. "Do you guys have first aid kits?"

Nodding, he grabbed his friend and went back to the clearing. They picked up speed as they moved.

Keats poked me in the shoulder and I turned in the direction he pointed. Percy was parked on top of the prostrate redheaded lumberjack. "Look, Edna. Percy's just sitting there, grooming."

"Ivy, really?" Justine had leaned in to listen. "It's news that your cat is grooming when men have fallen all around you?"

It was news indeed that my cat wasn't pronouncing anyone dead at the scene, but I couldn't explain that to Justine. I could only imagine the play that story would get in her rag.

"Yes, Justine. For us, that is news."

"Why? Don't you have bigger worries right now?"

"We're worried all right, but these men will get the treatment they need."

"But for what?" Justine pressed. "They must have been poisoned."

"That's my guess, too," I said. "Maybe they were using chemicals in the bush. Why don't you go see?"

She rolled her eyes. "Nice try, Ivy. You'd be happy if I passed out in there and was never found."

"Only half true. I'd come and save you, like I always do. But you might just find a real scoop in there."

One of her sneakers slid under Fleet and nudged him. "I think the big news is out here."

"Stop that right now, young lady," Edna said. "And I do use the term loosely. Never kick a man when he's down with poison." Perhaps it was a coincidence that she waited till Justine bent closer before bellowing, "Poppy Galloway, bring that kit, STAT!" The noise not only startled Justine, it made Fleet's eyes flutter open and he groaned.

The next few minutes became a blur, as Edna, Gertie and Poppy mixed and administered activated charcoal, while Jilly, Violet and I propped up the ailing men. The two healthy lumberjacks came back and helped, too.

By the time the ambulances arrived, the activists had dispersed, perhaps to avoid being blocked by emergency vehicles.

After briefing the paramedics, Edna joined us, checking to make sure Justine was fully occupied being an impediment to the authorities.

"How did you know to give them charcoal when the poison is unclear?" I asked.

"I guessed how it got in and while charcoal doesn't always help, it rarely hurts." She winced a little. "Except for the frontline staff cleaning up later. Sometimes there's an eject sequence that won't be a picnic with so many large men."

"How were they poisoned?" Jilly asked.

Edna gestured around the clearing. "Take a good look, Jillian. Use your powers of deduction."

Jilly did just that. Then she pressed both gloved hands to her forehead. "Oh. Oh no."

"What?" I said, clutching her arm.

"The stew. The only men who didn't get sick chose quiche."

"Exactly," Edna said. "And here I was lamenting they didn't leave a morsel of beef for us."

"This is awful." Jilly's voice was a hoarse rasp. "Everyone will say my cooking is toxic. The inn is doomed."

"Simmer down or I'll turn Gertie's fire extinguisher on you, Jillian. Nothing you did to your signature dish could take strapping men down that fast."

"But what then?" I slapped my pocket. "Was it the rat poison?"

"Unlikely," Edna said. "The required dose would have made the stew inedible and no one complained about the taste."

Jilly continued to moan. "How could this happen?"

I patted her arm. "I'm guessing someone slipped into the chip truck when we did our group walkabout before lunch and doctored the stew."

"There wasn't a bit left to test," Jilly said. "How will they figure it out, Edna?"

"Dorset Hills has a good toxicology department. They'll have the men back on their feet in no time."

My best friend's eyes had filled with tears. "Not before our reputation is ruined. Again. I should never have left the food unattended. What cook does that?"

"A chip truck newbie who doesn't expect a killer to infiltrate?" I asked. "If anyone's guilty, it's me. I shouldn't have asked all of you to explore the site with me."

"Like you could have stopped us," Gertie said. "The only person at fault is the poisoner."

I glanced down at Keats. "Is the poisoner still here?"

He mumbled a negative. His tail was down but perhaps that had more to do with missing the crime in the first place. While we were away, the toxic mice had played.

"It could have been anyone," I said. "Even the two men who chose quiche."

I turned back to the busy scene of paramedics working over the men. Some patients were already being transferred to ambulances. "This was very nearly the carnage our activists shouted about. If there's any bright side, it's that the mayor can't turn a blind eye anymore. First Dawes and then this. I'll try her again later, after—uh-oh."

Acting Chief Skowby and his henchmen, Fenway and Gibbons, were coming our way, while two of Kellan's officers carried Justine back to her car. Her sneakers kicked wildly, and I wondered how long it would be before her footwear choice caught up with her. Real winter would circle back and take her down eventually.

It struck me now that the new police executive team had presence, although I didn't want to admit it. In another life, I probably would have found them attractive, particularly Deputy Chief Fenway. Technically, Skowby was better looking, but at least Tye Fenway smiled now and then, while Gibbons didn't make decisions about his facial expressions without first checking with his colleagues.

"Mrs. Galloway," Acting Chief Skowby said, "I understand you've poisoned a small army." The comment was directed at Jilly and somehow the title felt diminishing. "That was efficient, but probably not great for your reputation as a chef."

Her earlier panic had subsided enough that she could straighten her shoulders and meet his eye. "I'm sure your diligent police work will prove I'm innocent of that horrible accusation, Chief Skowby."

His stare was unflinching. "The only men left unscathed skipped your beef stew, from what I hear. How do you explain that?"

I answered for Jilly, although she seemed to be doing fine on her own. "Are you kidding? What would we stand to gain from taking down a lumber crew—some of whom we're hosting?"

"I heard you wanted to interfere with this project," he said. "Went straight to the top about it. When you didn't get the answer you wanted, you derailed it in one fell scoop."

His lips twitched over his play on words and it was the closest to a smile he'd come.

"I doubt this will slow the project one bit," I said. "Fleet might be the best in the biz but any crew can clear-cut a forest. With all due respect, sir, you're wasting time taunting us that could be used to figure out what really happened. Someone obviously got into our truck while we were taking a walk before lunch."

"Hard to prove," he said. "Maybe you could do that for me, Miss Galloway. Rumor says you're resourceful."

I hated when men like him called me "miss." He was only a few years my senior, so it was meant to diminish me. But I had to look cooperative now that we really were implicated. "I'd be happy to try, sir." I jabbed a gloved index finger in a triangle. "Security cameras, and there may be more. How about giving me access to the feed and I'll serve that proof to you on a silver platter?"

"I've got a better idea. How about you ladies head home? You'll need to find your own way because we're impounding your toxic take-out tank."

I couldn't help smiling a little and wondered briefly if I might like him under other circumstances—say a time he wasn't trying to oust my fiancé and enable a corrupt agenda. "Fine. We'll go. But then you don't get to know what we know."

He crossed his arms and struck a classic cop pose. "That's not how this works. The information highway goes one way."

His deputy stepped forward. "Chief, let me handle this. They're probably quite rattled over what happened. From what I've heard, Ivy and Jilly are clever, capable women. Doesn't seem likely they'd risk their business with such a blatant ploy."

Skowby looked at his sidekick and gave a slight shrug. "I admit I'm hard-pressed to think of a good reason they'd compromise the careers of officers Galloway and Harper."

The word was another pinprick to my heart. "*Chief* Harper. Unless we missed your formal appointment, that is."

"I'll worry about my title and you worry about staying out of trouble. Go back to the farm and I'll be in touch."

"Awesome," I muttered, turning away. Poppy was already heading for her sedan and we followed. It was a good thing we'd cleared our personal belongings from the chip truck before they strung up yellow tape.

"Ivy, wait." I turned to see Fenway coming after us. "Do you really have more information? It'll buy me some time before coming over to question you. We've got a fair bit of work here."

"Where's the rest of the staff?" I asked, lagging behind my friends. "Asher would be happy to give you a hand here."

"I'm sure he would but that's not in the cards. At least right now."

The qualifier softened me ever so slightly. Perhaps Fenway could talk his boss down from his high horse.

I pulled the box of poison from my pocket and handed it to him. "I found this in the woodpile and assumed it was meant to target the fox. I showed it to the paramedics, of course."

"Anything else?" he prompted, with a smile. "I have the feeling there is."

I checked my other pockets and came up with Fleet's phone. "Oh, right. This fell out of Fleet Jurgen's hand when he fainted."

His head tipped almost impishly. "Did you get nosy with it?"

"I wish I had time. It was madness here till you arrived. Anyway, I'm sure a man like Fleet would have a password on his phone."

He did, and I'd cracked it easily. A man like Fleet should have chosen something less obvious than "choppers." I hadn't been able to do more than take some screen shots but there was time for review later.

"Nothing else?" Fenway asked.

I shook my head while watching the last of the ambulances pull out. "I truly hope everyone's all right. No matter how upset we are over a casino going up next door, we'd never hurt the workers."

Fenway smiled and it looked genuine. "I've heard nothing about a casino."

"What about a brothel?" Edna asked, falling back to join us. "That was everyone's next best guess."

"Brothels are illegal here, Miss Evans. As you can probably guess, the plans for this land are—"

"Above your paygrade?" I guessed.

"You got it." His smile really was quite nice and one of my sisters would fall prey to it if they weren't careful. "I wish I could give you a ride but it's not too far to walk."

"It's a few miles on the highway," I pointed out. "Not the safest jaunt on a winter day."

"We'll take the bush." Edna gestured to our usual trail. "Be home in a jiffy."

"You'll take two trips with the car," Fenway said. "I suppose at your age it is a hike."

I held up my hand to my friend. "Edna, don't. Deputy Chief Fenway is seeing you as a regular senior instead of a skilled field medic who helped men in need today before paramedics arrived."

"I only wish your sister had stocked more activated charcoal in her kit," Edna grumbled. "I always advise carrying enough for an army. This will tide them over."

"Forgive me if I don't congratulate you until we've confirmed you aren't responsible," Fenway said. "The fact you came equipped with an antidote doesn't prove anything."

"We don't need to prove anything, because you will." I threw him a bright smile. "Given Chief Harper's stellar record, you must be excellent investigators to cover for him. Temporarily."

"I like to think we are." He looked a little smug for Keats' liking so the dog took a small lunge at the officer's cuffs.

"Sorry, Deputy," I said. "I think my dog wants you to go and clear our names. Linger and it won't end well for your uniform. Chief Harper spends a lot on mending his cuffs."

"Ow! Hey!" Fenway hopped and then moved away. "He'll regret that."

Keats circled back and I gave him a pat. "I hope he knows more about investigating than he does about dogs. Because the only thing you'll regret is not drawing blood."

## CHAPTER FIFTEEN

The three cops turned to watch as Poppy pulled her car around, so rather than overcrowd the sedan, Jilly and I followed the others on foot.

Once we were out of sight, we climbed in, too. The seating was both precarious and uncomfortable. We chose the back to be less visible from the police reinforcements I expected to pass on the way home. That meant splitting my weight between Gertie and Iris, while Jilly sat squarely on Edna.

"Stop squirming, for pity's sake, Jillian," Edna said. "It's a rough enough journey without that."

"Tell me about it," Jilly said. We'd both had a few good thunks to the head, despite Poppy's careful piloting. A lane dug in winter was bound to deliver a rocky ride.

"I should think I earned the front seat after my heroic efforts," Edna said.

Violet turned and frowned. "It's no party up here with two pets who can't keep their balance. I'm going to need a medic for the lacerations."

I did my best to brace myself on the door. "What a day. Everyone could use a quiet afternoon."

Keats mumbled from Violet's lap that he was ready to go another round.

"We need to do something," Jilly said. "I don't trust Skowby to clear our names. Who knows, maybe they're behind the poisoning? Tarnishing us reflects poorly on Kellan and Asher."

"Now you're sounding as paranoid as me," Edna said. "Besides, whatever's going on with this project, the mayor's involved somehow and I doubt she'd let you take the fall. She owes Ivy too much."

"A fact she's conveniently forgotten," I said. "But in all fairness, we owe Meryl, too. She's the one who sent business our way when no one else would take a chance on the inn."

"And here we are in the same predicament," Jilly fretted.

"Jillian, it's bad enough your skinny rump is slicing my legs without your whining piercing my eardrums. There are no whiners in the trenches. And if I'm carrying your husband and Kellan, I can't carry you, too. I know full well you can cook your way out of this crisis."

I expected Jilly to snap back but instead, she subsided. "You're right. I won't take this lying down. I'm a warrior."

"That's the spirit. We'll put our heads together over dinner and come up with a plan. Hold the toxins, please."

Jilly actually laughed. "You got it. The meal I was going to serve our guests will blow your combat boots off."

"Remember I'm wearing a nice wedge today," Edna said. "Hold the explosives."

By the time we reached the farm, I was marveling again over how my amazing friends—and even my family—could joke together through the most awkward moments, this ride being one of them. Laughter and camaraderie made everything bearable, and in this case, even enjoyable.

A knockout dinner wasn't guaranteed for me, however. As I clambered out of Poppy's car, I saw Veronica sitting beside the driver's door of my truck. Unlike Keats, she was gracious enough to allow me to draw my own conclusions and then move a few yards away.

"Where are you going?" Jilly called after me, as I walked to my truck and let Keats inside. "Skowby said to stay here."

I smiled at her before climbing in. "He told me to come back to the farm, which I did. He didn't say I had to stay here. My life revolves around those subtle distinctions. I'll be back before dinner."

"You bet you will," Jilly said, scooping up Percy. "Because I'm coming with you, and without me, there's no dinner."

"Excuse me?" Violet said. "I'm capable of making a meal. It may not blow boots off but it'll fill a hole."

"I'll join you, of course," Edna said. "I'm sure you were planning to extend an invitation."

"Someone needs to stay behind and sample Violet's fare." Gertie touched the shoulder of her poncho, where Minnie usually rested.

"You're unarmed, my friend," Edna said. "I don't feel good about that. Head over to my place and choose a little something dangerous. You know where I keep the treats."

Gertie laughed. "I do indeed, but there's something closer, remember?"

I glanced at Edna as I shut the door. "Are you stashing weapons on my farm? Where innocent animals could get hurt?"

"Don't be silly," Edna said. "We know your hysterical thinking on the subject." She got into the back of the truck. "We also know precisely where the property lines fall."

"Is there a—? Never mind." I started the truck and rolled down the lane. "I trust you and Gertie. What I don't know can't get me into trouble with Kellan."

"Oh, if only that were true." She cackled from the rear. "It's lovely to stretch out and relax, but it would be nice to know where we're going. If it's into battle, there's a full set of fatigues in my go-kit. Stashed it in your truck this morning, just in case. Nowadays, I feel so vulnerable in street clothes."

"What you're wearing is fine for this occasion. I thought we'd drive down to check out Orono County, home of the choppers, and see what we can learn about Fleet and his crew. They were lying about the pool hall and I bet that's the tip of the iceberg."

"I guess he's been knocked off the suspect list in Croaker's death," Jilly said.

I nodded. "Probably. Seems unlikely he'd take a hit of poison to throw us off the trail. He looked pretty miserable before he went down."

Edna adjusted again to accommodate Percy, who was in need of a nap before our next stop. "I guarantee he's still regretting that stew but it won't be long till they're back in the trees. Two or three days, tops."

Keats offered a mumble of encouragement and I smiled. "Should be enough time to figure things out, although I don't feel like we've made much progress."

Jilly slouched in her seat, a sign she was downshifting from red alert to amber. "At least we don't have guests to worry about. I doubt the crew will come anywhere near me after they're discharged."

I held up crossed fingers. "They'd be in our way, particularly with their expanding fan club."

"I feel sorry for all the single women in Clover Grove," Jilly said. "I hadn't realized quite how hard it is to find a good man, at least organically."

"It's no easier online, according to my sisters. They've pretty much given up, which is a shame."

"Another vote for the Clover Grove Culture Revival Project," Jilly said. "It's been hard to prioritize culture between business and the business of staying alive."

"Lumberjacks seemed like a good dating option at the outset. Too bad we're surrounded by corruption. Cops might be the only reliable source of quality men. Present chief excepted."

Edna heaved an exasperated sigh. "We talked about hormones

earlier and the value of putting them on ice. Your sisters should spend that energy on learning valuable survival skills. Like I always say, romance and offspring have no place in a bunker."

I caught her eye in the rearview. "Do they make baby camouflage?"

"They do, and I have some onesies in my hope chest for you girls, presuming you'll ignore my advice, as usual." She fanned her fingertips. "Never mind. To your original point, if it's so hard to find eligible men, why is Dahlia's dance card overflowing?"

I flinched, which was no doubt Edna's goal. "I've wondered that myself. It's still true even though she's stopped looking."

"Maybe it's a generational thing," Jilly said. "Hazel Bingham says all the good guys leave town in search of fame and fortune. Maybe they circle back when it's time to retire and find Dahlia."

Mom had formally disbanded her "rotation" a few months after my father returned to Clover Grove but I doubted he was the reason. They were civil to each other but I never saw them make idle conversation. His turf included barn and pastures; hers the inn and the entire town. It was easy for them to coexist in different spheres and overlap only for celebrations, during which they were pleasant. Perhaps his presence tamped down her flighty exuberance, and if so, I was grateful. We probably had Dad to thank for driving Mom deeper into her passion for designing clothing from reclaimed fabric. It was an odd family dynamic, but somehow it worked, even with Asher living there, Poppy and two of my nephews working in the barn, and Daisy helping to run the inn. Still, this week, with the rest of my sisters hanging around, I'd had moments of feeling as smothered as I did while living as a high-rise exec.

Keats put his paw on my arm and mumbled some comfort. I wasn't trapped. Indeed, if I played my cards right, I might never see the 30th floor of a building again, let alone get stuck in an elevator, which happened so many times I had nightmares about it. As if there weren't enough repressed experiences to relive while asleep.

"You okay?" Jilly asked.

I touched Keats' ears and nodded. "It was cramped in the chip truck today. Still don't love crowds, I guess."

"Better get over that before the end comes," Edna said. "Crowds mean you're less likely to get picked off by the enemy."

Jilly ignored her. "What about at home, Ivy? Are Asher and I crowding you?"

"Absolutely not. Don't tell him I said so, but I feel safer with him there, despite how he takes over the family room with his gear. He prowls by night and with Dad often sleeping in the loft, it's a pretty good security system."

Edna cleared her throat conspicuously. "I presume you're putting good neighbors in an elite category."

Smiling over my shoulder, I nodded. "You bet. No one is quicker in a crisis than my surveillance team next door."

"I was thinking of taking down a few more trees to clear the view." She sounded mollified. "This crew made me lose my taste for it."

"Same for my woodpile. Chopping was such a great outlet before the choppers."

Jilly cracked her window at Keats' request. "Those protesters today were crazy, but I saw their point."

"Yeah. I don't like the woods personally, but the plants, animals and birds deserve better. There's enough legit development in our area without indiscriminate clear-cutting. If there's no accountability to the public, where will it end?"

"You know where it will end," Edna said. "Why do you think I'm prepping?"

Jilly laughed. "It's a leap from over-clearing to the end times."

"People like you always downplay the risks until it's too late, Jillian. One day you're cooking at a double range, the next over a campfire lit with your own calloused hands."

"I've cooked a meal over an open fire, Edna. Tell her, Ivy."

"Simple, fast and tasty," I said. "I especially liked the bonfire blueberry buckle."

Edna paused to digest this tidbit. "It's hard to surprise me, girls, but you've done it."

Keats drew in a gusty snort and turned to catch my eye. "Here's another surprise," I said, taking the next exit. "My dog recommends a pitstop to rest and refuel."

## CHAPTER SIXTEEN

There was never much rest at our destination, and to my knowledge, no fuel, either. Sterling Fable, my dad's uncle, had never offered us so much as a box of crackers. Hospitality wasn't his strong suit, and finding him on the porch in sweatpants and a bathrobe that barely concealed a rifle showed little had changed.

I let the pets out of the truck and they raced up the stairs, fighting to be the first to say hello. The gruff old man was among their favorite people, which irked Mom to no end. She had a more combustible relationship with Sterling than my dad, probably because they aired the dirty laundry my father refused to take out of the family hamper.

"Hey, Uncle Sterling," I said. "You're looking well."

He scowled at me and lifted the rifle in an idle threat. "How would you know? You haven't seen this old man in a dog's age." Looking down at Keats, he cracked a smile. "No offense to your pup."

"We saw you at Christmas," Jilly said, going in for a hug, regardless of rifle. "You stayed for days, so it's barely a month. Plus I know Asher's been down a couple of times."

"Only because he needs to escape the estrogen," Sterling grumbled as he led us to the door. "Little does he know how much he'll value it later." He waited till we passed in front of him before adding, "Well, not Dahlia's. Or Edna's, if she has any left."

"I don't. Takes work to run it off, though. Whenever it seeps back in, I head to the firing range. Add a few days in a bunker and I'm good as new. You should try retraining your hormones, Sterling. With all that whining, it sounds like testosterone is on the wane. Exposure to these girls and their ticking clocks will deplete your vitamin T even more."

I looked at Jilly. "Remember when we were respected executives? Feared by men and women alike? We were sharks."

She laughed. "Miserable sharks, although we didn't know it then." She pressed another hug on Sterling and he didn't argue. "I wouldn't trade places with former Jilly for the world."

"What about you, missy?" he said. "Got a hug for your favorite uncle?"

"You know we're not a hugging family, but I suppose I can cough one up for my only uncle."

"Only one you know about." He took the hug and settled into his recliner, propping the gun against the arm beside his cane.

I sat across from him on the loveseat. "Excuse me? Are you hiding more family?"

"Visit more often and you might find out."

"Offer us something to eat and we might visit more often," I said. "I promised these two refreshments if we stopped in. It's been a long day."

He flicked his fingers from Jilly to the kitchen. "See what you can rustle up, Toots, but don't poison anything. I may be old but I still like being on this side of the turf."

Her cheeks burned as she walked away. "You heard already? In Fleetborough?"

"Can't fault our rumor mill for being slow. We have a high-speed infrastructure. Probably knew almost before you did."

"It wasn't us," I said. "Just for the record."

"Not deliberately, I'm sure. Bad for business. But if you were going to let food spoil, those choppers were good targets."

I slid to the edge of my seat. "You know Fleet Jurgen?"

"Just by reputation. Good chopper, shady character. Goes with the highest bidder regardless of the project. Wasn't surprised to see him cut down in his prime with all the trees he killed before their time."

Jilly's head poked out the kitchen door. "He's not dead, Sterling. Edna treated them on site."

He turned to give Edna a frown. "Do you need to play hero every time? It wouldn't hurt you to hold back a little. Let nature take its course."

"That wasn't nature," Edna said. "And I hold back nothing. Personal mission statement."

"We were just heading down to Orono County to see what we could learn about the crew," I said. "Sounds like you can make it easy for us."

"It's not easy in this kitchen," Jilly called. "There's nothing but cheese and a jar of olives. How do you survive, Sterling?"

"One of those meal services for frail old men. Plus the diner in town."

"Cheese and olives sound good to me," I said.

Jilly came out with a tray. "Score! Found some broken crackers. Only a year out of code."

"Dinner of champions," Edna said, as Jilly handed the tray around and then joined her on the couch. "Spill it, Sterling."

Instead of answering, he tossed bits of cracker to Keats. My dog wasn't a mooch but he enjoyed using his skills in any context. The higher Sterling tossed, the higher Keats jumped, adding unnecessary twists and spins. He reminded me of an aerial Alvina with her dance performances.

Touching down, the dog tossed me a blue-eyed glare, as if

sensing my disloyal comparison. This dog demanded to be judged on his own merits alone.

"Enjoy your game," I said. "Sterling is playing with us, too."

He tossed Keats a few more bites before finally going on. "You won't learn much in Orono because they don't live there. They don't live anywhere, really. Constantly on the move through the hills, following the next job."

"So he lied about driving straight to Clover Grove from Orono?"

"And plenty more, no doubt. Bet the only thing he was honest about was their skills."

I leaned back in my seat. "So he's just an ax for hire?"

"More or less. But they were holed up in Brenton for a couple of weeks this time, according to my sources. There was a call out for more choppers. Something big is happening."

"There were two crews on site today."

His silver eyebrows went up. "Only two? Where's the third?"

"Just two, thank goodness," Jilly said. "Maybe the project got downsized."

"Heard there's a crew at the Big Snooze Motel. Five men."

"The place my dad stayed?" It made me uneasy to think about how I visited him there before we started healing the rift. However, it also reminded me of how far we'd come.

"Still stays sometimes. That's how I know."

Now Jilly slid forward. "Why does Calvin stay there? There's plenty of room at the inn. Plus he owns the old Galloway house."

"And has a cot in the loft," I added.

Sterling waved a dismissive hand. "It's not my business where he stays, but if you were him would you want to share a roof with Dahlia?"

"Even I don't want to share a roof with Dahlia," I said, and we all laughed. "What I want to know is why Dad didn't tell me about this phantom third crew."

The bathrobed shoulders rose and fell. "Maybe he told your brother. You know, the one with the badge."

"The cop who's been sidelined to highway patrol," I said.

"Don't think that hasn't stung. Maybe your dad hoped it would get Ash out of the doghouse with Skowby. Or maybe he didn't say anything at all because no one asked."

I crossed my arms and fought the urge to pout. "Why do things need to be so twisty in this family?"

"It's baked into our DNA," he said, grinning. "Pouting is not."

My arms uncrossed. He had a point. "What do you know about Skowby?"

"Not much, and I've worked my traplines for intel. I suppose there's a reason they brought him in from the foothills. Hardly anyone's heard a word." He sighed. "In general, bad news travels fast, as you discovered today."

"Well, there can't be any good news about a man who'd happily shove a stellar chief out of his role."

"If Harper can be ousted, it's not Skowby doing the shoving," Sterling said. "Sometimes, a cop like Kellan gets moved out of the way."

"What's that supposed to mean? He's a decorated detective. The youngest chief in all of hill country."

My uncle glanced at Edna. "Remember this when you get your next hit of estrogen. Hysteria clouds rationality."

"Oh, I know. If I spend too much time knitting, it creeps up again. Then I need to replace the click of needles with the clash of swords."

Jilly came to my defense. "Ivy is far from irrational. She came here for help, didn't she?"

Keats gave a mumble and Sterling laughed. "Thought so. Look what the dog dragged in. Two hysterical women fretting about their beloveds."

"And trying to solve a crime," I said. "Two, as of today. Skowby whitewashed Dawes Croaker's death but he can't ignore seven men getting poisoned."

"He can if he takes orders like a good cop." Sterling's smile faded. "I won't say you don't have cause to worry. Crime is escalating in the region and with your men sidelined, you need to start thinking with your head, not heart. I've given you a start, no?"

Staring at the ceiling, I mused aloud. "About that third crew... Maybe the main site is a decoy. The property is huge. Triple the size of mine. They're cutting somewhere else."

"And bringing their own meals." He grinned again. "You ladies took the bait and drove over in a truck so that higher-ups could keep an eye on you. Bet there's a lot of security cams."

I rubbed my face with both hands. "We got played. It's embarrassing."

"Don't be so hard on yourself," he said. "That's my job. At least when Edna's too busy knitting to see the forest for the trees."

She bristled. "Sterling Fable, watch your mouth or I'll take out the teeth you have left."

Dropping both hands to Keats, I found him waiting. "Maybe they duped us into catering, but I stand by my decision to go. Question my rationality if you must but don't impugn my dog's. Or Veronica's."

He rolled his eyes. "Do I want to know?"

"She's the fox who led me to the old Harlow land in the first place and then again today. Keats and Percy endorsed the plan." The cat got in my uncle's face and swished a "so there."

By the time he'd sneezed Percy away, Sterling was smiling. "Well, what now?"

"Now we figure out who poisoned the crew, to clear our names," Jilly said.

"Plus we need to find the other site." I got up and started pacing. "This isn't about building a house or a casino. It's about what's buried on the property."

"Now you're cooking with gas," he said. "If they let you near a stove."

He grinned at Jilly and she scowled back. "How about you stop teasing us and start working those traplines?"

"Maybe it's above my paygrade," he said.

It felt like fire to gunpowder. "If I hear that phrase one more time, I'm going to—"

"Throw a hissy fit?"

Hissy fits came from a more primitive part of my brain. I needed to stop fretting about Kellan and find my way back to rational thought if I wanted to solve this crime. "Uncle Sterling, could you please take us to visit Palmer Harlow at his retirement home?"

He shook his head. "I promised not to spring any more surprises on him. But I'll call him tomorrow and see if he'll talk to me about the Spanish gold."

"Spanish gold?" Jilly and Edna chimed in over me.

"How lovely, a choir," Sterling said. "Might just be a hill country legend, but as a boy I heard Levon Harlow, Palmer's old man, lucked into pirate's treasure—a claim contested by Frank Swenson, the reigning crime lord of the day. As the story goes, Levon buried it good and deep on his land. If it exists at all, no one's found it and Levon's corrupt son Dutton looked long and hard." He shoved his recliner back one more notch. "Palmer had no interest in any of that. Like me, he learned a small life is a safe life."

I got up and forced an awkward second hug on him. "There's nothing small about your life, Uncle Sterling. I want to be just like you when I grow up. Only with plenty of estrogen and a dose of hysteria."

"Get out of my house," he said. "And take those stale crackers with you. Don't come back until you've got a pot of stew in the truck."

Jilly followed me to the door. "I'm never making stew again. Or chili, for that matter. My lumberjack recipes are being retired."

"Get right back on the horse, Toots. Some of us like to live dangerously."

I let the pets out and turned back. "You'll call when you learn something?"

"I'll go one better," he said. "Let's go cave diving."

Edna snorted. "You use a cane, old man. It's a liability on the dance floor, let alone in the bush."

"Oh yeah? I'll find that gold while you sit by and knit us a safety net."

She went back and shook his hand. "Game on. Then I'll crochet a sling to get you back to your recliner, where you belong."

# CHAPTER SEVENTEEN

L ibraries were near the top of my list of happy places, although they'd drifted below barn, pasture and manure pile. In childhood, I spent many happy days hidden in the stacks of the Clover Grove library and now I was growing fond of our librarian, Dottie Bridges. I'd managed to shelve my resentment over her aiding and abetting a murderer who set her sights on me. Crime-solving truly benefited from forgiveness. You never knew when someone who'd done you wrong would steer you right.

Thelma Tilrow and I got off to a better start. Sure, she'd put me through my paces, but she knew about me from her best friend Dottie and had ultimately come to my aid. More than that, she had put her life on the line for my beloved Keats. To me, that was more important than saving my own hide. Without him, well... I wouldn't go there. Despite being here, where it nearly happened. Specifically, we were heading up the ramp to the red schoolhouse that held the Thistledown library. I shivered as I walked in the door but the smell of old books went a long way to counter the trauma. Too bad they couldn't bottle that smell because a whiff would come in very handy in precarious situations.

Thelma was at command central, her check-out desk, and didn't lift her crown of stiff gray roller-set sausage curls. "Good evening, ladies. I expected you. That's the only reason the door is unlocked after five. I tend to be more cautious these days."

One could hardly blame her, after a killer staged an invasion with my dog and held her captive. She had offered herself in exchange for Keats, but the man needed to surrender a specific hostage to his crime lord and that was my dog.

Keats presented his ears to quell my nerves, but the fanning white tuft on his tail suggested those memories hadn't sunk their teeth into him as they had me. For the most part, old news was exactly that for him and facing a bath was more emotional than reentering a crime scene.

He moved away from me with an indignant grumble, perhaps sensing my traitorous thoughts.

"Well, hello handsome," Thelma said, her normally severe tone light. "It's good to see you in fine fettle."

"You don't hear the word fettle often these days," Edna said. "Shows your age, Thelma. If the roller set hadn't already done it."

"It's no worse than your perm, Edna," Thelma said. "If you're not worried about what those chemicals are doing to your faculties, keep taking the easy route. I value my acuity enough to heat up my rollers twice a week."

So many of my senior friends enjoyed trash-talking each other that I wondered if it was their way of connecting without getting sentimental. It was good for their acuity, too.

Jilly went over and hugged Thelma. We'd only seen her once since Christmas but expected to be down here more soon. Keats' breeder, Maud Gentry, lived close by, and his littermate, Frost, was expecting puppies any day. "How are you?"

"Waiting eagerly for the big day, as I'm sure you are, too. Will you take home a puppy, Jilly?"

Keats gave an annoyed mumble. There was only to be one dog in

Jilly's life right now. He had no desire to mentor an upstart niece or nephew.

"Not this time," Jilly said, automatically opening her arms to receive Percy. "I've got my hands full as it is."

Thelma spun on her stool and got up, without using her cane. She seemed to get a little spryer each time we met and I wasn't sure she really needed it now. "I'm sorely tempted, but a puppy is hard work and I have several pressing projects. It would be good to complete my life's work before my life... completes."

"Those projects are what's keeping you going, I expect," Edna said. "Don't complete them too soon."

They exchanged a nod of mutual understanding. I had much to learn about living from the many strong seniors around me. This was another gift that came with my new life in farm country. Back in my corporate tower, there were few staff over 60 and sadly, instead of being valued for their wisdom and experience, they were often "put out to pasture." As the HR manager, I fought to serve them better, but it was an uphill battle. Wilf, my boss, found cause to let many a mid-lifer go, despite being close to that point himself.

Thelma snapped her fingers. "Ivy? Wake up. I don't have all night."

There was a crash in the stacks and we all turned, startled. At least, three of us were startled. Thelma looked annoyed.

"I thought we were alone," I said. "It's after hours."

"It is and we are." She picked up her cane and waved it around. "Books have been falling off the shelves for no earthly reason, lately. It's always the lower shelves, which aggravates my sciatica."

"Probably the floor shifting," Edna said. "This place is even older than you."

Thelma merely pursed her lips, and if she noticed Percy had puffed in Jilly's arms, she didn't let on. Keats looked wary but also curious. If I let him, he'd have gone into the stacks to explore. But Thelma was right. We didn't have all night.

"You probably heard from Dottie what happened today," I said.

Her tight curls bobbed slightly. "I'm aware of the latest shenanigans in Clover Grove." She held up her cell phone. "I remember when we'd have to wait days for snail mail and now we videoconference often."

"And yet you were filling out file cards when we came in," Edna said.

Thelma smiled. "I like technology but I don't trust it. Important work still gets done by hand and I find it soothing. I would expect that's why you're here. About one of my hand-drawn records."

"Drawn is the operative word," I said. "That night when—" I stumbled over the words. "When I broke into your office, I saw a map on your desk."

"Quite likely, yes. Cartography is one of my hobbies. Better than jigsaw puzzles and more useful in the right hands."

"It fell into the wrong hands that night. Justine Schalow snuck back there and took photos."

She gave me the same look of disdain Dottie often shot my way. It was likely something they learned in librarian school. "Oh Ivy, I wasn't born yesterday, as Edna frequently points out. I never leave my window unlocked when critical documents are on my desk—not even when a crazed killer is coming in the front door. What that reporter photographed was something quite different from what you're after."

"But you shared it with Kellan, too."

"I shared something with Kellan, but it wasn't the fantasy map Justine got." Her curls almost vibrated with silent laughter. "Oh, to be a fly on that fool's shoulder as she tries to make sense of it. If there's any justice in the world, she'll get lost and never be found."

"Too little justice, I'm afraid. I've lost her several times on the back country trails and she never stays lost. I have to give her credit for persistence."

Thelma beckoned. "I've had more experience learning the art of obfuscation. The map she saw will keep her busy for quite some time."

"Not the bunkers, I hope," Edna said, pushing ahead of Jilly and me. "Justine doesn't deserve an easy ticket to what I've spent years mapping."

"Bunkers aren't my primary focus. I'll leave that to you and Buckley Brackens." Once we were inside her office, Thelma locked the door behind us. Then she checked the window and drew the curtains. "What you see now must stay a secret between us to the very grave. Mine or yours. Understood?"

Jilly and I gave solemn nods but Edna followed hers with a snarky, "Quit the buildup. Like you, I'm on borrowed time already."

Thelma propped her cane on the desk and walked to a built-in bookcase. She pressed carefully on two points and the shelves swung open to reveal a large safe. "I'd ask you to turn. The combination is private."

When she gave us permission to turn back, she was already walking to her huge oak desk with a long tube under her arm. Removing the lid, she unfurled a large document and rolled it out on the desk. Then she secured the corners with bronze paperweights in the shape of cats and dogs.

We didn't wait to be invited to peer over her shoulder at the map. After a few minutes of staring, Jilly said, "I don't have a clue what I'm seeing here."

"I do," Edna and I chimed together. I pointed to a spot just past the midpoint. "That's Runaway Farm. And that"—I shifted my finger— "is where Dawes Croaker died. Thelma has marked the spot. All the dots must be bodies."

"Try harder," Thelma said. "And don't even think about touching it."

The dots were in various colors but there was no legend to break it down for us. On closer inspection, I saw there were two dots at the point Dawes died. One was black and it overlapped with another in a shimmering gold.

"Gold," I said. "Gold! And the body is black?"

"And a gold star for Ivy."

"That's what Dawes was looking for when he fell under the cable skidder's blade," I said. "Thinking back, the earth around him was disturbed. I was afraid he'd— Well, struggled."

"The death would have been instant," Edna said. "He was rooting around for something and Thelma thinks he found it."

"I don't think, I know. It doesn't get the shimmer treatment unless a trinket appears on the market."

"What market?" Edna asked. "Treasure Hunter Weekly?"

"I wish it were that simple, although modern technology helps. If you know your way around the dark web, you see patterns. My intelligence on what's hidden in hill country is far from complete but it's proven reliable so far."

"Dark web?" Edna was suitably impressed. "Even I don't go there."

"It's not without risk, to be sure. My young hacker friend is a boon."

I pulled out my phone and flipped through the photos till I found what I wanted. "Look familiar?"

Thelma stretched the image with fingers marked with healing slits. Even librarians of her caliber got paper cuts, it seemed. "Ah, yes. A Spanish coin dating back to the sixteenth century, I believe. I saw some of those on the market. Where did you find it?"

"Around Mr. Croaker's neck. Does that mean the rumors Uncle Sterling heard about pirate's gold on the Harlow land are true?"

"Looks that way," Thelma said, pulling out a notepad. "Must have been a small cache. A shadow cache. There were a few jewels, as well."

"Shadow?" Jilly asked. "What does that mean?"

Thelma pointed to several spots on the map that quickly fell into my mental landscape. "Gertie's property?"

"Exactly. And if you'll recall from your discoveries"—a mumble interrupted her and she nodded before continuing—"Keats' discoveries, of course, they were of various sizes and values. It was common a hundred years ago to bury small stashes as decoys, in hopes that marauders would be content with their find and move on. Working with Chief Harper, I believe many of the large caches remain buried, including the very gold you mention."

"You're working with Kellan on this? Why didn't he say so?"

"Because it's highly privileged information and having a little knowledge is extremely dangerous in hill country."

"Is that why the killer invaded your library?" I asked. "Did he suspect what you knew?"

"Doubtful, or he would have taken me up on my offer to ride along in place of Keats." She looked down at him and sighed. "It was the dog he wanted and for the very reason we discussed. His talent for finding treasure."

Keats gave an indignant mumble that no doubt suggested he'd never work for a criminal.

"I know, buddy," I said. "But others don't. They were counting on Stockholm syndrome—where the captive eventually sides with the captor to stay alive."

They'd had the same plan for his sister, Frost, and perhaps their dam, Annie, who had disappeared after Keats was taken and still hadn't been found.

The dog gave me a look with his brown eye that verged on pleading. I'd made him a promise that had yet to be fulfilled, because I didn't know where to start. Kellan had promised to find Annie, and with his departure, there was no progress.

"What's going on?" Edna asked. "You and that dog are locked in a mind-meld of some sort. It's rude, to say the least."

"Sorry. Being here has brought up some memories, that's all." I held out my hand to stop Thelma from rolling up her map. "Wait! Please let me—"

"No photos, Ivy." Thelma's voice was terse. "Not even for Chief Harper, and he's the only one in law enforcement who's ever had access. This document never leaves my office, digitally or otherwise."

"But I'll never remember all that detail."

"You don't need all that detail. Besides, Dottie said you had a stellar memory, at least in your youth. She credits that for your academic success, not superior intelligence."

"Dottie's not wrong," I admitted. "It was partly luck, although I did my time in the stacks. After the concussion, my memory can be fickle."

Thelma unfurled the map again. "Take a mental picture and see if the magic still works."

My eyes wandered and she redirected me to the Croaker land. "But wait, Thelma. There are spots on my property. In several colors."

She rolled up the map again. "If there was anything worth knowing about the farm, I imagine Keats and Percy would show you."

I leaned on the edge of her desk and rubbed my eyes. "Thelma, if you're right, it's everywhere."

"What's everywhere?" Jilly asked.

"Gold. Bunkers. Death. And more."

Percy underscored the comment with a sweep of his paw over the map's tube.

"If I'm right," Thelma said. "That's the key, isn't it? I've created this over a long career with questionable intelligence and help from good librarians like Dottie. But there is plenty of guesswork involved."

"Some of the dots on the Harlow-Croaker land were so tiny I couldn't tell if they were gold. More like a mustard color."

"Exactly. Unconfirmed intel. No shimmer."

I grunted in frustration. "Too many to remember."

Thelma resolutely slid the map into the tube. "Patience, young lady. You're forgetting the most important thing."

"Which is?"

She tapped my hip as a signal to get off her desk. "You have fur-covered assistants to fill in where memory leaves off."

Right. Of course. Now I had a vague idea where to look for the third crew on the Harlow property and Keats was as good as ground penetrating radar. Hopefully, we wouldn't need to avail ourselves of Percy's special skill again.

The boys' tails were high as they left the office ahead of Edna and Jilly. I waited while Thelma put the map back in her vault and pushed the bookshelves into place.

"I love your office, Thelma. When I was a kid I dreamed of escaping to a place like this."

"As did I." She turned and we exchanged smiles. It was like the secret handshake of the nerd alliance. "I've been fortunate to make that come true and contribute in my own small way."

"Small? You saved my dog's life."

"So that he can save even more." She picked up her cane and tapped me gently with it. "Do be careful. You already knew his value to you but he's priceless to others, as well."

My hand went to my heart. "Frost and the puppies-to-be. They're at risk, too."

"Indeed. At my suggestion, Wendel Barrick and Rickie Merriweather are rotating on security. Maud will need new fencing when the ground thaws."

"Unless we can round up the current threats first," I said, leading her out and waiting while she locked the door.

"There will always be more. You know that." We walked down the hall and stopped. "What is going on out here?"

Percy was on top of a bookcase hissing and spitting, while Keats was in a point.

"You got me," Edna said, coming out of the aisle with several books. "The boys are bent out of shape for nothing."

My pets never wasted energy like this on nothing. It was something. Just not the type of mystery we could solve. "Thelma, call Janelle Brighton," I whispered. "Jilly hates talking about her woo-woo family but I wouldn't be at all surprised if Janelle and her dachshund could provide support here."

"I don't believe in ghosts, if that's what you're suggesting, Ivy." She said it loud enough so that Jilly could hear, probably on purpose. "I'm a woman of logic."

More books hit the floor with a series of thunks two aisles over. "Sounds like the romantic poets are going down hard." I grinned at her. "They deserve better, don't you think?"

"I think you need to go solve a real mystery," she said. "And don't come calling at whim to see my documents. Available by invitation only."

We walked to the front door and I thanked her. "You've given us a fighting chance, although I don't relish time in bush or bunker like some people."

Edna was "some people," and she rubbed her hands together as we walked down the ramp. "We deploy tonight."

"It's already tonight," I said.

"Barely sundown. You drive and I'll plan."

Jilly and I groaned as we got into the truck, but we'd both rise to the challenge like we always did. If there was gold in that forest we'd do our very best to find it before the bad guys closed in.

## CHAPTER EIGHTEEN

Norland's Hardware was still lit from inside when we drove down Main Street in Clover Grove.

"Do you mind if we pop in?" I asked, easing the truck into a double spot at the curb. While my stick-handling had improved markedly, I was always grateful to be parking after peak hours when there was more room and fewer spectators. "I want to ask about the poison I found at the woodlot."

Jilly opted to pick up groceries and Edna stayed in the truck to continue planning. Her map of the local bunkers would be key to surviving the expedition. Keats and Percy were happy to join me, judging by their tails as they preceded me across the sidewalk.

Thirl Norland, the owner, was stocking shelves when I knocked on the door. His bald head shone under the lights and his face lit up, too, when he saw me. He came over, unlocked the door and welcomed me in. "Ivy Galloway! A rare pleasure to see you."

We both laughed. Repairs weren't my strong suit and I hadn't made much effort to learn. In the early days at the farm, I'd helped Charlie when I couldn't avoid it. With Dad, Poppy and my nephews around more, I could always avoid it. I preferred to put my free time into manure, and more recently, chopping wood. The latter had lost its luster, but we were already set for power outages and the early stages of the apocalypse. I knew where to find more if I needed it.

"Hey, Thirl. Sorry to bother you after closing. Happened to drive by and see your lights on."

"Always glad to help our hometown hero. You don't get enough credit for your work, if you ask me."

I waved away the praise, knowing Thirl was well-positioned to hear public opinion. In a homesteading town, the hardware store was a premiere destination. Every transaction probably came with a serving of gossip.

"I try to keep a low profile, I really do. Trouble just finds me."

He quirked one eyebrow. I always wondered how people managed to operate their eyebrows separately. Was it a genetic quirk or practice? "That's not what Chief Harper says. According to him you run right at it."

"Yeah, well, maybe the truth is somewhere in between. Depends on one's perspective."

"The perspective of a protective fiancé is what I understand, having been one. Besides, Kellan and I go back decades." He pulled off his blue work vest and hung it on a hook. "Handy as a boy, unlike your brother."

I laughed. "Asher's more of a lily of the field. Doesn't do much around the farm but dance with the alpaca. With my dad gone, he never had a chance to learn home repairs."

Thirl walked back to the display of flashlights he'd been stocking. "Your brother knows more than he lets on. Kellan couldn't have done such a big renovation without another set of hands."

"It was a big reno? His place looks like something out of a design magazine. It's immaculate." The house was so nice inside and out that I wasn't terribly comfortable visiting. I never went anywhere without Keats, and Percy usually came along, too. That meant we blew into Kellan's pristine bungalow in a swirl of fur and claws.

"You never saw the 'before' shot. The place was a total wreck when he bought it and he worked hard for more than a year. Now it's a gem that'll easily bring him more than double. He would have flipped it and started over if you hadn't come home. He found a new hobby."

This time he winked and while I smiled, I was processing information I hadn't heard directly from my fiancé. Or had I heard it and not listened? Kellan invited me over often enough, and sometimes I wondered if he was disappointed when I suggested the farm instead. I never told him I was afraid to sit on his nice furniture and he never told me how proud he must be of the work he'd done. Turns out there were still things to learn before tying the knot.

"Thirl, I feel bad I didn't even know about Kellan's reno skills. I'm sure he worked hard to develop them."

The old man nodded. "Started young. With his dad out of the picture, he kept his mom's place up and I was happy to offer advice where I could. Done my fair share of home repair." He glanced around the shop. It had the classic worn wood floors and a distinctive smell I couldn't quite place. Motor oil, paint and chemicals, perhaps, but it was pleasant. "He still comes in to shoot the breeze. Always has good ideas for me. Before he left for college I kind of hoped he'd work here and take over when I retire. But Kellan chose a nobler path and I can't fault him for that."

"I bet he thinks your path is plenty noble. The town would fall apart without you. Quite literally."

He sighed and then shook off regret. "Just a matter of time before a big box store goes in. Seems like they're zoning anything now."

That was the segue I needed, and just in time, because Edna was getting impatient. One text was a warning. Two more would bring her barging in to tow me out with a winch from Thirl's own shelves.

"I'm guessing you're alluding to the build on the former Harlow land. Any idea what's going up? I hear everything from a casino to a brothel."

This time both eyebrows rose and I sensed he was a hard man to surprise. "Haven't been able to get a straight answer out of any of those men and they've been in and out for weeks." He gestured to a rack of checkered jackets that ran along one wall. "That Croaker fellow snubbed my gear. Said he was building his dream home, but with all those choppers, I'm gonna guess it's a dream high-rise."

"He wouldn't talk to me either. Granted, we got off to a rocky start when he shot at my fox."

One eyebrow did its thing. "Got yourself a fox, too? Kellan's going to be thrilled."

I laughed. "She's part of the satellite menagerie. I don't feed wildlife, but unfortunately, someone else does." Holding out my phone, I showed him a photo of the poison. "Found this in the wood-pile and wondered if Dawes bought it here." There was a movement on a shelf over the counter and we both turned. Percy was showing me where the poison was stored and it was fully stocked.

Thirl nodded. "Yeah, he bought some of that. Wouldn't hear me out that a red fox is normally too smart by half to take poison bait or even sick mice. The guy was frustrated he couldn't get a good shot."

"He was a terrible shot and thank goodness for that."

Studying the flashlights in his hand, Thirl seemed to hesitate. Finally, he looked up. "I don't often deliberately mislead a customer, but I did with Dawes Croaker."

I leaned against the counter. "Oh? How so?"

"Well, there are plenty of ways to kill a fox and here in farm country it happens whether I like it or not. And I don't, you see. My theory is that they've got as much right to be here as the exploding chicken population." He paused. "That didn't come out right. I don't endorse exploding chickens, either."

There was a twinkle in his eye and I couldn't help laughing. "So, what did you tell him?"

"It's more what I *didn't* tell him. There's a humane way to get the job done and if he was too lazy to look it up online, he wouldn't follow through on it properly anyway. So I sold him poison for rats, as you see, which no healthy fox would touch, and didn't bother to tell him about FoxBeGone, a popular product for those less squeamish than I am."

I stared up at the shelf, where Percy sat grooming his chest. "FoxBeGone? I don't see it."

"Exactly. I don't carry it, but it's not that hard to find if you know where to look."

"Veronica thanks you, because this box is nearly empty and she's still spry."

He offered a half-smile. "And that's the third box. Sold that one yesterday." Holding out his hand for the phone, he pointed. "See the price sticker? Marked it down first thing in the morning."

"Huh. Someone from the crew must have been after her, too."

"Maybe. But most lumber guys would know about FoxBeGone." He waited a beat and then added, "Not Mrs. Croaker, I guess. She doesn't use Google either."

My phone pinged again and I ignored it. "Marlene Croaker bought it? Are you sure?"

"Only sold one after the discount." He shrugged. "No damage done, except possibly to mice and like I said, a healthy fox would pass them up."

I stared down at Keats, who'd been wandering the aisles. If there was anything of particular interest, he didn't let on.

"How much of this stuff would it take to make a whole lot of grown men sick?"

"More boxes than I've got in stock. So many they'd never eat what your best friend was serving."

Of course he knew. He'd just been more tactful than most people. "That's what I figured, because Google is a very good friend of mine."

He laughed, but there was a rueful note to it. "I wish I had an easy answer for you. And those men. No matter the project, they're basically chainsaws for hire and didn't deserve a bellyful of trouble."

My phone pinged yet again, so I pushed off the counter and zipped my jacket. "What about FoxBeGone? Could that do it?"

"Possibly. It's potent stuff. Comes in meat flavor, so with a nice beef stew, it might go down easier. Your friend Google might tell you more."

Percy jumped to the counter and then my shoulder. "If anyone checked my searches, I'd have some explaining to do."

"I bet Chief Harper calls you to account often enough." He walked me to the door. "You might even miss that right now."

I paused with my hand on the doorknob. "I miss Kellan so much. And I'm worried about him." There was a slight quaver in my voice, probably because of Thirl's fatherly fondness for my fiancé.

The old man gave my shoulder a pat. "Me, too. Don't like this Skowby character and I said as much to Meryl."

"The mayor? Don't tell me she does her own home repairs."

He leaned over and opened the door for me. "Heavens, no. But she does play poker and better than her husband, too. I'm always sorry when she shows up for our regular game because it means I'm going to lose money."

The door closed behind me and he laughed at my expression through the glass. "Good luck, Ivy. Don't do anything Kellan wouldn't do."

I gave him a cheery wave and called, "What fun would that be?"

# CHAPTER NINETEEN

I hurried back to the truck amid a flurry of pings. By my count I was two pings over a Butter Tart 9 1 1, and the last thing I wanted to do right now was go to a family meeting. Scratch that. The last thing I wanted to do was spend a chilly night roaming in the woods, but duty called.

"Finally," Jilly said, as I let the pets jump in and slid behind the wheel. "We've been texting because you're about to receive a very important call. At least according to the caller."

My phone rang on cue, with the screen saying "unknown caller." The caller, however, was very much known as her voice rang out on speaker.

"Galloway, when I text, I expect an answer tout suite."

It was Cori Hogan, the tiny dog trainer who was a founding member of the Dorset Hills Rescue Mafia. Her touch with dogs was light and exactly the opposite with humans. Or at least this human. She expected me to roll over and take a hit of dominance lying down. I usually did. Resisting her was a waste of energy.

"Hey, Cori. Sorry, we're on the run here. It's not the best time to talk about your next deposit in the Runaway Farm bank." Curiosity quickly overcame me. "What are you trying to place so urgently?"

"Ivy, Ivy, Ivy. Always so suspicious. Sometimes I call just to shoot the breeze."

I pretended to give that a moment's thought. "I cannot recall any of those 'sometimes.' You're a busy woman and you always have an agenda."

"I suppose. Even when I don't I do. For example, in this case I'm just calling with some intel for you. Goal number one is to be of service. Goal number two is to make sure you're still of service to me. It's not easy to find a place for a python when you need it."

"No!" Jilly's voice was a strangled squawk and even Edna protested. But I sensed the twinkle in Cori's eye. Her style of teasing wasn't so different to Keats' nipping pant legs. She liked to see you jump and occasionally left a mark.

"You wouldn't bring a poisonous snake to a farm and put the very animals you re-home there at risk. So, tell us what you really want. We're in a bit of a hurry."

"I heard you have your hands full saving Jilly's reputation and of course we wanted to help. Everyone knows we're team players."

Jilly leaned into the phone. "I appreciate the offer but it isn't really your area of expertise."

"Oh ye of little faith. I can cook and I'm as capable of poisoning a crew as the next gal. Probably more so."

Keats gave a happy pant from Jilly's lap. Regardless of how much he understood, he just enjoyed hearing Cori talk. He was happy being subordinate to her, whereas he saw himself as my equal. Perhaps even my alpha.

"Okay, we're listening," I said. "If only because Keats wants to know what you've got."

"It's about the security cameras at the Harlow property. You're probably hoping the footage will clear Jilly, but it won't."

My friend slumped beside me. "How is that supposed to make me feel better?"

"Just because they were too stupid to set cameras up properly doesn't mean I was. They only got the front of that wreck of a catering truck, whereas I got every angle."

"Why did you have a cam on the site in the first place?"

"Because I like to climb and I like to know stuff. As you've so aptly noted, I rely on you to keep our rescues safe and if there's suspicious activity right next door, well... it's best to take a closer look. One day they're shooting at a fox, the next an escaped pig. Catch my drift?"

"Okay, what did you catch on your camera? Did someone come in the back door?"

"More ambitious. Came through the bush and climbed in the window when you were out for a stroll. Maybe they were making themselves a light snack, but they came out with a hungry look. And a splat, I'm happy to say. If they were doing what we think, they deserve bumps and bruises."

Jilly snatched the phone out of my hand. "Send it. This footage may stand between me and utter ruin."

Edna spoke up from the rear. "You think so now but when I got shoved out of the school board it led to the most fulfilling passion of my life. Without that misery and desperation, I may not have started prepping."

"While I applaud that, I don't want to see Ivy and Jilly suffer," Cori said. "Mainly because if they suffer, Keats and Percy do, too. And what do you call the fox? Valencia? I bet even she suffers."

I shook my head. "You've got the site bugged, too? Better turn up the sound because it's Veronica."

"You'll be plenty happy with the sound when you get the clip. But it's not for delicate sensibilities. Sending it over now. Big file so it might take a minute."

"Tell us what else you've seen. Any idea what they're building?"

"Sadly, no. They work with a military-like precision. Admirable, but it leaves much to the imagination."

I refreshed my inbox repeatedly before her email arrived. It did take time for the video to load, and all heads came together in the cab of the darkened truck as we watched someone climb out the smaller side window of the chip truck and hit the ground with a thud and a volley of curses.

Jilly straightened in her seat. "Well, that was unexpected."

"See? I love surprises. Don't you love surprises?"

I gave Cori the laugh she craved and deserved. "Not when they come in fur and feathers. Or especially scales. But this surprise, yes. Stick around and I may just tell you I love you."

An abrupt click confirmed I'd discovered one trick for dominating the tiny trainer, but she'd always find a way to get back on top.

---

EDNA PRESSED a doorbell in the shape of a fat daisy. Without waiting a polite interval, she did it again. And then once more, even though we could all see the lights flicking on inside. Someone was coming but Edna was in a hurry. She'd set the time and rendezvous point and we only had an hour to take care of this and collect our gear. "It couldn't have waited till morning?" she said, although the train was rolling down the track.

Jilly gave her the side-eye. "It could not. I don't trust Skowby to do it right."

"I don't trust him to do it at all," I added, looking down at Keats and Percy. "Work as fast as you can, boys."

A wooden door swung back to reveal Aster Crooks behind the screen. She was wearing a floral bathrobe and terry cloth turban. Without fluffy hair to soften her features, she looked more foxlike than ever. No disrespect to Veronica intended. What looked very pretty on an actual vixen didn't translate well to a middle-aged woman. "It's late and I'm tired," she said. "What could you want at this hour?"

Edna rolled her eyes. "It's half past eight. Not too late for a few questions about saving the environment."

"I answered plenty when Officer Gibbons visited," Aster said. "Explaining the value of wild flora to a man like him was utterly exhausting, but part of my role as head of the club is to educate. I think he left with a fresh understanding."

"That's great," I said, switching on a good smile. "We do know the value and while these aren't wild, perhaps they'll ease your pain."

I held out the bouquet Jilly had bought at the grocery store to lift our spirits at the inn. It was too nice to just give away, but if all went as planned, we might get it back.

Aster's thin lips twitched as she considered refusing. She decided against it and the door cracked open. I tried to shove the flowers in bloom-first and that made her open it wider. Her sleeve came up and showed swelling, scratches and a large purple bruise. "That's no way to treat flowers, Ivy. Even murdered ones like this deserve better."

The dog and cat easily slipped in under her indignation and she shut the screen door again. It made me uneasy to see them trapped, but if we had to force our way in to free them, we could and would.

"You're very welcome," Edna said. "Too tired for manners, I see. You wouldn't have lasted long strapped to an oak tree, Aster."

"I can pull out the stops when necessary. I'm fit for my age."

I amped my smile up a notch. "We noticed. It couldn't have been easy hoisting yourself through that little window. No wonder you're exhausted."

She fell back a step and her eyes dropped to the flowers. "Window? I don't know what you're talking about."

Jilly touched my arm and picked up the interrogation. "There's no use being coy, Aster. You climbed into the food truck when we were out and dropped poison into my stew. Now seven men have been hospitalized and the police have suggested it was my fault."

"Did you think about the fallout before dropping FoxBeGone into the pot?" I asked. "You're lucky no one died."

"The only death was my reputation," Jilly said. "It won't do much for my husband's either."

Aster buried her pointy nose in the bouquet. "I've never heard of FoxBeGone, and anyone could have done what you're suggesting." Her words were muffled by fragrant freesia. "Are you pestering Melvin, Claudette and Pierre like this? We're equally concerned about the harmful consequences of clear-cutting."

"Normally we would," I said, "but the video saved us a lot of bouquets. I'm sure you can appreciate not wasting good flowers on the innocent."

She looked up with narrowed eyes. "There's no video. The cameras on site caught nothing, according to Officer Gibbons."

"Lucky for us, we have a very clear shot of you landing hard and cussing out whatever flora and fauna survived the frost," I said. "Lucky for the men, too, since we could alert the hospital to the poison and they can target treatment better. And lucky for you in the end, because one man was hanging by a thread."

"Attempted murder is an easier charge," Edna said. "You might get out of jail in time to see the last of the wildflowers around here. Although with the way the world's going, I wouldn't count on it."

Aster let the bouquet fall to her side. "I don't believe you. If you had any such video you'd have sent it to the police. Officer Gibbons was lovely. He came in for tea."

"How nice," I said. "Can we have our flowers back?"

The door opened again and when she passed them out, Edna shoved her boot in the gap. It left enough room for my pets to slip out. Keats raised his paw in a point to confirm my suspicions.

Jilly punched a text into her phone with enough force to break a nail. "You can have tea again with Officer Gibbons while he reads you your rights."

"Enough of this foolishness." Aster kicked Edna's boot out of the screen door and slammed it. "I've never heard of FoxBeGone."

"They'll say differently at the hunting supply store near Brenton," I said. Thirl Norland had made a few calls and confirmed that information. "Although I expect they'll find you planted empty boxes at the homes of your fellow activists. I doubt you used it yourself."

Edna turned to me, eyebrows rising. "She didn't use FoxBeGone?"

"Of course, I didn't," Aster said. "That's stupid."

"Stupid for a plant expert like you," I said. "Much better to make an educated statement about logging. I researched the leaves you left in the woodpile and it looked like wallflower poison—fatal to Australian livestock and lumberjacks the world over. The toxin is very similar to sodium fluoroacetate, which is of course used in—?"

I gestured to Jilly and she supplied, "FoxBeGone. Obviously."

"Harder to taste, I'd imagine," I said. "And probably to trace."

Aster's lips curled into a snarl that looked like confirmation to me. "This isn't Australia, in case you hadn't noticed."

"You've got a greenhouse. I can smell the tropics from here." Noticing sirens in the distance, I picked up the pace of the discussion. "Gotta hand it to you, Aster. Poisoning a crew was so much bigger and bolder than tying yourself to a tree, yet you got off unscathed except for some bumps and bruises."

She put her hands behind her, almost as if rehearsing for handcuffs. "Sounds like they got what they deserved."

"What about us?" Jilly said. "We could have eaten that stew, too."

"But you didn't." Aster sounded almost disappointed. "Count your blessings and choose the right side next time."

The sirens were louder now, and lights flashed up the street. "What about Dawes Croaker? He was sick when I met him.

Couldn't you have left the poison to do the job? Why crush him, too?"

Her eyes were small and feral through the screen. "No comment. I'll wait for my lawyer."

"They're hard to find around here," I said. "Surprising, when there's so much business."

Deputy Chief Fenway strode up the walk, officers trailing in his wake like goslings. I didn't recognize the others, which meant Skowby was bringing on even more outsiders. Maybe he sensed mutiny among Kellan's staff and was cleaning house. My stomach twisted, knowing Asher could be on the chopping block, too. With five or six new faces, they wouldn't need everyone. It was a small-town force, no matter how big the crime rate.

"Hey, Deputy Chief," I called, heading down the front stairs. "Don't drink the tea if she offers."

Fenway sent the new officers ahead and pulled us aside. I showed him the video and told him about the discussion, omitting only the part about Keats and Percy doing their walkabout inside to locate more of the leaves we'd found in the wood pile.

"Aster's behind the poisoning," Edna said, "which means you owe Jillian Blackwood an apology, young man."

Fenway rolled his eyes. "It was reasonable speculation given the circumstances."

"Speculation grinds good people under the heel of gossip," Edna continued. "Citizens might forget you carted off Aster Crooks, but they'll always have this vague association between Jillian and dangerous stew. A public apology from the police would go a long way to help."

He shook his head. "You guys are too much. Maybe Chief Skowby will be kind enough to hold back on publicly chastising you for confronting a suspect. He sure isn't going to apologize for generating gossip when you do that just fine on your own."

"Still," Jilly said. "You could have done your due diligence before speculating. Our friends in neighboring towns heard within hours."

"Blame your local reporter," he said. "I found her hiding behind your killer kitchen on wheels. She was eavesdropping on us."

That much was true. Cori's camera had captured Justine Schalow in the bush and the confrontation as she was escorted away a second time.

"Well, I bet you could make a statement to the Tattler to counter your slander," Edna said. "It's the least you could do."

He tired of the fight. "Go home. And this time, stay there. We'll be investigating all night whereas you can get a good rest."

"We just handed you Croaker's killer on a silver platter," Edna said. "Made your job easy-peasy."

"She may have poisoned him but do you really think she could operate that fancy tractor?" He pulled off his hat and the messy mop left behind made him decidedly less intimidating. "Oh wait, that calls for speculation, which leads to gossip."

"You're not funny," I said, as we backed down the walk.

"Some people think so." There was a flash of even, white teeth much nicer than Skowby's. "Like your sister."

I held up my hand. "Don't go there, Fenway. My sister—and I don't want to know which one—will be getting an earful about loyalty. We're on Team Harper."

"Ah yes, the Galloway family fiancé. I'm sure he appreciates that." I wanted to hate Fenway but his tone was teasing. "I don't imagine Harper likes it when you bypass him and talk to a suspect, either. From what I heard, he's a good cop."

"He is, and you're right." I turned and followed the others to the truck, glancing back at the deputy. "But what he really hates is when we get the scoop on him."

"Drive safe, girls." Another flash of white teeth suggested he knew the word would get under my skin, and it worked.

I let my pets into the truck and took a few deep breaths before turning the key. The last thing I wanted to do in front of Skowby's special sidekick was stall.

Of course, it was the first thing I did.

Also, the second.

I kept my head high as I rolled off. If I didn't actually see him laugh, I could tell myself it didn't happen.

# CHAPTER TWENTY

E dna was too busy planning our mission to taunt me about my driving, for which I was grateful.

"Forget about it," Jilly said. "It's been a long day and about to get longer." She peered over her shoulder. "Now that we know who killed Dawes Croaker, couldn't we save this outing till daylight?"

Edna didn't even look up from her phone. "Never put off till tomorrow what you can do while the cops are busy and the crew bedridden. Never been a better time to go looking for a secret logging site."

"That's a good point," I said. "It's nice knowing everyone's looking the other way. Before long, they'll realize Aster Crooks didn't actually kill Dawes and go back to calling his death an accident."

"What do you mean?" Jilly said. "No comment is as good as a confession, right?"

"She may have poisoned him, but she didn't drop the blade." I glanced at Keats and Percy in Jilly's lap. "At least, according to my pets. They left dissatisfied—even disgruntled—so I'm guessing the case is far from closed in their minds. Aster probably has an alibi."

I expected more of an argument but Jilly just sighed. "I noticed the boys were puffy as we left. Still, I clung to hope that we could avoid bunker diving on a winter's night."

"Fear not, Jillian. I've plotted a route that will avoid those very pitfalls. I enjoy bunker diving as much as the next prepper but daytime is always preferable. While Buckley and I have plenty of them mapped, we know there are more."

Jilly groaned. "Guaranteed we'll find a new one tonight. It's like the horror version of an Easter egg hunt. I'm going to hammer whisky when we— Hey! You missed the turnoff for the farm."

I gestured to Keats, whose paws were on the dash as he stared intently into the darkness. "Figured we should keep moving while the police are busy. Besides, it'll be even harder to leave a warm house and its whisky. I'm sorry about your flowers. They're likely to be casualties of a cold truck."

"Speaking of cold... We're not dressed for the bush and Edna's the only one with the go kit."

"You see?" Edna sounded gratified. "That's what I'm always trying to tell you about preparedness. There's nothing like a chilly butt to underscore my point."

Jilly turned to make a snippy retort but I shook my head. "Don't take her bait. Edna's got a fully stocked bunker we can visit."

"Oh yeah?" Edna said. "What makes you think so?"

"I see the shipments delivered to the post office at Mandy's store for you. That gear's gotta go somewhere. I think you've sprinkled bunkers all over, just like the Easter eggs Jilly mentioned."

Edna cackled. "Ten eggs for you, along with winter combat gear. You'll be as comfortable as if sitting by your fireplace."

"That's a bigger lie than the Easter bunny," Jilly said, although she sounded relieved. "Let's just get this done. What's going to happen when we find the site? Is there a plan?"

I shrugged. "It's one of those plan-as-you-go adventures. We'll find it, photograph it and take it from there."

"Maybe Kellan could take it from there." She stared at the side of my head. "When did you last fill him in?"

I thought about it. "Not sure. Time's gotten away on me. He didn't answer my last texts, anyway."

"In other words, too long. So put a heart-to-heart on the agenda. It's bad enough I'm keeping Asher in the dark, but he's in a sticky situation. Did you notice all those new cops? What if Skowby lays everyone off? It will kill Asher."

Edna's gloved hand came through the seats and gripped Jilly's shoulder. "I worry about your husband's capacity to survive an apocalypse, but getting turfed by Skowby will not kill him."

"His whole identity is about being a cop." Jilly's voice was tearful. "It's how he defines his worth in the world."

I shook my head. "You underestimate my brother. He's highly adaptable and as charming as all get-out. Besides, he defines his worth in the world by scoring you as his bride."

She shook her head. "With men, their work is so critical." Keats turned on her lap and stared at her. "What?"

He gave a mumble of clear disgust and turned back.

I laughed. "You've been told. Asher is not going to be a casualty of this regime. You might question Edna and me, but do you dare doubt Keats?"

Her pause was long enough to earn another mumble. "I guess not. But I know you worry about the same thing for Kellan."

"I worry, all right. But we're all doing the best we can to restore this town to order, aren't we?"

She nodded and her protests subsided. After a mile or two, she said, "Tye Fenway seems like a decent guy. I guess Skowby is smart enough to hire some sugar to offset his salt."

"Maybe, but I still don't want him dating my sister. It's Violet, I bet. Poppy's gotten wiser since being burned last year and Iris is wary, too."

Keats refused to weigh in on matters of the heart, but Edna did. "I saw Fenway talking to Violet at Mandy's when I was picking up one of those many packages you mentioned. Thought she had more horse sense but your sisters are desperate."

"Edna, don't say that," Jilly said.

"Aren't you the one always saying how hard it is to find men around here? With fifteen years and a little patience, those pesky hormones could be buried under a nice marker in the Clover Grove graveyard of broken dreams."

I raised my hand. "Edna, you and Jilly are my family, but my family is also my family. Don't put me in the position of roughing you up."

We all laughed and even Keats joined in briefly. But then one paw came up and he whined. I followed his gaze and the headlights showed movement in the bush at the side of the road. The pines rippled and swayed, making me wonder if it was a bigger animal than Veronica, with even more white fur. Keats must have thought so, too, because his own tail shot up straight, like an exclamation mark. He pawed at the window, then turned to scratch my leg, and repeated the maneuver, whining throughout.

"What's going on?" Jilly asked.

I slowed the truck to a crawl. "Something's got his attention. Veronica, maybe?"

Sure enough, the fox emerged from thick brush and trotted along the shoulder. Then she plunged back in at a 90-degree angle.

Keats' tail didn't just relax; it plummeted. My hopes did, too. For a second, I really thought there was another animal in there. A stray dog, perhaps.

I patted his shoulder and he moved away from my hand, pressing his nose to the crack. "Veronica seems to be telling us we're nearly where we need to be."

Just ahead was a thread of a lane that looked barely big enough for a fox, let alone a truck. There were tracks in the light dusting of snow, however, and just ahead we found another pickup.

"Buckley," Jilly said, with relief. There was safety in numbers, particularly when the extra hands came armed. Like Gertie, who jumped out of the truck ahead of him, Buckley was carrying a rifle. So was their other passenger, my great uncle.

"How nice of you to put on some pants, Sterling," Edna said. "I mostly see you in a bathrobe."

"Tell me more," Buckley said, grinning. "I miss all the best gossip."

If it hadn't been so dark there was a decent chance I'd have seen Edna's rare blush. "And here you told us you buried those hormones in the graveyard of broken dreams, Edna," I said.

Buckley laughed. "Not true. Pay me enough and—"

"You will not," Edna interrupted. "Because when it comes to a salacious tale, I can sling harder and higher than anyone, trust me."

Keats gave a sharp yap that echoed back from the bush, in a very different tone.

"Veronica," I said. "The fox is telling you to postpone the banter, as entertaining as Jilly and I might find it."

"I'd like to find some warmer gear," Jilly said. "You mentioned a fully stocked bunker."

Buckley switched off his truck headlights and closed the door. Another light came on, which turned out to be a single beam attached to his hunting hat. He gestured with his rifle. "Follow me. The bunker is right this way, although fully stocked is a stretch."

"Excuse me?" Edna was outraged. "You are not acquainted with my local bunker."

"Wanna bet?" His light shone in her face and made her squint. "I make it my business to get acquainted with the neighborhood."

Much to Edna's chagrin, he led us to a well-concealed crevice that widened into a cave. There were several tall, slim cupboards with the doors hanging open.

"Dagnabit, you jimmied my locks, Buckley Brackens. You could have had the decency to close them again. Spent good money on that gear and don't care to supply riffraff."

"Came by earlier to speed things up. It always takes ladies so long to decide what to wear."

Edna hurled harsh words at him and clothing at Jilly and me. We pulled camo snowsuits on over our jeans, and then grabbed hats and gloves with little heating packs. There were even boots in our size and tiny, high-powered flashlights.

"Nice," Jilly said, twirling. "The right outfit really does make the occasion."

Keats refused to participate in the fun, pacing restlessly instead. Percy, however, explored every nook and cranny of Edna's retreat. The cat clearly wasn't experiencing the same sense of urgency as my dog. Once more, I thought of the ripple of cedar trees before we turned in. Had Veronica been alone or with a companion of more interest to Keats? Perhaps our time wandering out here would tell the tale, or tail, in this case.

Outside, there was a clash of leadership. Not between Buckley and Edna, as I might have expected, but Veronica and Keats. The fox wanted to go in one direction, the dog another. Percy seemed to side with the fox, which was strange indeed. The cat had been considerably more wary of Veronica than any of our other animal friends, and rightly so. Now, he walked halfway across the clearing toward the fox, and then peered back into my flashlight with eerie eyes.

"Looks like you've got yourself a problem, Ivy," Edna said. "I guess you'll need to let the humans make the decision this time."

I expected Sterling to agree but he shook his head. "Keats has never steered you wrong yet. I trust him."

Gertie added her vote for Keats. "I trust him, too."

"It's foxes I don't trust," Buckley said. "They're known to be sly, no?"

"Folklore," I said. "Veronica's on a mission, and I sense she knows these woods better than even you veterans. Let me have a word with my dog."

Buckley let out a foggy puff of exasperation. "This isn't the time for one of your woo-woo meetings of the mind."

It was exactly that time. I did not dismiss intel from my pets easily, but I suspected it was less disagreement about direction than a matter of different agendas. There was only one thing I could think of that would turn Keats' focus from our mission, and my own intuition aligned. Unless I was very much mistaken, there was another dog in the vicinity and if I was right about its identity, I could see how he would be torn. But I didn't want to raise it with the others without so much as a clear visual.

At the side of the clearing, I knelt by my dog. "I know what you're thinking, buddy, and trust me, I do want to find out if we're right. Could we do that after we've found what Veronica wants us to see? It may lead us to Dawes Croaker's killer and while both situations are important, that seems more urgent. But if you really think this is the best route, I will ask the others to split off and we can follow your lead."

He looked at me with his blue eye and then turned to direct it into the bush. His tail had already been down and now it nearly scooted under his belly. He didn't need to mumble for me to know that whatever he'd hoped to find was now out of range anyway. His ears drooped too, and when I tried to pat his shoulder he moved away.

My heart sank into my new thermal-lined combat boots and a chill set in. I'd never seen my dog so disappointed. But as he trotted back to the others and joined Percy, his tail began to rise. Then he looked at me and mumbled a distinct order to get moving.

"What was that about?" Jilly asked, falling back to walk with me. Maybe it was the coward's route to follow four seniors into danger, but I was fine with it.

"Well, it's just a hunch, but Keats thinks—"

"Stop babbling," Buckley called, making us both jump. "This is a secret mission, is it not? Silence is the first order of secrecy."

"Then why are you yelling at us?" I countered.

"She's got a point, Brackens," Sterling said. "And since we've broken the first order, I'll mention that I spent an hour or two outside the Big Snooze Motel earlier. Only saw four choppers. Maybe one's already bailed."

"What did Palmer Harlow have to say?" I asked.

"Confirmed his father Levon was as corrupt as they come. Didn't trust his own sons enough to tell them the whereabouts of pirate's gold, if it actually existed. He liked stirring things up, even in his own family, and pitted the boys against each other. Palmer, as you know, wrote off his family and has no interest in whatever is found. However, he's concerned the Harlow history may be causing more violence today and hazarded a guess or two at where they might be clearing the land." He directed his flashlight after the fox. "She's heading in the right direction."

Based on what I remembered from Thelma's map, I had to agree. It was nice we didn't need to break the librarian's confidence to say so. Even Edna kept her lips sealed, which must have been hard given the friendly rivalry.

We all fell silent after that, probably mostly because we had to watch our step. Between us, there was plenty of light but the footing got more and more treacherous. The thought of the earth opening and engulfing us in a bunker kept my throat in a vice. It had happened to several of us before and it was a wonder no one had broken a limb.

"Ivy, you're up," Buckley said. "The fox is slowing and I think she wants your attention. Don't ask me how I know."

Veronica stopped walking and turned to face us. Then she picked her way up a small but steep cliff that was partially covered in snow.

"We'd better rope off," Edna said. "Otherwise, some of us will be bunking with the crew at the hospital."

Percy and Keats found an easier route. I followed slowly and carefully, staring around. "We can get up this way. It's just steep enough to— Uh-oh." I paused and then hissed. "Stop. Stop. Lights out."

Surprisingly, Jilly was the first to climb up behind me despite the darkness seeming more intense in the aftermath of so many lights.

"Belly." The single word came from Edna below. It was quiet but it carried.

Jilly and I dropped, even though the ground was covered in pointy rocks. "Just punctured my spleen," she whispered.

"You can live without that. Edna does."

"Quiet," Edna said, and Keats emphasized the command with a nudge.

Veronica had gone down the opposite side of what turned out to be a hill of rock. She trotted toward a well-lit rectangle about the size of two tennis courts. It was cordoned off with plywood and topped with what appeared to be an electric fence.

From our vantage point, we could likely see all there was to see. The trees within the rectangle had been cleared right to the ground with most of the stumps chipped out. Overtop, a few dozen ground-thawing blankets lay side by side.

"It's an incubator," I whispered to Jilly. "They're trying to hatch golden goose eggs."

Her shoulders shook a little. "Don't. This is serious and we're at the front of the line. With the electric fence we can't get a closer look."

The prospect of electrocution was definitely daunting. "I'm not going to leave without trying." I started to get to my feet, and then Keats mumbled a quick negative. The fox tilted her head this way and that, much as she had with the mouse on the first day we adventured together. Then she did a dramatic pounce that seemed more for show as she turned to stare up at us.

We started a reverse belly crawl over the rocks until we could roll down the hill. Thank goodness for padded snowsuits. Edna and Buckley hoisted us to our feet.

"Retreat," I said, signaling Keats to lead us back to safety. "I heard an ATV coming. Someone's ready to pounce."

## CHAPTER TWENTY-ONE

The next morning, Keats did his chores with grim determination instead of his usual verve. Normally, we both loved our morning and evening routines, and when we had to forfeit them to others it left us feeling a little unmoored.

He mumbled something edgy like, "Speak for yourself."

"I am speaking for myself." I released the goats and followed as he drove them to their pasture. It was a lackluster trot compared to his usual romp. Little pleased him more than an attempted escape, and every day offered that hope. Once in a while he got his wish and could do a proper roundup with all the sheepdog flourishes. It was like a barnyard slot machine. You never knew when you'd hit the jackpot and that intermittent reinforcement kept him alert.

The thirst for dopamine didn't work today. He was looking for a bigger hit. A massive reward. And he was mad at me for denying it to him.

Letting the sheep out, I almost wished one would make a run for it and let him work out his frustration. Instead, perhaps sensing his fuse was short, they walked sedately to their pasture without so much as a hoof out of line. On his way back, he favored me with a blue-eyed glare.

"I promised we'd take a closer look and we will. You know as well as I do that we had a mission bigger than us last night. One that affected public safety. Still, I'm willing to head back today if you think it's wise." He switched to give me some brown-eyed love. "We have to play our cards right to win both games. Let's take a little more care than usual. With Kellan gone, I realize how much I unconsciously depend on him to ride in and rescue us when the chips are down. I wouldn't take half the risks we do without him."

The dog gave a pant-laugh as he herded me to the truck. Not only would he take the same risks without Kellan, he'd take even more. Kellan may be my safety net but he was an unwelcome lid on Keats' ever simmering energy. Percy, who leapt onto my shoulder as I passed the donkey pasture, probably wasn't affected either way. Like most cats, he had complete confidence in his decisions of the moment.

Veronica was sitting in the middle of the driveway about 10 yards away. She didn't move as I let the animals into the truck. Nor did she move when I turned the key in the ignition. Even when I rolled slowly toward her, she held her ground.

I rolled down the window. "Fine. I get it. We'll hook up with you in an hour where we parked last night."

Whether she understood or not, she got up and faded into the trees. Despite her coloring and the sparse foliage, she seemed to be able to blend at will. I'd enjoyed that feeling while wearing Edna's camouflage last night, but I didn't intend to adopt it all the time. I was willing to carry my freak flag in overalls, but not army gear. Not yet, anyway.

Keats had his paws on the dash, urging me on with excited mumbles. Nevertheless, I turned right into Mandy's parking lot. "Sorry, buddy. I need fuel for this mission. It's probably going to be a long day and we should stop here first."

He grumbled complaints and refused to get out of the truck.

"Suit yourself. Percy and I are going in."

By the time I got the cat into the carrier and started closing the doors, Keats was trotting up the front stairs. Perhaps he realized he stood a better chance of speeding me up by staying close enough to nip my calves.

Or perhaps he'd caught a whiff of a customer who'd beaten me to my favorite spot at the counter.

"Oh," I said, so startled that I nearly dropped the cat carrier. "Mrs. Croaker. Good morning. Mandy isn't usually open at this hour."

Marlene turned her eyes back to her huge bowl of coffee. "The lights were on so I asked to come in and drown my sorrows."

Mandy gave me an apologetic shrug and signaled that she'd deliver my order. She knew better than I did what I needed.

I put the carrier under the closest table and took a stool at the counter, leaving an empty one in between. It wasn't enough for Marlene.

"I want to be alone, Ivy. Isn't that obvious?"

"You're sitting in the window of a popular place. That doesn't sound like a bid for solitude. You have plenty of that at home."

She scowled. "It's possible to want to be alone in public. Maybe that's beyond small-town comprehension."

"Well, I worked in a big firm in Boston for a decade so I can grasp the concept. I suppose it's not that comfortable at home for you, with your husband gone."

Her right hand fluttered and then settled on the counter, as if the big sapphire ring weighed it down. "That's not home. It's a sterile short-term rental. And while it does feel empty, Dawes wasn't around much even before... what happened."

"It sounded like he was laser-focused on building you your dream house. I guess that took all his attention."

She stared at the ring and gave a dismissive sniff. "You know nothing about marriage."

Mandy slipped coffee and a plate of pie in front of me so unobtrusively it was like they'd appeared by magic. I pulled out my phone and took a picture of the pie, making sure to catch Marlene's ring in the frame. Then I shot off a text and set the phone down, pressing record, just in case. "Maybe not, but I know a lot about pie. You should try some."

"I never eat sweets. Sugar is as addictive as gambling."

I carved off a forkful and then smiled as I raised it to my mouth. "Hit me."

"Don't tempt me. You've done nothing but cause trouble since we got here. I bet Dawes would still be alive if you hadn't picked a fight with him." She took advantage of my chewing to fire off her accusations. "You flustered him so much he fell under his own equipment. Now I'm a widow because of you."

I swallowed. "Seriously? How is it my fault? He was unsteady when we met, but that's because you poisoned him."

"Me! Aster Crooks is the one poisoning people. Chief Skowby told me so last night."

"Skowby doesn't know you got to Dawes first. You fed him the regular rat poison he intended for the fox. Then you replaced it the next day."

She shoved my plate. "That sugar is rotting your brain. Why on earth would I do something like that to a man building me my dream house?"

"Because you found someone else to carry on the project. A newer model. Like you said, marriage isn't easy."

"It isn't." She used her thumb to twist the ring on her finger. "It takes more than rat poison to get out of it."

I took another bite of pie and checked my phone. Thelma had answered almost instantly. "You're out of it now and your rings are gone. All except for the one you got from Fleet Jurgen."

Her hand clenched instantly, with the sapphire inside. "Why would you say that? I barely know the man."

Dozens of texts and calls round the clock said otherwise. His phone log suggested their relationship was far more than professional, and now Thelma had confirmed that the ring was available on the dark web not long before Dawes died. Fleet had likely bought it for his lady love as a promise of riches to come.

"Just a guess," I said. "As you say, I know nothing about marriage."

She used her left hand to hoist the bowl of coffee. "Dawes and I were working things out. That's what the dream house was all about. He wanted to move away from the place we'd grown unhappy."

Little did he know they'd moved toward the affair rather than away from it. I shoveled in more pie and chewed. "Did it help?"

"Not as much as he hoped. When you get to my age, you find some things aren't worth saving."

I washed the pie down with a big gulp of coffee. It was still scalding but the pie diffused the heat. "So that's where the poison came in."

"I didn't poison anyone. That stupid tree-hugger is under arrest for doing just that."

"The autopsy report will tell the tale." I poked at my pie, wondering if the report would come to light. It should have been back by now. "It's the kind of thing that might worry Fleet, right? He'll be sensitive about toxins after nearly dying. I suppose he'll always have doubts after this. Maybe he'll want that ring back."

Her mouth worked and she reached for a stack of paper napkins. "I would never poison Fleet. He'll know that. I'd never poison anything but vermin. That box was meant for exactly what it says. The fox was getting in the way and would have been killed in the long run anyway. If not by me, then the crew."

"She's trying to protect her territory. You and your crew are pillaging it."

The napkins dropped on the counter and her fingers closed over the ring again. "Building a house is not pillaging."

"We've all heard the rumors about what's buried on the Harlow property. You and Dawes were excavating with a purpose." I reached out and tapped her fist. "That ring is lovely and I would imagine there are more."

She shook off my hand and turned the ring out again. "You really shouldn't be slinging accusations like that around, Ivy. Clover Grove isn't nearly as sweet as that pie."

I tried to inject a little sugar into my classic HR smile. "Marlene, is that a threat? Did you slip a little rat poison into my coffee?"

Gathering her things, she dropped the pretense. "It's not a threat but a warning. This isn't about me. Dawes and I only got the property because we agreed to certain terms." She stuck her purse under her arm and directed a palm at me. "Don't ask because I don't know more. We were told only what we needed to know to get the job done. Fleet, too."

"That doesn't make you innocent," I said. "Any of you."

Her smile was cunning. "All you can pin on me is buying rat poison and that's not a crime."

"Maybe not, but it's criminally cruel."

"From what I hear your fox is fine. For now, anyway." She stepped away and then turned. "Eat your pie while you still have the appetite for it."

## CHAPTER TWENTY-TWO

I found the site we'd left last night in such a hurry without any trouble. Keats gave a ha-ha-ha as he pushed himself off the dashboard, where he'd been navigating. There was little need for GPS with him around. I only ran into problems when he didn't want to go where I wanted to go. Plus on the back country trails, where the routes were designed for the express purpose of losing people. Even clever canine people.

Another clever canid was sitting waiting for us. It was possible Veronica liked hanging around here because the mousing was good, but I doubted we'd find a fox in the same place twice by sheer coincidence. She had more to show us today and hopefully things would go better. I'd kept the camouflage gear from Edna in the truck and I put it on now, while Keats paced impatiently. Veronica paced on the other side of the clearing in the opposite direction, giving me the dizzying feeling of being stuck in a game of chance like the ones at the fall fair Asher liked so much. Only Percy stayed calm, sitting on the warm hood of the truck and cleaning his paws. It seemed a pointless task when they were about to get dirty again. The snow that kept those paws pristine was nearly gone in the bush. He stopped his work and gave me a little mew, perhaps reminding me that he was a cat. His life's work, aside from crime-fighting and cuddling, was staying clean.

I took his cue and came to the hood so he could step daintily onto my shoulder. A ride would reduce wear and tear on his pedicure, and also keep him out of the fox's way. Neither had shown particular interest in the other, but it was best not to tempt nature.

"All right, let's go. Double mission today, fur folks. Veronica, I sense you want to visit the dig site again and I'm all for it. But I also promised Keats we'd poke around for another trail." She stared at me from a distance of about five yards. I appreciated that she rarely came closer without a barrier in between. This time her amber eyes seemed to meet mine with intent and I said, "We're both pretty sure we saw you with a dog last night. Possibly very dark with splotches of white. Ring a bell?"

She turned away and Keats' tail drooped immediately.

"That wasn't a no, buddy. She just isn't going to make it easy for us."

His mumble was utterly despondent. I didn't even know his voice dropped to that register. He sounded helpless and hopeless, which didn't jive with his personality.

"Keats, you know we don't even like easy. We're all about tough puzzles and we don't need a fox to solve them. Why would she want to? There's nothing in it for Veronica, whereas evicting these literal gold diggers will salvage the forest for her and perhaps kits, come spring. We can't expect a wild dog to behave like a domesticated one."

The fox trotted ahead of me, checking over her shoulder periodically. There was something in her eyes that looked either pitying, contemptuous or both. To her, heart-to-heart conversations were probably for lesser canids.

"You do you, Veronica," I called. "We've got a good thing going here, and I doubt you'd be hanging around if you could do the job yourself."

Keats dug deep for a pant-laugh that heartened me. I was worried about the mystery dog, too, and could only hope that we came upon its scent while doing Veronica's bidding. If so, Keats would let me know.

The walk to the logging site seemed far shorter in daylight but the hill was just as treacherous when I crawled up. A tearing sound told me I was likely on the hook for replacing the snowsuit.

It was a relief and a disappointment to see nothing had changed except the heating blankets. They'd all been black last night, but today some were blue or green. Perhaps that had been the purpose of the ATV trip. The bonus crew was still hatching a dig and the ground wasn't ready.

"Nothing to see here," I said. "Except for the security cameras. Luckily I'm out of their sightline but I wish I could steal them." Keats mumbled and I agreed. "Probably wouldn't tell us much. We know who the crew is and where they're staying. The key is to question them and learn the identity of the showrunner. Based on what Marlene said, whoever's bankrolling this project probably crushed Dawes Croaker. Maybe he wasn't holding up his end, or maybe he talked too much. Hard to say. But now we know there's a kingpin and we'll find them."

Since there was no one around I took an easier route down and was about to walk back to the truck when Veronica gave a sharp yap. Keats gave that strange yap back—a feral sound I hadn't heard from him before we met the fox.

"Got it. New plan."

The fox led us in a wide arc around the dig site and deeper than ever into the forest. Were we even on the former Harlow land anymore? It seemed incredibly vast and the bush was dense and aggressively spiky. I always had the sense that the forest worked for the bad guys and repelled the good. If it could eject me now, it probably would. Fortunately, I had a fox in the lead and she knew the easiest route. Many would have been easier for a fox alone, but she seemed to select ones I could handle. Even so, Percy gave up clinging to my shoulder and jumped down to make his own way.

It was the cat who ultimately announced that we had reached our new destination. Climbing a hillock, he caught my eye and gave a single sweep of his paw over the frozen earth. Keats joined him and went into a point.

Following on hands and knees, I flattened in a hurry. About 30 yards away was another secure site that had been razed to the ground. Outside the fencing, huge old oak and maple trees lay strewn around. The wood was of no interest to the men who uprooted them. The trees were discarded like trash.

Percy swept the ground again and I saw the cable skidder that had ended Dawes Croaker's life. It may have been its evil twin but it couldn't have been easy to find identical machines of that vintage.

It wasn't in use at the moment, however. Nor were the shovels lined up along the inside fence. Tarps covered a few areas in a patch of land far bigger than a football field. Seemed like overkill to me, considering the impact on the ecosystem. Pulling out my phone, I took plenty of photos and mapped the location carefully. The mental image of Thelma's map was already fading in memory but there had been gold dots here—the mustardy shade, whereas the crew was hoping to hatch shimmer.

"This is the real dig," I said. "The one they have highest hopes for. I bet they used ground penetrating radar to find something."

Keats mumbled a question and I answered. "I'm not going any closer today. Not alone, buddy." His next mumble sounded a bit hurt. "I know I'm not alone with you guys, but the stakes are too high. If I get caught here by police, Skowby will follow through on his threat to toss me in jail. Worse, I could get caught by the crew and end up like Dawes. They've been digging recently. It smells like fresh earth, or at least freshly thawed earth."

I backed down the hill and by the time I straightened, Veronica was heading back the way we came.

"See?" I told my dog. "Even the fox wants me to be mature and resist temptation."

He mumbled a saucy comeback.

"Yeah, sure. She who hesitates finishes last. But she also finishes alive. Like it or not, my friend, I'm a whole new Ivy. Daredevil no more."

# CHAPTER TWENTY-THREE

The harness cut into me through the snowsuit as I dangled from the long arm of the tree-cutting crane that night. I regretted laughing at Rob the lumberjack a couple of days ago, since I was the bait on the fishhook now. I didn't see any humor at all in swinging nearly 20 feet over the dig site.

Keats grumbled something into my ear. A complaint about his doggie backpack, no doubt, combined with a distaste for heights. This dog preferred four on the floor. I wasn't a fan of arboreal rides, either, but since we didn't trust the new Skowby regime to investigate properly—if at all—someone had to go up and over, and I was nominated.

Fine. I nominated myself, but the options were few. Even if Uncle Sterling and Buckley had been available I would have felt terrible strapping them into this contraption. They were staking out the crew at the Big Sleep Motel so we could investigate in peace. Not that there was much peace to be had with the roar of the crane's motor below.

Jilly had also opted out of the mission because Fleet and his crew had been discharged from the hospital that afternoon and ordered by Skowby to stay at the inn until he'd resolved the poisoning incident to his satisfaction. None of the men had much energy so I doubted they'd give her trouble. Poppy agreed to spend the night but the enthusiastic female fan club had vanished. Poisoning had apparently dispelled the powerful lumberjack pheromones. Even Mom had relocated to her apartment in town.

That left Edna and Gertie, both of whom were more than willing to take this death ride. Someone had to stand guard, however, and that was Minnie, in Gertie's capable poncho. And most important of all, someone had to operate the machines and the only one who could do that was Edna. It was a specialized skill set she'd gained working summers on a farm and later as a medic on a remote logging site.

I was in good hands. It just didn't feel that way.

The cherry picker trip to nab the cameras had been a breeze in comparison to the crane, in part because Keats wasn't riding along. It wasn't that he was heavy, but the weight of responsibility for his welfare certainly was. A responsible owner would not take her beloved dog on such a perilous ride. An irresponsible amateur sleuth? That was another matter entirely. I needed Keats and Percy inside and only one of them was capable of climbing in on his own. Edna had disabled the electric fence but there was also a high and heavy layer of the most aggressive barbed wire I'd seen in my history of trespassing. It was like a high-security prison. But the safeguards didn't deter my nimble cat and he was already waiting for us on the ground.

Keats offered further testy commentary and I cut him off with a grumble of my own. "Look, you wanted me to do something earlier and now we are. So much for my newfound maturity."

There was an ache in my chest that didn't come only from fear. I missed Kellan so much right now it hurt. If he were here doing the policing job right, I wouldn't have to take a risk that seemed extreme even to me.

The thought of his reaction if he ever heard about it made one leg spasm and sent me spinning in a circle. I choked back a squeal of terror with marginal success.

"Quiet up there," Gertie called, over the motor. "We nailed the cameras we could see but there could be more."

"I'm trying," I called back. "This is the scariest thing I've ever done."

Gertie tossed her braid over her other shoulder and grinned. "You've faced down a dozen killers. How is this worse?"

"Because my feet were on the ground and bands of steel weren't slicing off my limbs."

Edna was wearing ear protection but accurately interpreted the conversation. "Quit whining, soldier," she bellowed, probably louder than she intended. "It'll all be over in a few minutes."

I just hoped it wouldn't be permanently over.

She lowered us slowly and with great precision over the small "landing strip" we'd identified. Most of the ground was covered in tarps of various colors, so it was impossible to know what had been excavated. Mounds of soil had been moved out with a shiny new bobcat that Edna was itching to try out, but it wasn't part of the plan.

That plan was simply for me to explore the site with the pets and figure out where the men were digging and whether they'd found success. It would be a bonus if Keats and Percy could outguess them. But first, I had to land safely and move the tarps to see how to get around.

The descent was painfully slow but necessarily so. Getting deposited into a deep hole wasn't going to help the cause. A shudder ran through me as I thought about falling into what might turn into a grave. One of my many recurring nightmares was about being buried alive, sometimes in a coffin, other times not. Without the help of an expert shrink, I interpreted that as a fear of returning to the confines of my former life as a miserable HR exec. Trapped. Bullied. Despairing.

Keats' tone changed to become more encouraging. Even this

strange ride was better than what came before. Maybe, if I took a few deep breaths and stayed present in the moment, I could actually enjoy it.

Nope.

And again nope.

There was no enjoyment to be found, but luckily, the journey was short. Edna let me touch down with such precision and skill that I didn't even wobble. She turned off the motor and called, "Release and go forth."

I knew the drill from our dress rehearsal and stepped out of the harness. Then I gently slid off the backpack and set Keats free. He shook and shook again, as if he'd been doused in water. Because of the special occasion, I hadn't made him wear a coat. My fear and his excitement were keeping us plenty warm.

Percy had started picking his way around the site even before we landed and Keats went in the opposite direction. I followed the dog, knowing he'd sense and avoid any cavities. Getting out my phone, I lifted each tarp and shone my light underneath to see holes in various stages of excavation. There was no sign of any buried treasure but I hadn't expected the crew to leave it, even with all the security.

When I had flung back all the tarps, I saw eight holes distributed across the large site. Two were quite deep, which Edna told me to expect. Once the heating mats thawed the layer of frozen ground, digging wasn't difficult.

Turned out the holes were the least interesting part of the exploration.

Keats chose a spot at one end of the field of destruction and went into a point. Not just any point, but an assertive, "landed something big" kind of point with muzzle high and eyes bright under the lights. Technically, it seemed to be half under the fence line, which made it easy to photograph.

"Score one for the dog," I called to my friends.

"Don't rest on your laurels," Edna called back. "There may be more."

Indeed, before we'd quite reached the other end, Keats snapped into another point. Not quite as assertive but still an affirmative. There was something worth digging for and thanks to him, we might be able to find it first.

Edna saw the point and rubbed her gloves in glee. She was ready to jimmy another machine, slice the fence and find some gold.

Maybe that would have happened if Percy hadn't made a discovery of his own. As with many of his revelations, it came with much ado about litter. The soil was loose under the tarp he'd selected so he was able to throw up a spray of grit.

"Oh no," I said. "Percy, are you sure?"

He added the other paw to emphasize just how sure he was. The double sweep was always definitive.

"Is that cat doing what I think he's doing?" Gertie said, coming around the perimeter to watch.

"If you think he's locating a body, then yes."

She adjusted Minnie on her shoulder and rubbed her eyes with her free hand as if hoping to wipe away the vision. Then she stared at Percy again and found him still sweeping, perhaps sensing we didn't want to believe and forcing us to accept his verdict.

Edna joined her, looking downhearted. "I suppose this means no digging for treasure?"

"Not unless you consider mystery bones a treasure."

She cracked a grim smile. "In a way, I do. But far less fun than pirate's gold. Are we going to exhume the remains? I brought shovels but we'd have to hoist Gertie in to help."

Now I rubbed my eyes as I thought about it. "It's one thing to walk in on Kellan with a femur under my arm and another with Skowby."

"But you can't just tell him your cat says there's a body." Gertie brought Minnie around and patted the long barrel, as she was inclined to do when in need of comfort. "Or can you? I'd like to be there when you do."

Keats cast his vote by easing Percy out of the way and starting to dig briskly. I was of two minds whether to stop him but a series of phone pings cast the deciding vote. Buckley and Sterling were letting us know the crew was gearing up to move.

If we didn't hurry, I could be trapped inside this pen with a dead body and a few holes big enough to contain mine.

# CHAPTER TWENTY-FOUR

I did my best to restore everything to its original condition and hitched a ride over the fence on the crane. It was quicker and scarier on the way out because Edna was in too much of a hurry to indulge my nerves. I wanted it to be over, too.

She backed the big machine into the tight spot where we'd found it, looking understandably proud as she jumped down. This retired nurse never failed to surprise me. Now, when she could be bragging, she was gathering equipment to beat a hasty retreat.

"Won't the crew notice the equipment is warm?" I asked, watching Veronica pace. The fox was probably eager for us to get going.

"If they get here before it cools," Edna said. "Buckley and Sterling have a few tricks up their sleeves."

Gertie checked her phone. "And a pen knife, apparently. The crew had a puncture that will slow them down. Plenty of time for us to make a getaway."

Light snow was falling, which brightened our path but would also show footprints unless the crew faced more than a flat. I was sure between them they would be quick with a spare tire.

"Four flats!" Gertie's voice perked up after her phone pinged again. "One spare. They're stuck for the moment and it won't be easy to stay undercover while getting those replaced."

I was grateful we had a little more time to figure out our next move, and fell into step behind the others while I mused.

"You going to call Skowby?" Gertie asked, not long before we reached the truck.

Edna spoke for me. "Of course not. He won't believe your cat raked up a dead body or that your dog knows where the treasure is really buried."

"Skowby doesn't deserve custody of that gold," Gertie said. "You know who does?"

"Chief Hottie, obviously." It had been quite some time since Edna used that term and it stood out now. I sensed she was missing Kellan, or at least the sense of stability he brought to the region. As a wild card, she probably liked playing off the staid cop. "I don't suppose Ivy can ask him to come home."

"If he could, he would. I haven't heard from him in nearly two days." The heart emojis he sent weren't worth mentioning to Edna and Gertie but they'd done me a world of good. I trusted him implicitly, but I sure didn't trust the situation. He had little control over his fate right now whereas I still had a modicum over mine.

At least I hoped so.

"Let me sleep on it," I said, as we got into the truck. "I could try a vague story on Officer Fenway, but it won't fly without real evidence. There isn't a whiff of woo-woo in either of these men."

"That's for sure," Gertie said from the back seat. "Their loss. I love the woo now."

I gripped the wheel tighter. "The treasure is one thing but the body in the ground another. The earth was tamped down well but still loose enough for Percy to send dirt flying."

Edna moved around in the passenger seat to give Keats more room, while Percy opted for the back seat. "Recent, then. A lumberjack who mutinied, perhaps."

"That was my first guess," I said. "Sterling thought they were one down from the original five."

"The police aren't doing their job if they don't know who's missing in the community," Gertie said.

"Or maybe they do." Edna's voice was quiet, perhaps expecting to be shot down by a soon-to-be wife of a cop.

After a long pause, I sighed. "That occurred to me, too. Skowby seems to be turning his back on what's been happening on the Croaker property. Would he also ignore a murder?"

Keats was strangely silent on the subject. His eyes were trained out the passenger window and he tapped Edna's arm to get her to open it. Less than a mile from where we'd parked, he sniffed deeply and let out a loud, keening whine.

"What's got his knickers in a twist?" Edna asked, patting him with a glove. He shrugged it off and gazed at me with pleading eyes. I didn't even know his blue eye was capable of that expression.

He wanted to pull over and plunge into the bush to search for the mystery dog and I may well have done so, if not for the fear of the logging crew getting their hands on another vehicle. They were resourceful and possibly capable of committing and concealing murder. Still, it broke my heart to turn him down again and the truck slowed nearly to the point of stalling.

Gertie's finger came through the seats and poked me. "Ivy? You falling asleep? Maybe I should drive."

I shook my head, feeling the weight of Edna's stare. "Ivy Rose Galloway, what are you hiding?"

Pressing the gas a little harder, I touched Keats and he leaned away from me, too. Picking up speed meant a no. "Keats and I thought we saw a stray dog in the woods last night. We're worried about it running loose at this time of year. I tried the lost pet sites and didn't find any recent posts."

"It's not that late and I don't mind looking around," Edna said. "Keats isn't a whiner as a rule. It must be something."

"I'm in," Gertie said. "I owe Keats a lot and I hate to think of a stray out here."

My heart filled with warmth over my good fortune of finding friends like these two quirky women. They were tough on the battle-field and soft when it came to animals. My kind of people.

Keats' gaze turned into a glare of challenge. His friends were on board. What about me?

I probably would have folded under the pressure, if not for the fox. Veronica emerged from the bush and loped along the shoulder, pausing to make sure we were following.

"She has other plans, buddy. I promise we will look around again when we get on top of the current situation."

He turned a cold shoulder and it chased away the warmth I'd just savored.

"Someone's in trouble," Edna said, patting Keats again and getting a noticeably warmer reception. "I've got a spare room if you need it, my furry friend."

His next look my way was a deliberate taunt and he mumbled something that sounded like, "Dare me."

It bothered me terribly to be on the outs with him, but strange as it seemed, I trusted the fox.

She wanted us to go home to the farm.

The answer to our questions must be there.

## CHAPTER TWENTY-FIVE

I spent the night in the barn, waiting for that answer to arrive. There was no reason not to go inside the inn, other than that I didn't want to be waylaid by Fleet and his crew. I figured they had to know about the shadow sites, and perhaps even the body. I could not pretend to be a gracious hostess in those circumstances. What Jilly didn't know right now would help her cater to the recovering team, with Poppy's help. In response to my text, she sent Daisy down with food and my laptop. My eldest sister, who'd been reading me all my life, knew better than to ask questions. After giving me a motherly hug, she left for the night.

I wondered if Keats would carry his snit so far that he'd go up to the house, but he settled for resting on a hay bale in the corner of the barn and turning his back. Percy climbed the ladder ahead of me and spoke harshly to the barn cats my dad collected. There were six of them now, and they were lined up on a blanket on top of more bales of hay. They had the decency to leave the cot to the humans, and tonight it was empty. Dad was here more often than not and I wondered if he'd gone along with Sterling and Buckley. He liked to keep a low profile, but he was also very close to his uncle.

"All ours," I told Percy, sitting on the cot with my laptop. It was plenty warm enough without a blanket thanks to the heat rising from the livestock. Eventually I had to unzip my snowsuit, but the flush of heat burning my face and ears probably had more to do with my efforts to access the data on the security cameras. Finally I woke Cori —a skilled hacker—and got her to help me out. She was so decent about it I decided to wake her more often.

At some point sheer exhaustion bowled me over and if it weren't for a noise downstairs and a rumble from Keats, I may have snored through the arrival of the answer to my problems.

Rarely did answers of any kind come into my life with a song, as they did early that morning. Asher was singing loud enough that he didn't hear my footsteps as I walked to the edge of the loft. Below, he gave Keats a pat and went over to his favorite farm resident, Alvina the alpaca. Giving her a deep bow, he invited her to dance. She had a stall of her own for this very reason. A girl needed room to freestyle if the opportunity arose and my barn cam told me it arose often. Asher frequently joined her after his night shift to shake off his worries before heading inside. It was a wise strategy that left him smiling.

I was smiling, too, from the top of the ladder and when he finished singing "Dancing Queen," I applauded.

That caused him to jump higher than ever and Alvina mirrored the move in her stall.

"What are you doing up there?" he called. "More of your sneakery."

"It's not sneakery if I own the place. Besides, wasn't Keats your first clue?"

He shrugged. "I figured he had a livestock emergency. Or sometimes a guy—even a canine guy—just needs a little space. It'll be hard to come by up at the house."

"That's partly why I didn't go in." I climbed down the ladder and jerked my thumb at the door. "Mind if we take a little ride?"

"A ride? Now? It's my bedtime."

"Come on, I'll buy you a coffee. Mandy will let us in and you normally have some java when you get home."

"Probably sleep better if I didn't," he said. "What are you up to, Ivy? You've got that look on your face."

I gave him an innocent smile. "What look?"

"The 'I swallowed a big secret and it's turned into an exploding alien' look. I think Kellan coined that one."

Keats gave a pant-laugh at me, not with me. He was still miffed about last night.

"It's just something I want to discuss privately."

He shook his head. "Uh-uh. You want to drag me into one of your crazy exploits. The kind that'll lose me my job."

"On the contrary, what I have to say might just earn you a promotion." I tried my smile again. "Or maybe it's just something important about Jilly." I started walking outside. "Can you stand not knowing?"

He could pass up the promotion more easily than information about the woman he adored, so he trailed after me grumbling complaints. "I'm driving so I can escape. I know without a doubt I'm going to regret this."

Half an hour later, sitting in the truck outside the abandoned railway station with an empty coffee cup in his hand, I could tell he really did regret this.

"You let Edna Evans lift you with a tree crane? Are you totally insane? Kellan will freak." His hands rubbed his face over and over, and I realized he looked older now. My brother was perpetually youthful but this past month had aged him and it wasn't just the night shifts. "All I can say is I hope I'm in your will. Jilly and I could take over the place. Only without the guests."

"Alvina would love that," I said. "I'll look into it when you've finished investigating."

"I knew it. You want me to throw my badge out the window, let

Edna hoist me in and start randomly digging holes on someone else's property."

"Well, not exactly. Although it wouldn't be random. Keats and Percy have a strong track record for locating the good and the bad. However, I don't think any of us should be going in there without an army."

His hand came up. "You can amass an army in three simple texts. Forget it."

"Let me rephrase that. I think what you're suggesting is too risky for anyone, especially someone with a badge."

Now I had his attention, although his blue eyes were wary. "What do you mean?"

I took a deep breath and dropped the bomb. "I think Skowby's in on it."

"In on... what, exactly? Spell it out nice and slow, twisty sis, because I'm running on scraps of sleep."

I passed him the rest of my coffee, which was a major sacrifice, even for my favorite sibling. "Is it possible Skowby's ignoring crimes and greasing the wheels to make this dig happen? I can only assume he'd be in for a cut of whatever they find. Uncle Sterling and Thelma Tilrow agree that it's probably a sizable fortune. The crew may have used ground penetrating radar but their targeting is off. We have an opportunity—probably a short one—to beat them to the punch." I rolled my window down and took a few breaths. "And prevent anyone else ending up as filler."

"Ivy, you can't just make accusations like that about the chief of police, even if he is only acting." He patted my arm gingerly. "I know you're probably emotional over what's happened with Kellan."

If he'd used the word "hormonal," I might have socked him in the jaw. That's probably what he meant.

"I am not emotional!" Regrettably my tone was emotional enough to make Keats pant-laugh again. "Has something happened to Kellan I should know about? I haven't heard from him lately."

Asher leaned back and shook his head. "Me either. I only meant you're shook up. Not thinking rationally."

I pulled my laptop out of my bag. "I figured you'd need proof and luckily, I have something to show you."

He downed my coffee with a gulp and stared at the screen. "What am I seeing? It's pretty grainy."

"Security cam feed. Edna sent me up on the cherry picker to grab them before I swung into the site."

"You stole the—never mind. This just gets worse and worse. I don't know how Kellan— Wait, what's happening there?" He touched my screen. "Looks like Skowby."

"Sure does." The man in question was in street clothes with his back mostly turned but he had the bearing of the chief. Even from the rear, he exuded attitude. "There's sound, too."

I turned the volume to the top so that he could hear three men arranging a meeting. I'd been able to zoom in on one crew member's phone and see the destination was the Big Snooze Motel, where they were staying. Granted, they may have moved on after their Land Rover was vandalized. I wouldn't mention that quite yet.

Asher hit replay twice before sliding down in his seat. "I don't get it. Why is the chief meeting privately with lumberjack dudes? It looked..."

"Clandestine?"

"Exactly. You know all the big words." He sat up a little. "Here's another one for you. Corruption. That's what you're alleging, Ivy. Corruption on the police force."

I started to nod and shrugged instead. "I guess that is what I'm alleging. But all I've got is this footage and a hunch. So, I was thinking we could work on this together. Build a case."

Asher opened the driver door, hopped out of his own truck and started walking along the dirt road toward the farm. I released the pets and went after him. "Ash. All you need to do is poke around a little. Find out if Skowby ticked all the right boxes in Croaker's death. He dismissed it too quickly as accidental. Did he order a full autopsy? Follow up on the results? Or is the report MIA?"

"Are you kidding me?" He walked so fast I had to jog to keep up. "I'm not going to poke around his case files. That's treason."

"I'd just call it due diligence within a corporate context. Nothing more. I did it all the time at Flordale." I caught his sleeve to make him slow down. "Flip this in your mind. How about you search for information that proves Skowby's innocence? That's you being a good cop and a good employee. When I was in corporate, a big part of my job was watching Wilf's butt. Not literally, but he was always crossing the line and I saved him from trouble a lot. I'm sure you and Kellan give each other reality checks all the time."

"I don't need to tell Kellan how to do his job. Best chief in all of hill country. Probably the state."

"Agreed. So, you've never, for example, suggested that letting me trespass or dig up old bones was a bad idea?"

He glanced back at me. "Of course. I told him you're a bad idea in general. Wouldn't listen and now he's putting a ring on trouble. There's still time to convince him he's under the influence of your voodoo, by the way."

I decided to let that pass for the greater good, but he'd pay for it later. "If you've advised Kellan in any capacity, that's you having your boss's back. Whether you like Skowby or not, shouldn't you do the same now?"

His stride slowed slightly. "Is that how you turned into a fake detective? Using your sneakery in Flordale?"

"I suppose. Being in HR, I just never took anything at face value. I learned early that people lie. Not everyone, but enough that I was always on the lookout for a workplace mystery. There would be the staffer disappearing at odd hours, or clocking too much overtime, or calling in sick too many days. I never considered any clue too small to turn over and take a look. Corporate sleuthing, as it were. Some-times it turned out to be nothing and other times a major fiasco. If I hadn't left, I guarantee I'd have found that my colleague, Neil, was sharing company secrets with competitors."

My brother let me catch up. "He was the IT guy, right? Since when are you so good with IT, by the way? Hacking into security cameras?"

"I can't be all the things. Private consultants helped me out many a time and now I have clever friends." I walked alongside him but didn't look up. He needed to come to this decision himself. Keats wasn't so subtle and gave Asher a cheeky mumble to hurry up, while Percy scaled his back to settle on his shoulder. "I made a career out of questioning everything and everyone, and now I do it for free."

He churned his hair, while Percy tried to get a pat out of him. "I know you're trying to drop a big fat hint with all your twisty mumbo jumbo. You've been trying to confuse me since the moment you could talk."

I laughed. "Mom says I talked late. So late she took me to Doc Grainer to see if I had a developmental delay."

Asher finally cracked a smile. "Little did she know you were already talking to me in some fake language that only I understood. It was a mixture of grunts and cackles."

"Grunts and cackles! That's insulting. Either way, you understood me."

"But one day I realized I was getting bamboozled. So I—uh— acquired a nifty stuffed dog that you'd been eying at the gift store and put it on my highest shelf to see what you'd do."

The memory whisked me back to his bedroom of long ago. All the girls had to share but the golden boy got his own room. "You literally dangled that shoplifted treasure over me. It was cruel."

"What was cruel was you jerking my strings with your mumbles." His smile turned into a grin. "You sounded like the dog you ended up getting."

"My strategy must have worked, because you gave me the purloined stuffie, didn't you?"

"Only after you finally asked for it using real words, like I knew you could all along. You were manipulating me from the jump, Ivy."

His diversion had worked so well that I was curious. "So then I just dropped the charade of being unable to talk?"

"Nope. You started speaking English with me and continued faking with everyone else. I kept your secret. There was no harm done and I knew you really just didn't want to talk to Mom. None of us did back then."

I sighed. "Because she didn't listen. I guess after six kids I was lucky she even noticed the delay."

"She didn't. That was Daisy."

Keats gave me a poke in the shin to let me know I was the one being bamboozled today. Asher had led me as far as he could from the notion of a dirty cop. I wasn't the only one capable of sneakery.

He was satisfied enough with his ploy that he circled back for his truck, allowing me to keep up.

I, in turn, circled back to the matter at hand. "What I was trying to say earlier is that protecting your boss is a good thing. Especially if that boss is truly Kellan. If Skowby is clean, great. If he's dirty, I imagine Kellan would be back in his office fast."

That would play to my brother's fierce loyalty to his best and oldest friend. Plus, his career was going nowhere fast under the current regime and his driving force in life was making Jilly proud. I counted on these things to get him to do what I couldn't. Even the most ambitious amateur sleuth couldn't easily expose police corruption.

When we reached the truck he handed me the key, along with Percy. "You drive and I'll jog home. I'm tired of listening because I know you're just trying to wear me down. It's another one of your old strategies." He loped away with his easy, athletic gait, knowing I couldn't possibly keep up on foot or risk hitting him on the highway. Glancing over his shoulder, he called, "I'm not the kid you duped way back when, sis. You can't just make me do whatever you want anymore."

With a flick of my fingers, I sent Keats after him and soon Asher was dodging, weaving and in true peril of a face-plant in gravel. Maybe I couldn't get my brother to do what I wanted, but Keats could and since the dog was an extension of me, I still won.

# CHAPTER TWENTY-SIX

There was little I enjoyed more than hearing my brother scream like a schoolgirl, and it was worth every uncomfortable moment of hiding in his rear footwell under a blanket with two pets as the evening chill set in.

I let Keats and Percy have the pleasure of springing out first, waiting till we were so far from home that he wouldn't turn back or eject us on the highway. It was a matter of careful timing, because I didn't want to end up crushed in the ditch, either. But I knew exactly where he was going, and when he hit the four-way stop on a side road, Keats took a peek and signaled we were good to go. Percy took aim at my brother's head and Keats waylaid his sleeve.

Then I hoisted myself onto the rear seat and said, "Whew. I'm a little stiff. Guess I'm not as flexible as I was when I started bamboozling you."

"Are you crazy, Ivy? Wait, don't answer that. I know you're crazy. But this time you could have killed someone, and your pets."

"It was well planned and executed with sheer joy."

He made the turn slowly. "And what is the purpose of this invasion?"

"Isn't it obvious? We're coming with you to stake out the meeting and catch Skowby in the act."

He pulled over, deciding whether to proceed. "What makes you think I'm doing that?"

"Astute observation. Instead of going to bed this morning, you disappeared for a few hours and I saw your truck down at the station."

"You tailed me?"

"My truck voodoo isn't good enough to tail you, so I just took a roll by on a hunch. Lost you after that for a while but when I over-heard you call in with a family emergency, I knew it was game on. I'm your emergency."

"You spent the whole day monitoring me?"

"I've spent worse days, trust me. I still got my chores done, and now I'm ready to solve this mystery together, brother. For Kellan."

He stared at me in the rearview. "You're impossible. And just so you know, I am going to try a lot harder to talk him out of marrying you. He deserves a nice girl."

"That he does, and it's your job as best man to see he's making the right decision. If you can change his mind, it's for the best and I'm not worried."

His shoulders sank at the failed ploy. "I can't take you along, Ivy. It could be dangerous. As Kellan's best man I owe it to him to keep his fiancée safe."

"I owe it to my fiancé to keep *him* safe. They've redeployed him who knows where and are probably pulling his job out from under him. After all the great work he's done here. I'm going to watch this meetup, brother. If you turf me, you can bet I have a plan B."

My plan B included Edna and Gertie, and he knew it would. I counted on his wanting to keep me under his supervision. I wanted the same thing. With the possibility of police in the mix, I was batting out of my league.

He drove on, letting the grim set of his jaw do the talking. Turns out he'd picked up a few things working for Kellan.

A mile down the road, he turned off into a farmer's field and rolled along the side until there was enough brush to hide his truck. "Wait here. I mean it, Ivy."

"I am not waiting in a field while you go on by foot." I opened the door. "If you're walking, we're walking."

"It's miles, you idiot. We're not walking. I've arranged other transportation."

Keats was already out and I let him follow. "My dog will make sure you come back."

The only answer was a rude gesture but I cut him some slack. He'd had zero sleep and was probably feeling in over his head, too.

I barely had time to get worried before a beat-up gray sedan bumped toward me. The windows were down and Keats was in Asher's lap, panting happily. "Get in," Asher called. "We're on the clock."

"Who loaned you the car?" I asked, getting into the passenger seat with Percy.

"I have friends. They don't ask as many questions as you do."

Once we were on the main road, I tried again. "I'm assuming you learned enough today to make you suspicious."

"I'm keeping an open mind and so should you. We may be going to a lot of trouble to see a bunch of lumberjacks having a beer. They're fully entitled to work on the old Harlow property if that's what Marlene Croaker wants. She owns it now."

"Yeah, but you found something or you wouldn't be taking the risk of getting your friend in trouble by Skowby recognizing this car."

He could have stonewalled but he probably didn't have the energy. "I didn't find much. No one who makes it to chief of police is going to leave an obvious trail. But you were right about the autopsy report. It's not in yet, which is strange. Even more so, they sent

Croaker's remains down country, when there's plenty of capacity in Dorset Hills. I checked."

"Huh. He must have wanted to buy enough time to get the work done. A few more days would do it."

"Possibly. I also wondered about the identity of the body Percy thinks he found. A crackerjack arborist from Balsam Ridge is missing. Guy's a recluse who normally only works when he really needs the cash and has no friends or family to report the disappearance."

I knew Balsam Ridge, a tiny town an hour's drive from Fleetborough. "You sent Uncle Sterling to look for him."

He scowled at me. "I'd never send an old man into that situation. He was already on it and drove over with Buckley Brackens."

"Those cranky hermits are bonding," I said. "What did they find?"

"A hungry dog in a run outside, for starters." Ash patted Keats, who'd stayed in my brother's lap, possibly to diss me. "Sterling took care of that, don't worry. There was food in the fridge so it looked like the chopper planned to come home soon. Otherwise, the place seemed untouched except for a missing hard drive from an old desktop."

"Maybe someone removed the digital trail after they turned him into fertilizer."

"Again, we'll keep an open mind. But it did make me curious. If Sterling could figure out the guy was missing, why couldn't their local police?"

I shivered, which brought Keats back where he belonged. "I sure hope corruption hasn't spread that far."

The grim set of Asher's jaw returned. "If it has, I'm surrendering my badge. That's why I'm here, Ivy. To make sure I committed to a worthy cause. There are plenty of other ways I could support Jilly and a family with less risk and stress."

"Definitely. But policing is your calling, just as it is Kellan's. It would be such a shame to have that work sullied."

He held up crossed fingers. "I just hope what we find today restores my faith in justice."

What we found when we reached the Big Sleep Motel, however, was nothing. Well, not nothing. There was a stack of tires by the dumpster that confirmed the lumber crew was rolling again. Unfortunately, the slashed tires were probably why they'd moved. By this point, they may have discovered the missing security cameras, too, although I doubted they could even imagine we'd gained access to the footage, let alone the dig site itself.

I sighed. "It's a bust."

Asher looked at me in mock disgust and addressed his question to the dog in my lap. "Does she always give up that easily? It's only strike one."

Keats gave a happy pant and pawed the dashboard. "Swing again, brother. You were always good at baseball."

"I'm good at all sports," he said, turning the car around. "And games of chance. Even poker. The rest of you Galloways always underestimated me."

He wasn't wrong about any of it. "I'm sorry. We probably did, but remember, Mom didn't notice I wasn't talking till nearly age four."

"Can you really blame her? There was a constant din in our house."

Houses. We moved several times after defaulting on the rent. "Yeah. I still blame her."

A smile appeared as he gunned the car up the street. "For better or worse, she made us what we are today. Would you change anything?"

I shook my head. "Guess not. Now, where are we going?"

"There's an abandoned motel a few miles away. If I didn't want to be seen, I'd hole up there."

"If they really don't want to be seen, there are countless bunkers."

He took a hard right and headed down a poorly maintained road. "Guys like them don't do bunkers. Not for the cut they're likely to get from any profit. Only true eccentrics can stand that hardship. Imagine if you got trapped underground."

I didn't have to imagine it since it had already happened. At least some of those true eccentrics got me out.

"What if it's strike two?" I asked.

"It's a hit." He flicked a finger to the passenger window. Inside a fenced farm field, an auburn streak kept pace with us. There was enough snow left to make Veronica noticeable in the failing light. "Isn't that your fox?"

Keats mumbled a suggestion to the driver and Asher slowed down. At the next breach in the fence, my brother plunged over a gully and into the field. He turned out the lights and I hoped Veronica would stay out of our path.

The next half mile was a rough ride in the old sedan but we made it to a grove of squat pines, by which point the fox had vanished.

"Stay in the car," Asher said, grabbing a bag from the back seat and then opening his door.

"As if." I got out and followed him into the trees. On the other side, we could see a long, low and very decrepit building. The faded paint on the sign read, "Stay a Day Motel." That was probably as long as anyone could ever stand staying there. It was in the middle of nowhere and had a creepy vibe.

Keats went into a point and Asher pulled out a camera with a telephoto lens. "There's the Land Rover. Put the wrong tires on it. Guess they were desperate. There's another car, too. Not Skowby's."

"Can we get any closer?"

The camera lens moved back and forth. "Don't need to. They're coming out. Inside's lit up with candles like a séance. Guess the power line's cut." The camera clicked and clicked. "Binoculars in the bag."

I bent to grab them. "Maybe it is a séance. They might need help from beyond, because they haven't found the gold yet. Edna sent a drone over the site to check."

He turned for a second, which gave me a chance to nose in front of him, and our lenses jockeyed for the best view through the branches. We both became very still suddenly. Then I slid back in time to see my brother's broad shoulders slump. His ideals had plummeted to a very dark place. "Skowby," he said.

"Yeah. But all it proves is that he's here meeting with a lumber crew. Can we get close enough to listen?"

Asher shook his head. "No cover. Even if there were, it's not safe. For now, we know enough." He refocused the camera and took more photos. "The chief of police is at a derelict motel meeting with a crew doing suspicious work. With your security footage and the other anomalies, it's enough to escalate the matter."

"You think? I could see it creating more trouble for you without being conclusive."

He pulled me back into the trees and hissed, "Land Rover's on the roll and coming in hot. Get in the car."

Seeing Dixon Skowby here wasn't enough evidence.

The bullet that hit the fender as we drove off felt conclusive.

The second, even more so.

The third, fourth and fifth? Overkill.

# CHAPTER TWENTY-SEVEN

Asher drove straight across the field with the lights out. "Ivy, grab the pets and get down."

For once, I did as I was told, more for the pets than myself. Keats grumbled as I shoved him into the footwell but Percy was happy to cover his green eyes with his tail and pretend it wasn't happening.

"Are they following?" I asked.

"Land Rover's still looking for a way into the field. But if they're firing on us, they will. Make no mistake."

"Do you know where you're going?"

"Basically, yeah. But your fox has other ideas. She's running alongside again. Guiding me further south than I would have gone. Can I trust her?" He reached over and held my head down. "Just use your words. Real ones, okay?"

"Yes. Veronica is risking her life. Honor that by trusting her."

He moved his hand off my head and pressed harder on the gas. "You're so weird. How did you get so weird?"

"We've already established how that happened. What I want to know is how you can be so cool after gunfire."

"The idea is to expect it and plan ahead. I knew where I'd run. The only wild card was the fox. I hope she knows what she's doing."

Keats mumbled something comforting and I saw my brother's fingers relax ever so slightly on the wheel. "She does. Are they in the field yet?"

"Yeah. Both vehicles are pursuing."

"Should we call someone? I mean, this is bad, right?"

He gave a humorless laugh. "It's bad. Who do you call for help when the chief of police is shooting at you?"

"The *real* chief of police," I suggested. "Kellan."

"Oh, I will once we're safe. For the moment, expect the ride of your life."

"Yippee. The back country trails. Good thing I skipped dinner."

"That's where I was headed and your fox has gotten us there much faster. She found another breach."

I let him focus as he rolled down a ditch and up the other side. There were several quick torturous twists and turns that let me know we'd arrived on the trails my brother knew well. He'd been driving back here since before he had a license. "Can I sit up? Two of us are getting carsick." Percy was making retching sounds that only made me feel more nauseated.

"Okay. We've lost them for now, and probably for good. I can't imagine any of them know the trails like I do." He turned on the lights and sighed. "Only Kellan does. Dad, probably."

"Don't count Mom out. She gets around back here pretty good. Edna and Gertie, too." I eased myself back into the passenger seat and stared over my shoulder. "I think they're still there, Ash. Look at Keats."

The dog was puffed and growling. He wanted to prop his paws on the dash to take over navigation now that the fox had gone, but I held on tight. These trails were a rollercoaster.

"Fine," Asher said, turning out the lights again. "If that's how they want to play this... buckle in."

I did just that, clutching Keats with one hand. Then I grabbed hold of a cracked vinyl handle and said, "Hope none of us heave in your friend's car."

"Relax. I got this."

He did have this. Kellan always sat back during a challenging ride—calm, cool and composed. My brother, on the other hand, was the sporty type, chest forward, chin out, urging the car on like a race-horse. Indeed, the car moved with power and ease that defied its beat-up exterior.

Keats gave an encouraging mumble and I translated. "We're losing them."

"About time. Now, use your phone light." Asher leaned forward even more. "Just for a second. I think I'm where I gotta be."

I flashed the light around quickly and he steered into a skinny opening, where the trail was even rougher and all uphill. Instead of slowing, he actually pressed the gas harder.

"This is it," I said. "The place where nightmares come true."

"Au contraire, twisty sis. This is my signature trail. Every hill country boy's dream come true. A route absolutely no one knows better than you. Guaranteed to get you out of any trap."

"Your signature trail? Are you kidding?"

He laughed. "Took me decades to carve this out. Started at four-teen and finished... well, maybe by forty. Most private trails are a lifelong project, especially since it grows over almost as fast as you clear it. Rock slides, floods, downed trees... All part of the fun."

"And you call me crazy." I let out a breath and then gasped as he took a hairpin turn and headed down again, still without light.

"Fear not, I know this terrain. That's what I think about when I'm stressed. When I can't sleep. I run the trail over and over in my head. Watch this."

Instead, I closed my eyes and listened as water splashed from below. "Do not ever bring Jilly here," I said. "Not if you really want children."

"Why? I'd like her to see it. I'm just waiting for the right moment."

"The right moment is not in this lifetime. You risk paralyzing her ovaries. She would never trust you with her kids. I mean it, Asher. In this way I know your wife better than you ever can."

He slid down in the seat and turned on the lights. "Bummer. My proudest accomplishment wasted."

I laughed. "Hardly. You just saved my life and earned bonus points from the real chief of police. But your private trail should remain the bit of mystery that adds spice to every marriage."

He laughed, too, and slowed to a pace I could handle. "I'll leave it to the next lifetime... unless the apocalypse comes first."

"Oh, man," I said. "I hated every minute of that, but I have to admit I was really happy to be riding with you tonight."

He took one hand off the wheel and patted my head, as if I were that mumbling kid again. "Thanks, sis. I feel bad for putting you in a position of getting shot at."

"I put myself into your back seat, remember? If you'd waited long enough to dump me, we'd have missed them. But your friend isn't going to be too happy about the dents in his car."

"Doubt he'll care." I noticed a small smile playing on his lips. "Doubt he'll notice. Doesn't know it's gone."

"Excuse me? You stole a car?"

Now his smile turned into a grin. "You're acting like it's the first time."

"It is the first time... since you became an officer of the law."

"Yeah? You sure about that?"

I thought about how Kellan and Asher used to "borrow" cars for drag racing. "Honestly. What would Kellan say?"

"That he hoped I picked my mark wisely and changed out the plates to protect the owner. Which I did." He patted the dash. "This baby's been up on blocks for two years, easy. I had to fix up a few things to get her running like a racehorse."

"Since when did you take up mechanics?" I saw the exact moment his grin turned guilty. "Asher, tell me you didn't rope one of our nephews into helping you steal a car."

"There was no roping involved. Sutton was paid well for helping me get a friend's car running."

"What if he'd been seen? Daisy would kill you."

"It's not the kid's first rodeo, Ivy."

That shocked me into a brief silence. "Sutton steals cars?"

"You're thinking about this all wrong. It's not theft when you know the owner and want to give his wife's old car a free tune-up. In the law arena, we call that supporting a friend. Paying it forward. One day the guy will come to turn this girl over and find her purring. It'll feel like such a gift he won't see the dents in the fender. Glad it wasn't the window though. Hassle finding the right one for old models."

"Did you lift the key, too?"

"That I did not. A lot of people leave the key in the ignition. You've got to do your shopping early."

"This didn't happen today?"

He shook his head. "Months ago. After my last getaway car got towed before I needed it. You've got to monitor your traplines."

I digested this for a few minutes. "Does Kellan do this, too?"

The shrug was indifferent. "No one talks much about it. But in this environment, you'd be stupid not to have a plan, a backup plan and then another. Is Kellan stupid?"

"Obviously not, if he's chosen a gal like me. But if I may, given your light fingers, why did you give me such a hard time for stealing *your* car last fall? It was to save Keats. The very best reason."

"Ivy, I'd let you steal my truck to save your pets any night of the week. No questions asked, even if you stripped the gears and left the tank empty. The issue, if I may remind you, is that you stole my *squad car*. Left me at a diner holding a bag of burgers and made me a laughingstock among my peers. They're still riding me about it."

Keats made no attempt to conceal his canine laughter and I smiled, too. "I was desperate, brother. And tonight, I'm helping you get your pride back. Think what your peers will say about how you nailed your corrupt boss. You'll be promoted immediately and end up the boss of those jokers until Kellan gets back."

"There's a long way to go before that happens. At this point, I'm as likely to be fired as promoted. We don't know how high up the chain the corruption goes." He slowed on a steep hill and then paused, looking over the world of complex trails he loved.

I looked around too. He probably felt like I did when I gazed around the farm. "Higher than the mayor, I guess. What is higher than the mayor?"

He didn't answer, and I knew he was planning his next move. I decided not to push it. This was a serious problem that needed to be handled with supreme delicacy. That had never been my brother's forte, but I wouldn't underestimate him this time. Still at a standstill, he pulled out his phone and fired off a couple of texts. Hopefully this was the first step toward restoring justice in our region.

When we came off the trails not far from Runaway Farm, Asher spoke again. "I've decided a promotion isn't all it's cracked up to be. I'd rather have Kellan back and spend a little more time dancing with Alvina. I barely see my wife anymore." He gave my arm a light punch. "Besides, how could I move to another town and tear you two apart? I don't know who'd crack up first."

"Me. Hands down. Jilly is the lifeblood of the inn and a big part of my sanity program." I returned the punch. "But I'll never stand in the way of what she wants to do. Or you, either."

"Love you, sis."

We didn't drop the l-bomb lightly in our family. This was huge. A post-gunfire anomaly.

"Love you, too." To break the weighty feeling, I grinned at him. "Will you teach me how to set up getaway cars one, two and three? Without involving Sutton?"

"Let me think about that. I've got a few things on my plate and the first is getting you home. Then I'll return my borrowed steed and head into work. Probably better to show my face. It's turned into a legit family emergency, though."

"Just drop us at the lane. I need to walk off that ride. Your handling was brilliant but those hairpin turns get me every time."

I thought he'd refuse but he pulled over and stopped. "Ivy. Please promise me you'll let me handle this. There's a lot on the line and your animals are all safe. I know that's usually what sends you over the edge."

There was no point denying it. When I stole his squad car I was dangling from a precipice over a dark chasm. I would have done worse to save Keats. "I promise."

His eyes bored into me with the intensity, however brief, of my dog's eerie blue eye. "Promise for reals?"

I offered my hand and we shook on it. "For reals. No bafflegab or HR voodoo." I opened the door and let the pets out. "This is above my pay grade." I hated the expression but it felt like the right time to use it.

"You don't get paid," he reminded me, as I grabbed my bag and got out. I turned and hung onto the car while my legs steadied.

"I should, though. Clover Grove owes me, big time. But if I were on the payroll, I couldn't just opt out of the really tricky stuff, like tonight." I leaned down to grin at him before closing the door. "I trust you to figure things out."

"I trust you, too." His grin outshone mine by far. "But not really. That's why I put a police detail on the farm. For your protection. And my wife's."

"A police detail?" I grabbed Percy and set him on my shoulder. "How'd you do that without riling up Skowby?"

"Not his cops. My cops. The ones he fired without cause this week."

"Oh no! Kellan will be so upset."

"He's going to be upset about a lot of things. Let me brief him first, okay? I'll try to catch him now."

"You bet. I'm so exhausted I'll probably crash in the loft. If I see another lumberjack, I might just—"

His foot pressed the gas and the door slipped out of my fingers. It might have been an accident but when he leaned across the front seat and yanked it closed, I could tell it wasn't the first time he'd performed that maneuver while picking up speed.

I waited till his taillights were two red eyes in the distance, then started walking along the shoulder in the same direction. My legs were wobbly but that would pass. It was nothing to prevent me from moving on to our next mystery.

Keats trotted ahead of me, white tuft aloft. Then it sank... and rose again. This cycle repeated so often in our walk that I got worried and slowed down.

Circling back, he mumbled something I didn't understand. Maybe I was just too tired to commune with my dog.

He resorted to communing with me in a more primitive way, with a savage little sheepdog pinch to my calf.

And that was how things continued until we arrived on Edna Evans' front porch.

# CHAPTER TWENTY-EIGHT

The lights were on but no one was home. I walked around the house to confirm it. Edna was a night owl, if she slept at all, so she must be out on a mission. I texted her and when I didn't hear back right away, moved on to Plan B. I couldn't hang around waiting. The cops Asher enlisted would figure out soon enough where I'd gone and swoop in. It was better to take heed of the repeated sheepdog nips and keep it moving. I could text my friends on the way and arrange a meetup.

The only problem was a vehicle. Edna's main mode of transport was an ATV and riding that monster would be a sure way to get pulled over. Further, there was no subtlety on an ATV and I wanted to keep this low key. Calm, peaceful and— "Ouch! Stop that or the mission's off. I'm doing this for you, Keats. I could be snoring on the cot already."

Percy snarled at him, too. That was a rare occurrence but he didn't like being jolted around any more than I did.

I checked the shed with the ATV and found it padlocked and likely boobytrapped, too.

That left only one option and Keats drove me to it. "Really? You want me to take that? There's even less hope of arriving in one piece than on the ATV and it's almost as loud."

The herding arc tightened, driving me relentlessly toward the chip van. When the police finished their investigation, Gertie and Edna had gone to collect it but I thought Gertie took it home. Edna probably bribed her to leave it, since any set of wheels was an asset to a skilled driver without a license.

I hoped the key was missing, but Keats sniffed it out in a magnetized metal box over a rear wheel.

"Fine. I accept your challenge."

Inside, Keats perched quite happily on the passenger seat, whereas Percy disappeared into the back of the truck. The poor cat hadn't had a chance to recover from the back country adventure and now we were heading into another rough ride.

I rolled down my window before starting the engine. The fresh air would do us all good.

The truck shimmied and shook as I headed very slowly down Edna's lane and onto the highway. Gertie wasn't wrong about the big beast's strong desire to head into a ditch and die. I had to tug the steering wheel firmly and constantly to show him who was boss. This one definitely had a gender and was a stubborn male.

Keats mumbled general disagreement, possibly suggesting I was as stubborn as they come.

"Backatcha," I said. "This thing makes my truck feel like a magic carpet ride. If we have to hit the back country trails, I can assure you, we're toast. Get ready to run."

He was always ready to run, whereas I would most certainly fall into a ravine and perish. I wondered how many actual skeletons could be found in the trail system. There was no formal policing of the area, and now I sensed that was deliberate. If anyone needed a quick getaway, it was the police in this criminally quaint town.

The phone rang and I hit the hands-free button, despite the ever-present call of the ditch. "Hey, Edna. Where are you? I need help. Stat."

"Not Edna. And why do you need help?" The voice belonged to the man of my dreams and my heart filled with both joy and fear. I'd driven right into this one.

"Oh, it's just bedtime at the farm. You know how unruly Drama Llama can be."

"A clever evasion and more evidence of your—"

"Sneakery? Yes, I know, Kellan. You've obviously been in touch with your staff. Such a shame they've been fired. Good men and women who deserve better."

"I'll rehire them as soon as I get home."

"Are you expecting that any time soon?"

"Imminently, yes. I'm on my way to the airport to catch the next plane. If all goes well, I should make it by mid-morning."

"Really? That's awesome!" My voice hit a high note normally out of range for an alto. Keats sent me a look of searing disgust. I sounded like a giddy girl. "I can't wait to see you."

"Same. I was hoping you weren't doing anything stupid, but I can tell from the background noise you are. It sounds like you've fallen into a bag of hammers."

I laughed. "Feels that way, too. I take it Asher told you what happened?"

"Fast and furious," he said. "I called a couple of contacts and before I was even done Meryl Martingale was on the phone begging me to come home and get things sorted out."

Relief flooded through me and the right front tire hit the shoulder. Hauling hard, I got back into the lane again. "Is Skowby in custody?"

"He'll be questioned, along with many other people. The station is going to be full. That's all I'm at liberty to say."

"Oooh, you sound all chiefly again. It gives me goosebumps." I was teasing, but it was also true.

"I'm sure everything will be fine. Could you please turn around and go home? You got what you wanted. What could possibly be important enough to take you out now?"

"There's never been a safer time for a little outing. Like you said, everyone's being questioned. I'm going to check on my fox at our regular meetup spot. Veronica, remember? She was a superhero tonight. I'm sure Asher told you about how she led us out of danger into the trails. And more danger, from the perspective of a passenger with a queasy stomach."

"He actually tipped his cap to Veronica, which is saying something considering the stress he was under. What makes you think she's back already?"

"Foxes can run thirty miles per hour and she knows all the shortcuts. I'm sure she's home by now."

"If home is on the Harlow property, that's a hard no, Ivy. Who knows what opportunists will move in before we have enough staff on the scene? The mere whiff of treasure brings out the lowest of the low. In my renewed capacity as chief, I am ordering you—"

I missed the last words because Keats reached over and swatted the phone off the console. It ricocheted into the rear of the truck, where I could hear faint hints of my beloved's voice among the clatter of pots.

"If that phone is broken, you're in big trouble, Keats. We need it, both as a flashlight and to call for help."

His backtalk was also swallowed in the metallic din. I'd hit a bump and unleashed more clanging objects. Kellan had apparently given up the fight but Percy's yowl was decidedly miserable.

"Thank goodness, we're here," I said, forcing the truck into the slim road we'd made slightly wider by snapping bare branches on every visit. It trundled along rather nicely once we were in the bush and the lights were more than adequate for the job.

Finally, I pulled up at the spot where we usually met Veronica and there was no sign of her. I was more worried than disappointed. What if she had injured herself trying to save Asher and me?

"We'll wait." I glanced at my dog, knowing how that news would go over. "She'll show up."

Keats gave me a defiant stare. Then he crossed my lap at a bound and jumped out the open window. If he glanced back as he trotted toward the path into the woods, I missed it while scrambling to follow.

"Hey! Stop right there, John Keats Galloway. I'll join you, but not without Percy and my phone."

Relenting, he circled back, sniffing the ground and pacing anxiously. This time there was no doubt in his mind that we were onto something, and it felt decidedly more urgent than a couple of days ago. Percy rubbed against him but he sidestepped the cat. There was no appeasing or diverting Keats now.

His tension was contagious and I fumbled in the back of the truck as I searched for the phone. By the time I found it, I'd also discovered a bonus flashlight and a leash I'd left behind. I added it to the one in my pocket. With any luck, I'd be returning with a bonus canid, and it wouldn't be Veronica. The fox was a great friend but I didn't kid myself that she'd ever become domesticated. On this matter, I was with Cori Hogan. The day you turn your back on a natural predator is the day you lose an emu. With all due caution, however, I hoped we could continue to look out for each other.

Keats came to the van's back door and mumbled an impatient order to hurry up.

Jumping down, I pocketed the key. "For the record, I don't like your tone. No matter how difficult the challenges, we've always been respectful of each other. More or less. Cheeky sarcasm is not only fine but welcome. Rude demands are not. I'm out here alone and you know how much I dread the woods even in daylight, surrounded by friends. I'm doing my best, Keats."

He came over and gave my leg a conciliatory nudge. It was still meant to get me moving, but I accepted the gesture at face value.

"That's better. Now, lead on. You seem to have a plan."

I paused only long enough to text an update to Edna and get Percy settled on my shoulder. Then I plunged into the woods after my dog, muttering a monologue meant to calm my jangled nerves. While the human threats here were neutralized, the landscape was still full of hazards, manmade and otherwise. Normally, I would trust Keats to do his best to avoid bunkers and cliffs but he had never been more distracted.

Percy meowed in my ear and I responded by setting him down. As he ran ahead, it seemed like he wanted to pinch hit for his canine buddy. It was brave and bold of the fluffy feline warrior and I hoped he wouldn't catch a chill without his bomber. Their coats were among many things I wished I had time to collect before setting off.

When we got to the fork in the trail, such as it was, Keats turned left instead of our usual right. It was a relief to be moving away from the dig sites. The crew was detained, but if all went well, the police would move in soon to excavate and most likely exhume. I didn't want to think about that missing logger right now, or the dog he left behind. The man didn't deserve to become compost for the next generation of trees. The killer had counted on the forest to fill the vacuum they left, and that would have happened in a surprisingly short time. By next fall, the dig sites would show little sign of this unnatural disaster.

Keats circled back once more to collect me. I hadn't realized my pace had slowed. Being lost in thought could very easily lead to being lost for real if I didn't heed my pets.

After that I paid close attention. With every step, Keats got more agitated. His tail went up and dropped repeatedly. Worse, his hackles did the same. Percy's demeanor was more consistent, but no less worrisome. For him it was hackles all the way.

"Boys, hold up. I'm more than a little worried, now." I set the flashlight on the ground and reached into my pocket. "You're not going to like this, Keats, but it's got to be done." Indeed, he tried to evade the leash but I nailed him in one go. "Tonight, we follow Percy."

An indignant grumble continued for the next 10 minutes as he dragged me after the cat. That made walking much harder, especially as the temperature had dropped and there was a slick of ice underfoot.

"Stop pulling or I'll strap you on my back with the spare leash. Don't think I won't."

The next stretch passed more calmly, despite the dog's decision to keep his flags on high alert. He probably realized I was more help to him upright than passed out at the bottom of a gulley. Small cliffs rose and fell in the flashlight's glare. They were all starting to look the same.

Just as I wondered if we would ever "get there," we arrived. I knew it because Percy turned with a silent hiss. He came back to do a figure eight through my feet. I interpreted that as a warning to be very careful about what I was stepping into.

Keats, on the other hand, let out a shrill whine.

It came back as an echo, or so it seemed. When Keats stayed silent and the sound came again, I realized it wasn't an echo at all.

Either it was Veronica, or we'd found our stray dog.

Keats went into a point at the base of one of many small cliffs. Looking down, I saw an opening a little over two feet high and almost as wide. Was the stray dog trapped?

Walking closer, I stopped just over a yard away and dropped to my knees. Then I shone the light directly into the cavity.

A horrified gasp nearly choked me and I dropped the light.

# CHAPTER TWENTY-NINE

Percy batted the flashlight over to me and I directed the beam into the opening again. The cavity appeared to be quite deep. The border collie was well back from the entrance, but I could see enough for tears to well up. She was so like my own dog, only with far more black and two blue eyes that pierced my soul.

"Annie?"

She whined again in confirmation, although Keats' whine by my ear had done so already. His mother was trapped in that cave. And by trapped, I meant confined. About three feet inside there was a barrier of barbed wire and mesh. There was also a small side cavity just inside the mouth of the cave that was currently inhabited by a red fox.

"I'll get you out, Annie. Don't worry."

Groping inside my jacket, I found the wire cutters I always carried in the front pocket of my overalls and set them on the ground by the opening. I responded to Edna's text with our approximate coordinates and then slipped the phone into my side pocket. The flashlight was far brighter and I'd need all the help I could get in there.

I was no more a fan of small spaces than heights, but there was little choice in the matter. It was either me or Keats and he was very much willing to tear up his paws to free his mother. Thank goodness I'd leashed him.

"Stay back, boys. There's only room for one of us, and I need you to stand guard. Annie isn't there by accident. This trap is carefully constructed and will take some work to dismantle."

Keats refused to stay back. He desperately wanted to get to his mother and wasn't going to listen to me.

He did, however, listen to Annie when she gave a sharp yap of reproof. Then he retreated like a chastised pup.

I still didn't trust him to keep away, so I got up and looped the handle of his leash over a broken branch a few yards away.

"Just howl if there's a problem. Or meow, in your case, Percy." I lifted the cat into the same tree and he obliged by going higher still. "You'll have the better view."

With my own pets settled, I went back to the cave opening and spoke quietly to Veronica. "Look, I've gotta crawl in here and we're going to be in close confines. I'd appreciate leaving without fang marks or scratches, since my fiancé is coming home tomorrow. You're free to go. Let me handle this."

Instead, the fox backed further into her private cavity, amber eyes glowing. There wasn't so much as a growl out of her, so I took it as permission to proceed.

I had to crawl in on my belly, pulling myself forward with my left hand while keeping the light shining with my right. The wire cutters I nudged ahead, with each inch awkwardly gained.

"I hope Kellan doesn't hug me too hard because I'm going to be stiff and bruised from this workout, ladies."

Annie backed away from the barbed wire and crouched, waiting. Her toes were white and as I stared, I couldn't help noticing the remains of mice in a neat pile. Had Annie caught them in the cave, or had her feral best friend shared the spoils of the hunt? There was a gap in the wiring just large enough to support such generosity.

As I picked up the cutters, I groaned. "Right. Gloves. The barbs will get one of us."

Turning on my side in the narrow space, I managed to dig one out of my pocket, then reversed the move for the other. They were Edna's bulky camouflage gloves, not meant for finer work, but they would have to suffice. Pulling them on, I set the light in a good spot and examined the barrier. Was it set up to open like a gate? How did Annie's captor get in to feed her? Did they feed her at all? Tears started again and she gave a shockingly familiar mumble. It sounded like, "Focus." And also maybe, "Hurry."

So, I did. I stopped trying to find a mechanism of release and started snipping. The cutters were good and in no time I'd sliced an incision up the center. Annie had the patience to wait, rather than try to force her way through the opening. Continuing the project, I cut along the top and then the bottom, which allowed me to bend the wire open like a gate, turning the worst of the barbs against each other.

"Nearly there, Annie." I almost said "girl," but it seemed too familiar. This dog wasn't my girl. Maybe she wasn't even "girl" to Maud Gentry. She had an air of maturity and gravitas that probably wasn't simply the result of confinement.

I snipped away even more to make sure she'd emerge unscathed, muttering assurances to her that all would be well.

Maybe if I'd worked a little faster or talked a little less, I'd have heard a warning howl or yowl from outside. Or maybe the acoustics in the cave were such that it dulled external noise. Something made me look up and I saw Annie's hackles were high and her teeth bared in a snarl that made her black face wolflike.

I thought she was growling, but the higher pitched sound came from behind me.

Not Keats.

Not Percy.

That left only Veronica.

"What's going on?"

The answer came swiftly as two hands grabbed my legs above my boots and yanked.

It had been rough going in but was far worse coming out. My face slid along the dirt floor and while there was little time for reflection, I knew I wasn't going to look kissable to my returning sweetheart. If I ever saw him again.

The tight grip on my calves told me three things. The perpetrator was a man. He was large. And he was angry. None of which provided much assurance that my longed-for reunion was going to happen.

There was one thing going for me, however. I had managed to grab the flashlight on the way out. The better choice may have been the wire cutters.

I managed to choke out one word to Annie: "Stay." She was technically free to leave now. Whether she'd take orders from a stranger was anyone's guess.

When my chin bumped over the last rock and I saw light from someone else's beam, I gathered my strength. All I could manage in the clinch was a half-turn—just enough to shine my light in my assailant's face.

Then I started kicking.

## CHAPTER THIRTY

N o one likes a man in a balaclava. Even another man in a balaclava. It means you can't know what the other person is thinking.

In this case, I didn't have the luxury of even seeing his eyes, because he managed to boot the flashlight out of my hands. It clattered as it landed and spun around a few times, creating a light show on the trees. Maybe he regretted that move because his own light went out, too.

Even in darkness, I had a pretty good idea who it was. Thinking back, I probably knew even before climbing into the cave, but I would have done it anyway. First, I thought everyone was detained. Second, I would have tried to rescue that dog no matter how great the risk. I had made a promise to Keats months ago and nothing would have stopped me but a situation like this. Still, I considered it an intermission rather than the finale. While I had breath, I intended to use it for the cause. Annie deserved no less than my best effort.

Granted, getting hauled around by my feet wasn't ideal. But it also wasn't the first time. Myrtle McCain had done the same in my own barn and threatened to drag me to the dump behind a tractor. It was worse here, without the home field advantage. Plus, it would be harder for help to locate me in time. All I could do was hope that luck continued to work for me, as it always had before.

The attacker flipped me fully on my back, shifting his grip to keep my legs in a vice. Digging deep, I gathered what I could of my unflappable HR façade and smiled. "Hey, officer. Isn't it hot in that mask?"

I didn't expect the flashlight to spin around in my favor but it did. Perhaps a certain feline had come down to give it a bat. Either way, I was grateful because it gave me the reward of seeing surprise in his hazel eyes.

"Make that chief," he said.

"Really? You got a promotion today? Congrats."

"I'll have that title by tomorrow and you're going to help me win it."

I pushed myself up on one elbow. "How about you let go of my feet so we can get right on that?"

"How about you shut your trap and put these on, first?" He managed to grasp both legs in one hand and reach into his pocket for handcuffs. He was wearing jeans but came equipped. Tossing them on my chest, he gave a little laugh. "I trust you know how they work?"

"Yeah, I've seen a lot of these. So far I've managed to avoid them."

"That's a crime in and of itself, considering how you operate."

I took my gloves off and slipped one metal cuff over my left wrist, making sure it gave an audible click. He relaxed enough that I took a chance and kicked one foot free and thrashed like a mad woman. While he struggled to catch it again, I reached into my side pocket for the phone and pressed a number. Any number. By the time he nabbed my ankle again, I was snapping on the other cuff. "There. Are you hot now?"

He was breathing heavily, so I took that as a yes. "Try that again and one of the pets goes. I'm inclined to shoot the cat, but you can choose."

I didn't doubt him. "Could you please shoot me, first? I don't want to see that."

"Uh-uh. Too easy. When we're done, I'm going to stuff you in that cave and leave you to die a slow death, wondering what's happening to your beloved animals. I'll wall it up so thoroughly no one ever finds you."

My nightmares of being buried alive flooded back, but I swallowed hard and kept my game face on. "If you say so. Pretty sure my pets will track me down, though."

"By that time, your dog will be long gone." His next laugh was colder. "I turned his leash into a slip noose, so don't waste your breath—or his—by calling him. Wouldn't it be awful to know you choked your own dog out of selfishness?"

"Guess you're an expert on animal cruelty, having trapped a brilliant dog in a cave. Another ten minutes and I'd have had her out of there. The barbs were making it slow work."

"Exactly the point. I needed her handy, but secure."

"I'm surprised she's still alive. It's winter, in case you didn't notice."

"A mild one, but the cave is insulated, Miss Spy and Mighty. Didn't waste dog food on her, though."

"Why would you starve something you value enough to hide?"

He shrugged. "Wouldn't do what she was told—what I'd been told she's capable of doing after I paid a bomb for her. Figured if she got hungry enough she might be more cooperative."

"Whereas it actually made her more desperate to escape. That's how we realized she was out here."

"Didn't know about the other exit but I sealed that up after I caught her in a snare meant for the fox. Maybe she's motivated now."

"Dogs are motivated by love and kindness. Not abuse. She's never going to work for you without building that bond, Fenway."

I couldn't use his first name and wanted to take his title. Fenway it would have to be.

"Maybe not. But I figure she might work for *you*. Get up and we'll give it a try."

"I'm not going to work for you, either. You killed Dawes Croaker. And unless I'm much mistaken, you've dumped another logger in a shallow grave."

"It's a very deep grave, actually. The hole was already dug, you see, and it was easy to roll him in. Solved one problem. Guy was supposed to be crew lead but like Dawes, he wasn't motivated."

"Greed doesn't turn everyone's crank, I guess. Did the logger's qualms have anything to do with how you were treating this dog?"

"We're not here to debate dog training. They evolved to assist humans and that's what she'll do."

"I've got a better idea, and one guaranteed to work. My dog will help me help you. Leave Annie behind. She's been through enough."

This would accomplish twin goals. Keats would be free to help me deal with the attacker when we got the opportunity. Meanwhile, Annie could follow the fox to safety. I had the feeling Veronica had helped Annie escape the first time and there was a reason she was sticking around now.

Fenway pushed up his balaclava and it was unsettling to see that he was still handsome, when he'd revealed the ugliness inside. I wished people with serious character deficits showed it more obviously. It would make my life easier. At least I had pets who could see beyond handsome and clever.

"Just so we understand each other... you know I'm going to kill you anyway, right?"

"Sure. Once my dog shows you where the gold is, you can dig it up and then pop me in. One and done."

He stared down at me. "Are you insane?"

"Quite possibly, yes. You've had access to my record. On top of that, I imagine it's noted that Keats has revealed treasure before."

"That's why I'm here, actually. I heard about what happened to him in Thistledown and wondered why someone would go to such lengths to steal a dog. When I learned his mother was on the market again, I decided to get in on the action. She's been passed around but never delivers. A dud, I guess."

"Probably." It was easier to go with that than explain to a sociopath that dogs couldn't be switched on and off like a metal detector. "How'd you decide to dig here?"

"Everyone knows the Harlow history, so I bought the land and hired Croaker as the front man. Then I had to see what your human honey had on file." He smiled. "Bingo."

"You and Skowby got Kellan sent away so you could find the gold and split the profits?"

"No cop has that kind of power, and Skowby has nothing to do with it. I have friends in higher places who backed the enterprise."

"Since you're going to kill me anyway, would you mind telling me if it was the mayor? I like her and it would be so disappointing."

"She doesn't have enough clout, either. And no, I won't tell you more. Just in case you pull one of your fast ones. I wouldn't put it past you to throw yourself off a cliff and sprout wings."

"That would be so fun. But I'd never abandon the pets, even if I could fly."

"I'm counting on that. And if you behave, maybe I'll toss them into the hole after you to keep you company."

"You won't do that. You'll take the gold my dog finds and then move on with him to the next project. No matter what's buried here, it won't be enough for your friends in high places. They probably have a map of what's stashed in the region."

He frowned for the first time. "That would help but if a map exists, we haven't found it. All I had was case notes and a couple of Harlow's old cronies. It took ground penetrating radar to find this."

"From what I saw on our site visit, you're a bit off target. I can help, but we'd better hurry. Your window's closing because Kellan's coming back."

"Eventually, maybe. Don't get your hopes up."

"Eventually *tomorrow*," I said. "Have you spoken to Skowby lately? Your colleagues? Even cops get one phone call."

He let go of my right foot, yanked his phone from his pocket and cursed quietly. "Get moving. We're on the clock."

When he released the other boot, I sat up and then fell back. "My hands are cuffed and my feet are numb. Be a gentleman and give me a hand."

In that moment of sitting, I'd seen that Keats was free and poised to attack. I figured he'd chew through his leash and it was a relief to know he could defend himself. Percy, in all his fluffy glory, was good to go, too.

I had a plan, but it turned out to have one major flaw. I'd counted on two pets coming to my aid. Animals I knew well and whose behavior I could predict.

Instead, I got four.

As Fenway bent over me and grabbed my forearms, I went limp and flopped back heavily. It was enough to throw him off-balance. Then I said, "Now."

Just one word.

My voice was calm.

Then came the storm.

# CHAPTER THIRTY-ONE

P ercy launched first, shooting out of the tree and landing on the back of Fenway's neck.

Keats came next, hitting the cop between the shoulder blades.

Then a blur of auburn shot past my face and Fenway kicked out as Veronica grabbed his leg.

That left hands for Annie and she snagged the left.

I raised my cuffed hands in defense and started to scoot sideways.

Too late.

Fenway stumbled and fell on top of me. Worse, his head shot through my cuffed arms, pinning him to me.

I was flattened and then ground into the hard, cold earth as he squirmed and flailed, presumably trying to escape assault by the furry cyclone. My breath was nearly gone and I feared I would suffocate under a dirty cop instead of in a coffin, as I'd dreamed.

My vision was going dark when Fenway flipped us over so that I was on top. The more he thrashed, the more tangled he got and I worried he'd snap my arms like twigs. I caught a glimpse of Annie jumping from side to side, biting one hand and then the other.

Then my face got squished into Fenway's shoulder, leaving me to imagine the clawed, fanged fury. I'd heard men scream before but never from such close range. It was deafening.

He rolled me back over and tried to shake free but we were locked in a desperate clinch that may have continued for some time had lights not flooded the area and a voice rung out.

"Dagnabit, Ivy. If I'd known you were having illicit relations with another cop, maybe I'd have gone to my euchre game after all."

"Get him off her," Jilly yelled. "It's no time for jokes."

I thought it would take ages to find the key to the cuffs, but someone deftly snapped them. As always, my friends came equipped for anything.

Buckley and Edna flung Fenway onto his back beside me. "It didn't look like a bit of fun to me," she said. "But whatever floats your boat." Her words were teasing but her expression deadly serious. "Minnie? We need you."

Gertie already had her rifle trained on the cop. Sterling did the same with his. Jilly, who ran over to help me, was the only one under 80 in the group. I wasn't too far gone to be awed and amazed by my posse.

Fenway and I managed to sit up at the same time, but he wasn't going anywhere. When he lifted his head from his knees, I was the one who screamed.

His torn earlobe? Expected.

Scratches around the hairline? Also expected.

The disfigured nose? *Un*expected.

And the way he moaned as he rubbed his legs? Also unexpected.

"You'll want a rabies shot," Edna said, passing him a handkerchief from my gallant uncle. "They don't usually stitch dog bites, you know. Holds in the bacteria. So that'll scar pretty good."

"What's the old expression?" Gertie said. "Handsome is as handsome does. But they don't have ladies where you're going, Fenway. Or cosmetic surgeons."

My spotty recollection of the skirmish suggested Annie had a signature move even more savage than her son's. Maybe she'd never had a chance to use it before, but she probably would again.

"Where's Veronica?" I asked Jilly, as she sat down beside me. Percy came and settled into my lap, purring over a job well done.

"Ran off in a hurry. Looked fine." She was wearing her camo snowsuit, curls tucked under a matching hat with earflaps. It was the outward sign of her inner transformation. Maybe she could handle Asher's signature trail, after all. I shouldn't underestimate my best friend, either.

The four seniors hogtied the spent cop, exchanging comments and witticisms I wasn't ready to hear.

Luckily, there was a sweeter distraction and Jilly gestured to it.

Keats was utterly abasing himself in front of Annie, howling in what sounded like a blend of happiness and grief. Annie tolerated his frenzy for a few moments before putting one white paw on his head and pressing him down. My fierce warrior collapsed like a house of cards and rolled onto his back. Then she washed his face, which would have been adorable if she hadn't left a streak of blood on his white muzzle. At least he looked the part of the true hero he was.

I let them have their moment and leaned against Jilly. "Who did I call?"

"Asher, and he's on his way. We'd already deployed after your earlier text and know the terrain better. Thank goodness, the howling carried. At first I thought it was wolves."

"Ash and I staked out the wrong cop tonight," I said. "Maybe we could have prevented this."

"The wrong cop looked like the right one at the time. Turns out Skowby was already trying to figure out what was going on. When the secret lumber crew fired on you, Skowby tried to shoot out their tires and hit your car instead. Ultimately, they were detained by the officers he downsized, because the more recent hires didn't know the trail system. Now, everyone's cooling their heels in lockup, pending investigation."

"Acting chief no more," I said.

She smiled. "That title fell to Asher, and he'll get to enjoy it till the real chief is home tomorrow." Giving me a one-armed hug, she added, "It's the end of a terrifying chapter."

## CHAPTER THIRTY-TWO

The next day, I wanted to wait for Kellan to arrive before leaving, but it wasn't fair to Annie and Maud Gentry. I had called to share the good news while getting cleared at a Dorset Hills after-hours medical clinic and she told me another day wouldn't matter. I knew she was counting the hours till they were reunited, though, and when Kellan landed he would need to put business before pleasure.

I opted to blend pleasure with business, by taking Annie around the farm while doing my chores. She was a natural, of course, and escorted the sheep out with no help from Keats. Normally, the only dog he deferred to was Cori's border collie, but in this case he stood back meekly, mouth hanging open in a happy pant. Every so often he went into another frenzy of abasement and Annie mostly ignored him. I suspected she would do the same with Frost. She had more on her mind than grown offspring, or even pending grand-puppies.

I hoped the memory of her trauma would fade with time. Keats had faced plenty of hardship and generally lived in the present. Annie would have a good life again with Maud, and now there was an army behind her to ensure her safety.

"Darling, stop playing farmer and let's go," Mom called as she came down the front steps ahead of Jilly.

"I am a farmer, Mom, like it or not."

Her tinkling laugh drifted over. "That would be a 'not.' But I do love the inn and the constant diversion. You just never know what a day will bring."

"Some of the crew is still at the inn, waiting to be questioned. I'm surprised you'd choose Thistledown over the company of men."

She waited for me to open the passenger door of the truck, as if I were a chauffeur instead of her beleaguered daughter. "They bore me. Not men in general, but these in particular. All they seem to do is swap war stories about mighty trees they felled. No one wants to talk about important things. Specifically, me and my various fascinating projects. Can you believe it?"

"Nope. You certainly dominate my conversations."

"Thank you, darling." She buckled herself in. "Makes a mother feel cherished."

Jilly climbed into the back seat with all the pets. There was no way Annie was sitting on Mom and Keats wouldn't leave Annie's side, so my best friend gave up on her favorite coat and shrugged. "Dahlia told a few war stories about your exploits. They were suitably impressed that you swung in and out of that site on a crane. Rob gave you 'mad props.'"

I laughed as I turned the key in the ignition. "That one's going to stick with me for a while, no question. Rob doesn't seem like such a bad guy. I hope they weren't all in on it."

"Asher said some might go free," Jilly said. "Not Fleet, though. It sounds like he knew everything, and what's more, dragged Marlene into this. The Croakers were hiring for a much smaller build when they met, and Fleet got Marlene to talk Dawes into being the frontman here. Little did her husband know he was being sidelined in more ways than one."

I glanced through the seats. "She knew everything?"

Jilly shook her head. "Probably a pawn like some of the others. I don't envy the police in trying to tease all the strands out of this gnarled mess. We won't see much of our guys for a while, I'm afraid."

"More time for manure management," I said. "I'm hanging up my ax."

Mom pulled down the visor and checked her reflection. She was wearing enough makeup for a cotillion and the bit of red satin sticking out from her coat suggested she'd dressed the part, too. Dolling up was her way of blowing off steam after a crisis. Today's elaborate attire suggested she'd been very worried about me. In our family, warm words and hugs were hard to come by but if you looked hard enough, the signs flashed red.

Snapping the visor back, she said, "I hope you're going to clean up for Kellan's homecoming, Ivy."

I rolled down the lane, trying to avoid the potholes to spare my aching muscles. "I had a shower. I'm as clean as I get."

"It's bad enough that your face is scratched and scraped. You're wearing overalls. With a ponytail. This man's been gone a month."

"Twenty-seven days, to be precise." I turned onto the highway. "You'll recall I looked exactly like this when we met again after all those years, minus the scrapes. The guy likes farmers, what can I say?"

"There's no accounting for tastes, I suppose." She fluttered manicured fingertips between the seats. "Thank you for always making an effort, Jillian. That's why you're my favorite daughter."

"That and she caters to you hand and foot."

"Catering makes me happy, as long as it's not out of an old food truck," Jilly said. "You don't see me going anywhere."

Her words reminded me of what Asher said last night. "If Ash gets a promotion out of this, you go. Understood?"

"Darling Jilly, you must," Mom said. "You can't let Ivy hold you back from your dreams."

I took my eyes off the road long enough to glare at my mother. "I am not holding her back." After a few seconds I checked the rearview. "Am I, bestie?"

"On the contrary. You're both worried for nothing. Don't get me wrong, I appreciate that you care. But you're overlooking the fact that I'm living my dream. Running an inn and cooking elaborate meals is a big reason I left Boston."

"Then what about Asher?" Mom asked, more quietly. "He has dreams, too."

Jilly rocked Percy in her arms. "We talk about them, Dahlia. It's a moving target. I don't think your boy really wants to leave his family."

"You'll get tired of housemates, though. I certainly do, so I go back to my apartment."

"Not often enough," I muttered. Keats gave a pant-laugh that made me smile, too. It was the first sign he was returning to his normal self.

"Oh, darling, can you blame me for wanting to be among my children? I've always been what they call a—what's the new term? Helicopter parent."

Even Jilly couldn't hold back a snort. Dahlia Galloway wasn't even in the same airport when we were growing up under Daisy's propellers.

"Funny you should say that, Mom, because Asher was telling me yesterday you didn't realize I hadn't started talking till I turned four."

"Heartless slander," she said. "You were always mumbling to your brother in some private language. I suppose it was inevitable you'd do the same with your dog."

"Using the English language is an important developmental milestone, is it not?"

"Oh, darling, you were just trying to hoodwink me and I knew it. So I beat you at your own game."

"How so?"

"I gave you time to find your voice and when you hung onto the ruse, I took you down to Doc Grainer's office and asked Edna to give you a vaccine. You were entirely up-to-date, and she said so, but decided to play along. Edna's so good that way. She got out a syringe the size of a turkey baster and you let those words fly. All of them English, if not appropriate for a young lady. Or anyone, really."

I sputtered. "What? My first words were profane?"

"Very much so. You'd learned that from Asher, naturally, and I will admit I had no idea about the richness of your vocabulary. I was certain we were on the road to delinquency. I've rarely seen Edna startled but she was that day."

I shook my head. "Is this one of your tall tales? I'm sure she would have told me."

"Probably thought it was Poppy. She always got you girls mixed up and despite being the youngest, you were taller than your sisters. I was afraid you'd become a linebacker as well as a delinquent. Yet you ended up a master of corporate messaging with a handsome husband-to-be."

"Did I keep on talking after that?"

Mom pulled down the visor again, already bored. "I believe so, but honestly, once I knew you could drop a bomb at the right moment, I went back to worrying about Asher and Poppy. The need was more pressing."

Jilly spoke up from the back. "I love hearing these stories. It's so different from my family. Maybe that's why I can't see myself leaving."

I still worried I was holding her back. "What if you built a house on the property? Dad would be thrilled to launder his treasure for family. He can't seem to spend it on himself."

"You need your land for your ever-expanding menagerie. Besides, it would never be as nice as the inn Hannah designed."

"It's true," Mom said. "You've done very well for yourself, Ivy Rose. I hope you flaunt your success thoroughly at your upcoming class reunion."

"Class reunion? I don't know anything about that and wouldn't go if I did."

"The invitation came in the mail two weeks ago." She turned with a smug smile. "After a while the adhesive gave way and it opened itself."

"You're something else," I said, over Jilly's laughter. "I have zero interest in reuniting with classmates who never accepted me. I hated high school, in case you missed that, too."

"Same," Jilly said. "Definitely not my glory days."

"Really?" I caught her eye in the rearview. "I assumed you were prom queen and all that jazz."

"Again, my family. People knew something strange was going on even after Mom and I moved away from Wyldwood Springs. The weirdness clung like a bad smell. I only felt truly accepted after I became a Galloway."

Her words warmed my heart. "Then you'll understand why I'm not going to any stupid reunion."

"I understand you're not going alone, but of course I'll be with you helping you flaunt your success. And hand out business cards. The inn did take a hit with this lumberjack fiasco."

"Seriously? I really don't want to go. There were cliques and factions and plenty of people still live in town. It's been hard work avoiding them."

"Stop whining, darling. Embrace the new you and swan in with the chief of police on your arm, with your brother and best friend close behind. I'll do your hair and makeup. I still have time to whip up a dress. Vintage velvet, perhaps."

"Forget it. Can we just talk about Annie? And puppies? This is the only reunion I care about."

By this point, we'd turned into Maud Gentry's lane so there was no further need to fight off my mother's "prom mom" advances. It was just a small taste of what would happen when Kellan and I actually set a date.

Maud was standing alone on the lawn, arms crossed over her down parka. The winter chill had come back to our part of hill country and strangely enough, I welcomed it. All the thaw did was create mud and problems. There was no use fighting the seasons, I finally realized. You had to go with the flow.

Annie, so contained and composed, whined just a little behind me. I put the truck in neutral and turned to look. The stunning dog was trembling all over. Keats quivered in sympathy, and a vibration passed through me, as well.

I could see people inside, backs to the window, and understood that while they were all curious, they wanted Maud to have privacy.

Mom, on the other hand, was about to get out and crash the most important reunion I knew, with the possible exception of mine with Keats after he was stolen. He mumbled something reassuring and poked my arm. I reached up to touch his ears and said, "Mom, hold up. We're just going to let Annie out and take a little drive. Maud doesn't wear her heart on her sleeve, so this isn't for our eyes."

"Ivy, it's a happy occasion. That's why I wanted to come. To share Maud's joy."

"Boundaries, Mom."

I nodded at Jilly and then pointed up the lane. She got the message loud and clear. Opening the rear door, she let Annie sail up, over and out. Then she closed it quickly and turned away. All I saw was a black-and-white blur as I got the truck rolling again.

"Ivy Rose Galloway, you stop this truck at once. One boot is out the door."

"Bring it in if you want to keep it." She did, and I leaned across her to close the door while the truck kept rolling.

"Smooth," Jilly said. "You couldn't have done that a year ago."

"I couldn't have done that a week ago. Asher taught me last night."

Mom turned away from me. "Maybe he should move out. He's a bad influence on you. Always has been."

"Not so, Mom. There is much I can learn from my big brother. He was grace under pressure yesterday. Made me proud to be a Galloway."

Her posture softened. "What mother doesn't like to hear something like that? My children are finally showing Swingle genes."

Jilly laughed. "They always have. The girls look like Russian nesting dolls, remember? With you being the smallest at the very heart?"

Mom pulled down the visor and stared again. "I could empathize with Maud, you know. Every time you get into one of your situations, Ivy, it sends a stiletto through my heart."

The emotion in her voice surprised me. Was Dahlia Galloway experiencing a strange thaw like the one that just passed through Clover Grove? "I thought Jilly was your favorite daughter."

"Both of you were out in that terrible forest, and don't think I didn't know there was trouble. I paced before, during and after. Tell her, Jilly."

"It's true, Ivy. Your mom was drilling her stilettos into the hardwood long before I got Edna's text."

"Some day you'll know a mother's pain." Mom closed the visor again and put on her game face. "At least I hope so. I'd like more grandchildren. Daisy overwhelmed me with those twins. This time, I'm ready."

"Some day," I said, and Jilly's voice overlapped with mine.

"Bring me little girls, darlings. I can teach them all my mysterious ways."

I groaned as I rounded the block and headed toward the schoolhouse library.

# CHAPTER THIRTY-THREE

T helma's sign on the library door said, "Closed for one hour," so we headed back to Maud's house sooner than I might have liked. No doubt the librarian was one of the people waiting inside for Annie's homecoming.

"I thought we were giving them privacy," Mom grumbled. "I can never keep up with you."

I shrugged. "They had their moment, and I guess that's probably enough for now. Hopefully they have years together to reconnect."

Keats urged me on with grumbles of his own. He didn't want to miss another second of this family reunion.

When I finally parked, we found Maud, normally so reserved, sitting on the cold ground with Annie in her lap, much as I had so many times with Keats, after a crisis. Annie was very still, however, with her black muzzle resting on Maud's shoulder. The scene seemed more somber than joyful, but I knew that would change when both dared to trust the new situation.

Frost came down on the side of joyful, however. The gorgeous brown dog was racing in circles around the yard, albeit with less velocity than usual. She was carrying a heavy and precious load.

Mom patted her stomach and then pointed to Frost. "I hope that dog doesn't let herself go after this. Maternal sacrifice doesn't end with delivery, you know." She directed the same finger from me to Jilly. "Same goes for you. Heed my words, girls."

"If I have six pups like you did, I might cut back on pie," I said. "But I'm not worried about Frost. These dogs have so much drive it's unlikely she'll chunk out snoozing by the fire."

Our Thistledown friends were coming out of the house now, their coats hanging open. Maud's niece Louisa was in the lead, with her gray cat Fanny in her arms. Rickie and Madge Merriweather were right behind her, and Thelma after them. Wendel Barrick brought up the rear with his border collie, George, who despite having a mostly gray muzzle, was the pedigreed prizewinning sire of Frost's litter.

Keats shot ahead of us as we got out of the truck and joined Frost to run circles around the lawn. Always competitive with his sister, he charged past her, cut her off rudely, and flaunted his unfettered speed with cheeky yaps. Frost reached out to grab his tail and sent my dog tumbling into the hedge. He came out covered in twigs and mumbling something unfit for polite company. Luckily only I understood it.

Or perhaps not.

Annie left Maud's lap and walked over to my dog. This time when she pressed his head down with her paw, she didn't spare him a lick. In fact, she gave an impatient rumble that came just short of a growl.

"That's how it's done," Maud said, as Rickie helped her to her feet. "Watch and learn, Frost."

The discipline was brief, and the three dogs trotted toward the side of the house together. Frost and Keats were in the lead, tails high, as if giving their mother the grand tour of the property she'd never seen.

Annie turned and came back, peering at Maud with unforgettable blue eyes that were all the brighter for the darkness of her face. Her head tipped in a question.

"Yes, go," Maud said, wiping the last of her tears away. "Enjoy. The back is secure now, with a fence as high as a state prison."

"Aren't they sweet?" Jilly said, clutching Percy to her chest. The two cats were doing their usual indolent posturing while cradled like cherished infants. "They're a team already."

I smiled as the dogs disappeared together. "It's a good sign, right, Maud? That Annie is willing to explore after all that's happened?"

She nodded and shrugged, pretty much at the same time. It might have been comical with someone else. Maud's sense of humor had been driven underground by losing the dogs she loved, but it was still there. "These dogs are nosey by nature. I don't need to tell you, do I?"

Everyone smiled, and some of the heaviness lifted.

"Do you think you'll return to agility work?" I asked. "You said that was Annie's passion."

She shook her head. "It was just the key that unlocked her love of learning. There's no end of things to learn that don't take her into arenas and competition. We're sticking very close to home from now on."

"With plenty of backup," Rickie said. "Madge and I consider it an honor to serve and protect these dogs."

Wendel nodded. "Me, too. I'm about to be a granddad again, and I come well trained."

The conversation began to flow and I pulled Thelma aside to fill her in on what had happened. She let me talk, although I could tell from her prim smile she already knew most of it.

"Chief Harper called on the way home from the airport to ask about my involvement," she said. "First, he thanked me, and then chastised me. He thinks I put too much knowledge in dangerous hands. Specifically, yours."

"Did he, now? And what did you say to that?"

She patted her stiff curls gently with both hands. "I told him I was an excellent judge of character and if he chose to leave his post, I deputized myself to make decisions as I see fit. And then I suggested he not leave the kingdom unguarded again. We need him."

I laughed. "Thank you for that. I couldn't agree more."

The dogs came back around the house. Annie was in the lead now, while Keats and Frost battled for position behind her. They were an impressive trio—similar in size, posture and gait, if not coloring. I looked down at the white front paws they shared and shook my head. All six were covered in grime.

"How nice," Maud said. "With the cold, I thought the gardens were safe from excavation."

The word made me shudder but Jilly and I exchanged a smile, too. It was heartening to see the fur-family having fun.

Annie trotted right past Maud and came to me. I knelt on one knee to meet her. "What is it? Oh!" I turned to look over my shoulder. "Thelma, this might be in your purview."

I held out cupped gloves and the elegant dog dropped something into them. Although dark with both dirt and time, the object was very clearly an ornate antique key.

"How interesting," Thelma said, holding out her bare hand.

Annie nudged it away—not rudely, but assertively. She may as well have held down Thelma's coiffure with one paw, the message was so clear.

"It's for you, Ivy," Jilly said. "What do you think it means?"

The dog's blue eyes met mine at close range, and the silent communion went on long enough that Keats shoved in front of his mother. This time, Annie backed away. When it came to me, she yielded to his supremacy.

I looked up at Jilly and sighed. "Trouble is what it means. Maybe not now, but someday."

"Delivered right into the hands that saved her," Maud said. "Can't be that bad."

All three dogs mumbled in various pitches and their breeder's eyes widened.

"Yeah, it could," Jilly said. "That sounded unanimous."

# CHAPTER THIRTY-FOUR

To onlookers, my reunion with Kellan may have seemed nearly as frenzied as the one between Keats and his mother. There was so much hugging that we toppled right over in the mud behind the barn. Maybe it was no coincidence that the thaw had returned in time to pull us down. That said, flashes of white and orange paws told me he'd had a firm shove from behind. The move worked on Fenway and they deployed it again today without tooth and claw.

Either way, I ended up flat on my back with a man on top of me again. My ribs complained but the heart they held howled a happy tune.

"Sorry, sorry." Kellan tried to push off but his hands slid in the mud and he crashed even harder. A furry face looked over each shoulder and I laughed at my pets' delight, plus the absurdity of the situation. He tried again with the same result and gave up. "Maybe this is where it ends. With us being sucked back into the primordial ooze. Never getting a chance to experience the apocalypse with Edna."

I giggled helplessly, despite my aching muscles. Turned out the cure for being crushed by a bad cop was being crushed by a good one. The best one. "I thought you'd never come back."

"It was only a month."

"A forever month."

"Well, relax," he said, managing to get enough traction with his elbows to let my lungs expand. "If that's possible in our current predicament. It's all behind us now. I'm home and the bad guys and gals are getting what they deserve."

"Not all of them. Fenway said someone with more clout than the mayor was in on this. Probably behind all this. Do you know who it is?"

He shook his head. "Looking into it, but needless to say this needs to be handled with extreme care. Your undercover work with your brother will send them running. For now."

"Whoever it was had the power to overrule the mayor and redeploy you. How can you fix that from below?"

"Meryl and I have friends, too. Corruption is nothing new in hill country. This is just the latest eruption."

I gave up on keeping him clean and wrapped my arms around him. Keats pawed at my wrist, eager to have us up and moving so that he could menace Kellan's cuffs. "What if you had lost your job? I was so scared you'd be transferred permanently. Or worse, fired. What would we have done then?"

Shifting his weight to one side, he grabbed my left hand and held muddy fingers in front of my face. "What do these rings tell you? For better or worse."

"We haven't said those vows."

"Oh, I said them in my head long ago. First in high school and again when I saw you standing over the dogcatcher in that field." He gestured in the wrong direction and Keats gave a pant-laugh. Both pets were still clinging to Kellan's slippery uniform jacket. "Fine, Keats." Kellan gestured again. "It was that field."

Keats mumbled a "wrong again, honey." He hadn't had this much fun in ages.

My anxiety was still on overdrive, however. "What if you'd lost your job and I was faced with leaving the farm?"

"We'd have figured something out. Don't you think I could find another job to support the Galloway-Harpers? I have skills, you know. No one is more capable of hot-wiring a car, for example."

"More capable than Asher?"

"Who do you think trained him?" He propped himself up a little more. "Guess I do have something in common with Edna. I've been prepping for this my whole life."

"'This' being police corruption?"

"Prepping for crime-fighting, with or without a badge, I suppose. Make no mistake, if I got fired, I'd come right home and continue in a new way. Plus, I'd get a regular job."

Finally, stress started leaking out of me. As it did, it felt like I sank even deeper into the muck. Tonight it would freeze and leave the imprint of our bodies, something like a chalk outline only more romantic. With any luck, it would stay till spring and be a constant reminder of our strong foundation as a couple. If the worst happened, Kellan would come back and we'd make it work some-how. I wouldn't be forced to make the difficult choice between him and my animals. Hannah Pemberton had never recovered from leaving Runaway Farm. Maybe she should build a house here, too.

Smiling, I asked, "So where would you work if you weren't a cop?"

"Hardware store." He didn't miss a beat so I knew he'd thought about it before. "Thirl Norland will retire at some point and he'd love it if I took over."

"He would. Told me so himself. Apparently, you've been hiding your fix-it skills."

"Some preppers keep things under wraps. And with that in mind, a hardware store would be the perfect cover for underground ops. I'd have legit access to hunting supplies, toxins and the latest in surveillance and tracking technology."

"I see. So, you'd launch a hardware detective agency."

"The Undercover Hardware Detective Agency. Although I wouldn't sell my services until I'd cleaned up crime in our area. I've committed every open case to memory, you see. We could solve them together. You, me, and your fleet of furred or feathered assistants." His smile spread. "It would be nice not to worry about coloring inside the lines. A real chief doesn't get to freestyle that much."

It melted my very bones that he daydreamed about a future like that, although I hoped he'd always be respected for his work inside the policing arena. "I didn't think I could love you more, but your bedroom talk is out of this world."

"May it always be so easy to romance you." He gave a little jerk and I knew a tuxedoed puppet master was pulling his strings again. "Luckily, there's plenty of mud in our future."

"Dirty cops, dirty politicians and just regular farm variety mud. We'll be a power couple around these parts. Justine will need to pay for our story."

Jerking again, he shrugged Keats off and got to his feet with as much grace as possible in the circumstances. "Let's get you inside to thaw that butt. I don't want it falling off before the wedding."

He pulled me to my feet and that's when I noticed the audience lined up along the fences. Sheep, goats, donkeys, llamas and sweet Alvina. That wasn't all. Edna, Gertie, Mom, and all four of my sisters were watching, too. Asher was back on day shift and covering while Kellan took a break.

"In my day, a couple discovered in a position like that would be frogmarched to the altar ahead of a rifle," Edna called.

Gertie patted Minnie through her poncho. "I've got the gun for the job."

"Bring it on," Kellan said. "Today's as good a day as any."

"It is not, Kellan Harper." Mom's voice was shrill. "I have plans for your wedding and they don't include a mud-caked bride."

He shook his head. "Dahlia, you're kind of missing the point of Ivy. Do you even know your own daughter?"

"She gets all her girls confused," I said, and my sisters shouted agreement. "Jilly is easily identifiable, so she's slipped into the best daughter role."

Mom ignored that. "Just remember you'll be marrying all of us, Chief. It's a package deal."

My fiancé hesitated long enough to earn a nip in his uniform. "All of you, then. Till death do us part, Dahlia."

"Some will depart sooner than others when the apocalypse comes," Edna said. "I had doubts about you, Kellan, but after overhearing this hardware plan, I've reconsidered. You and Asher won't be as big a burden as I imagined, which might leave a little room in the bunker for Dahlia."

Mom's smile blazed. "A bunker should never want for a seamstress. I can patch four uniforms together by hand in the blink of an eye. Can any of you naysayers claim that?"

"Actually, no," Edna said. "You're in, Dahlia. No scarlet allowed, unless it's necessary bloodshed."

"I'll make my own style decisions until my body is colder in the ground than Ivy's just was."

They argued about it all the way up to the porch, where Jilly was standing with a steaming pitcher of what I hoped was cocoa. Better yet, spiked cocoa. Reunions were a cause for celebration, although there was no privacy allowed here.

Even Veronica was looking on from her favorite hillock beyond the donkey pasture. I sensed she was well-satisfied and would be continuing to keep a close eye on the farm and surrounding area. We were in good paws.

Kellan's arm dropped over my shoulder. "I hear we're going to your class reunion."

"You heard wrong. I wouldn't be caught dead at that reunion.

School was a nest of vipers and plenty of them are still in town gossiping about me to this day."

"But you could show off your cop fiancé. Doesn't that sound like fun?"

"Tempting, but no dice and you can tell Jilly so. Or Mom. Whoever put you up to this."

Keats gave him another nip for getting me riled and Percy launched from the fence to land on his shoulder. "Fine, let's keep on pretending we're just regular Clover Grove High graduates contributing to the community in the best way we know how."

I stood on tiptoe to kiss his cheek. "Perfect, Chief."

The crowd engulfed us on the stairs with laughter and hugs. It felt like a warm-up for our wedding day and it tasted far sweeter than cocoa.

A Halloween fundraiser takes a strange turn when Ivy and the gang visit a reputedly haunted house... and discover real horror in the pumpkin patch. Can a clever mouse lead them through a corn maze of clues to the truth? Dive into *Mouse of Ill Repute* to find out.

Interested in hearing more about my writing and my dogs? Join the Ellen Riggs newsletter at *ellenriggs.com/opt-in*.

# RUNAWAY FARM & INN RECIPES

## Crime-solver's Quick Cobbler

Ingredients

- 4 cups berries, peaches or other fruit
- 1 tbsp lemon juice
- 1 large egg
- 1 cup sugar
- 1 cup all-purpose flour
- 1/2 tsp salt
- 6 tbsp butter, melted

Instructions

1. Arrange fruit in a buttered 8-inch baking dish and sprinkle with lemon juice.
2. Stir together egg, sugar, flour and salt till the mixture resembles a coarse meal and sprinkle over fruit.
3. Drizzle melted butter over the top.
4. Bake in 350-degree oven for 35 minutes, until lightly browned. Let stand for 10 minutes.

Note: When crime-solving (or reading about it) leaves you criminally short of time, nothing is easier than this tasty dessert. You could very likely bake it over hot coals in a firepit... but why not crack open another book instead?

More Books by Ellen Riggs

*Bought-the-Farm* Cozy Mystery Series

- A Dog with Two Tales (Prequel)

- Dogcatcher in the Rye
- Dark Side of the Moo
- A Streak of Bad Cluck
- Till the Cat Lady Sings
- Alpaca Lies
- Twas the Bite Before Christmas
- Swine and Punishment
- The Cat and the Riddle
- Don't Rock the Goat
- Swan with the Wind
- How to Get a Neigh with Murder
- Tweet Revende
- For Love Or Bunny
- Between a Squawk and a Hard Place
- Double Dog Dare
- Deerly Departed
- Think Outside the Fox
- Mouse of Ill Repute
- Bee All and End All
- Sheep with One Eye Open
- Roo the Day
- Till Death Zoo Us Part
- Hit the Road, Quack
- One Horse Open Slay
- Beg, Burrow or Steal

*Bought-the-Farm* Mysteries - Boxed Sets

- Bought the Farm Mysteries - Books 1-3
- Bought the Farm Mysteries - Books 4-6
- Bought the Farm Mysteries - Books 7-9
- Bought the Farm Mysteries - Books 1-10

*Dog Town* Series

- Ready or Not in Dog Town (The Beginning)
- Bitter and Sweet in Dog Town (Labor Day)
- A Match Made in Dog Town (Thanksgiving)
- Lost and Found in Dog Town (Christmas)
- Calm and Bright in Dog Town (Christmas)
- Tried and True in Dog Town (New Year's)
- Yours and Mine in Dog Town (Valentine's Day)
- Nine Lives in Dog Town (Easter)
- Great and Small in Dog Town (Memorial Day)
- Bold and Blue in Dog Town (Independence Day)
- Better or Worse in Dog Town (Labor Day)

*Mystic Mutt Mysteries* Paranormal Cozy

- I Want You to Haunt Me (Prequel)
- You Can't Always Get What You Haunt
- Any Way You Haunt It
- I Only Haunt to be with You
- All I Haunt Is You
- Do You Haunt to Know a Secret?
- All I Haunt for Christmas
- I Haunt You Back